HAILEY NORTH

Perfect Match

AVON BOOKS
An Imprint of HarperCollinsPublishers

This is a work of fiction. Names, characters, places, and incidents are products of the author's imagination or are used fictitiously and are not to be construed as real. Any resemblance to actual events, locales, organizations, or persons, living or dead, is entirely coincidental.

AVON BOOKS
An Imprint of HarperCollins*Publishers*
10 East 53rd Street
New York, New York 10022-5299

Copyright © 2000 by Nancy Wagner
ISBN: 0-380-81306-8
www.avonromance.com

First Avon Books paperback printing: August 2000

Avon Trademark Reg. U.S. Pat. Off. and in Other Countries, Marca Registrada, Hecho en U.S.A.
HarperCollins® is a trademark of HarperCollins Publishers Inc.

Printed in the U.S.A.

WCD 10 9 8 7 6 5 4 3 2 1

To my perfect match:
thanks for your endless inspiration.

And in tribute to Nancy Richards-Akers,
whose generous spirit lives on
despite her untimely death.

One

"*Y*ou have sunk to new depths today, Lauren Grace Stevens."

"Arck! Arck!" The parrot on Lauren's shoulder screeched and bobbed its tufted head, obviously agreeing with the sentiments of the woman on whose shoulder he perched.

"The last thing I need at a time like this," Lauren continued, "is criticism from a feathered fiend."

The parrot lowered its head. Lauren sighed and scratched the beak of her only ally in New Orleans. "All right, I'm sorry I called you a fiend. It's not your fault I'm in the situation I'm in."

"Arck! Buy low. Sell high!"

Lauren smiled despite herself. The bird's former owner had possessed a magic touch when it came to the stock market. Not that even the fattest portfolio in the world could have saved Mrs. Plaisance from succumbing to pneumonia, an event that had triggered Lauren's own downfall from paid companion to her current state of street performer, earning tips in exchange for photos of her exotic parrot. Despite everyone's advice to the contrary, two months ago Lauren had taken yet another leave of absence from her doctoral dissertation to accompany Mrs. Plaisance to New Orleans. If only her dissertation advisor could see her now!

"Mom, can I pet the bird?"

Lauren smiled at the youngster approaching the spot she'd made for herself among the tarot-card readers, jugglers, artists, musicians, and mimes plying the tourist trade. It seemed visitors to the city were drawn to Jackson Square in New Orleans's French Quarter like lemmings to a Norwegian hillside.

"Only if the lady says so," answered the woman puffing along in her son's wake. She carried several shopping bags, but it was the bright purple bag with gold lettering that seemed to dance as the bag banged against the woman's thigh that captured Lauren's attention. Focusing, she made out "Bayou Magick Shop." Her artist's sense of style appreciated the beauty of the design, and she promised herself the treat of visiting the shop just to see what type of establishment put such effort into its shopping bags. Of course, she couldn't purchase anything, but possession wasn't her object.

"If Buster says yes," Lauren said to the boy, "it's okay with me."

"What kind of name is that for a parrot?"

"His," Lauren answered.

The boy swung back to the woman. "This is stupid. Why'd we come here? You know I wanted to go to Disney World."

The woman tugged at her hair and directed a glare at Lauren.

Lauren thought of her empty pockets and correctly interpreted the glance. Hating herself for her own duplicity, she said, "Just kidding."

"Yeah?"

"What would you name a parrot?"

The boy's eyes lit up. He studied the bird, then reached out a hand toward Buster's brightly hued wings. "Tweety. 'Buster' is for dogs."

How predictable. Two hours of working for tips had taught her more about holding her tongue than all her prior twenty-eight years of life. "Let's call him Tweety, then."

The boy nodded and held out a hand toward the bird.

"Buy low. Sell high!" With a show of his wings, Buster hopped from Lauren's shoulder onto the boy's. The child smiled, and Lauren did the same. In a few more minutes, she ought to collect enough of a gratuity from this pair to cover her expenses for the day.

"Wow, Mom," the boy said. "He likes me. Can I get a bird when we get home?"

The woman, who'd broken open a chocolate bar, paused with one square en route to her mouth. "No." The woman glared at Lauren. "Give it back. Now."

Lauren reached for the bird and settled him back on her shoulder. The boy fished in his pocket and dumped some change into the discarded popcorn box Lauren had placed next to her feet. Waiting for the mother to provide the real compensation, Lauren found another smile for the boy.

The woman popped another square of chocolate into her mouth and, without another word, hurried them away.

Two quarters winked in the sun.

Two quarters wouldn't get her a streetcar ride, let alone the art supplies she needed if she were to earn some real money and get herself out of the bind she was in.

"Good morning," said a deep voice from just beside her.

Lauren jumped. She hadn't heard the man approach, but only a foot away stood the most gorgeous male specimen she'd ever seen. A blond with close-cropped hair, he stood almost six feet tall. His lips were full and curved up gently, and she knew without knowing that they would be warm and firm to the touch. Above a perfectly shaped nose, blue eyes matched the dark blue of a suit she could have sworn was cashmere. It was all she could do to keep from reaching out to stroke the fabric.

"Hello," she said.

Buster, for once, said nothing, though he fixed one nonblinking eye on the man.

"I couldn't help but notice your parrot," the man said. "An African Grey?"

Lauren thought about the answer and wondered whether she should tell the truth. Would this well-dressed man wonder why a street performer possessed such a valuable bird? Lauren sure would.

"A real sweetheart," she said, scratching Buster's tufted head.

"Yes, I can see that," the man said, but oddly enough, he was looking at Lauren rather than at Buster.

The saxophonist leaning against the fence behind Lauren chose that moment to blow out a note that rendered any reply unnecessary.

The man stepped closer and spoke over a warbling version of "Summertime." "So are you a regular?"

Lauren glanced from the man to the fortune-teller seated beside her, then down at her feet. She sure hoped not, but what kind of answer was that? You're working for tips, she reminded herself, and flashed a smile. "Oh, yeah," she said, "like clockwork. Every day, rain or shine."

"Buy low. Sell high!"

"And I see you bring your financial advisor along with you."

Lauren chuckled. She appreciated dry humor.

"Tell your fortune?" Sister Griswold, the palm and card reader working next to Lauren, butted in. A veteran of the tourist-hustling business, the woman knew a mark with money when she spotted one.

Lauren sighed, recognizing the inevitable loss of her customer. The old woman had been kind enough to fill her in on the unwritten rules of Jackson Square, but had also warned her it was every entrepreneur for herself.

Well, it didn't look as if Lauren was going to make anything off this man. He carried neither camera nor map and was more than likely a local with some business to attend to in the French Quarter.

"Only twenty dollars," Sister Griswold said.

"Twenty—" Lauren gasped, then clapped her lips closed. The old woman had told her last three customers that she worked for tips and had collected no more than five bucks from each of them.

The man was gazing, not at the extortionate card reader, but at Lauren. "Is it worth it?"

The intensity of his expression puzzled her. But if she cost Sister Griswold this well-dressed customer, she'd never hear the last of it. Lauren nodded. Lightly, she said, "Who can resist a peek into the future?"

The man produced a twenty-dollar bill from his slim leather wallet, then settled into the lawn chair in front of the card table draped with a purple cloth. Sister Griswold shuffled the tarot deck in front of her like an experienced Vegas dealer, then abruptly dropped the cards in a heap.

Lauren tried not to stare too nosily.

"Not the cards," Sister Griswold said. "Give me your hand."

The man hesitated, then complied.

Seated in a webbed folding chair that had seen better days and certainly much-less-elegant customers, the man in the cashmere suit presented an incongruous picture. She wondered why he'd agreed to have his fortune told. He was dressed for business, and he didn't strike her as a man given to fanciful invention. Perhaps Sister Griswold sensed that, too, and had decided to pour on the theatrics for the money she was getting from him.

Lauren didn't set much store by either the card

telling or palm reading. Knowing how her own bad fortune had drawn her to the Square to scrape whatever money she could from the steady foot traffic of free-spending tourists, she assumed the other street performers pretty much managed in whatever way they could. The artists Lauren put into a different category. Artists worked wherever they could and had always had a tough time getting along in a world that valued function over beauty.

Lauren sighed and wished out of a restless curiosity that she could hear what her neighbor was saying. But the fortune-teller had lowered her voice and was staring with a frown at the beautifully tended hand of the man in front of her. Lauren assured herself it was simple nosiness, but she knew it was more than that. The blond-haired man was both intelligent and gracious, traits she admired in a man, traits that reminded her strongly of her father.

Buster chose that moment to walk down her arm and hop to the ground. His wings had been clipped so that he couldn't travel far, but he got around quite swiftly by a mixture of hopping, flapping, and skimming along the ground. To her surprise, he walked his way up the seated man's arm and settled on his shoulder.

Rather than object to the invasion, the man murmured something to the parrot, who continued to explore his new pal, sticking his head in pockets and moving from one shoulder to the other. Whatever Sister Griswold was telling the man seemed to have fixed his attention, as he now stared into the fortune-teller's eyes as if he'd walked into the future she described and no longer sat in the present.

Three children ran up to them, pointing at Buster. Lauren rose, reclaimed the parrot, and posed with him for the children, earning a grateful smile and five dollars from a harassed-looking woman shepherding her lively charges.

The folding chair clattered to the ground. The man's face had gone pale, and as he hurriedly righted the chair, he said, "That's not an experience I'd like to repeat."

"Bad news?" Lauren asked.

"Some good, some bad," he answered.

Sister Griswold reshuffled her cards. With a flick of her wrists, she spread the cards before her. "Such is the nature of life," she said. "For another twenty dollars, we can see which wins out."

The man shook his head. "I think I'll work that out on my own."

Lauren liked that. As a matter of fact, she liked this man, although he didn't seem to be able to stop staring at her in the same goofy way most men stared at her. Just once she'd like to meet a man who treated her as if she were as plain as dishwater and tried to see what lay beneath her face and figure.

"Will you be here tomorrow?"

"Buy low. Sell high."

Lauren nodded. One more day, two at the most. She couldn't linger too long in New Orleans. Her job as companion to Mrs. P. having ended once greedy relatives descended to fight over the spoils, she had no place to stay. If only she hadn't abandoned most of her art supplies in her dash to rescue

Buster, she could set herself up as a painter. Her work was every bit as good as the other artists displaying their wares in Jackson Square. But the Plaisance family had been on the phone asking the animal shelter to come get the parrot, and Lauren had not hesitated to act. She'd promised Mrs. P. to care for her bird, and she figured even in heaven—or especially from there—Mrs. P. was counting on her.

But now she had a double quandary. If the Plaisance family figured out they could sell Buster rather than merely dump him in the shelter, they might come looking for her, police in tow. So perhaps it was just as well she didn't stay in the Square.

Her funds were tapped out, and once again she'd have to fall back on her father. And she'd have to confess yet again that she hadn't finished her dissertation. Lauren sighed, thinking of how patient her father had been, and of the many schools he'd sent her to. If only he'd accept she was simply not Ph.D. material, his bank balance would be so much plumper.

The man glanced at his watch. Lauren recognized the expensive Rolex. Her father, she thought with an insight she tried to ignore, would approve of this person.

"Tomorrow?" he said. His expression remained more serious than it had been before his session with Sister Griswold, but at least he seemed to have recovered his composure.

"Tomorrow," Lauren said, her palms growing damp as an idea blossomed in her mind. And, too, the word *tomorrow* always made her nervous, and it was small wonder as her tomorrows usually brought trouble.

The man backed away, still watching her. She raised her hand to wave, then called, "Hey, I don't even know your name."

He smiled, then, still moving backward, called out, "Oliver." As he spoke, he rammed into a canvas mounted on an easel. The canvas and a bottle of water and paint splashed to the pavement. The irate artist jumped up, screaming.

The wail of the saxophone mounted, adding to the pandemonium. Sister Griswold jumped up, moving surprisingly quickly for someone of her advanced years. She reached his side and bent over him, clucking sympathetically and smoothing his jacket. Even Buster scooted over to take a look at the wreckage.

Lauren, though, remained rooted to the ground. "Oh, no," she whispered. It was always like this. Wherever she went, havoc followed.

Alistair Gotho pushed open the massive cypress doors guarding the main office of First Parish Bank and Trust. As he left behind the sunshine and breeze of the marvelous spring day and traded it for the hush and dimly lit interior of this bastion of money and tradition he shivered slightly. But he'd made up his mind.

At the New Accounts desk, he paused and asked for his brother. The woman there smiled nervously, and said, "He hasn't come in yet."

At that information, Alistair paused. His brother

had been running the family banking business since the death of their father a year ago. Alistair had the impression that nothing kept his younger brother from toiling ten- to twelve-hour days. According to their mother, who at the present was off on a month-long cruise to the Galapagos Islands, his brother was working himself into an early grave while Alistair pursued his own eccentric ways and did nothing to help.

Well, he was here to help.

But where was his brother?

The woman shuffled a stack of papers on her desk. Without looking directly at him, she said, "You're Mr. Alistair, aren't you?"

"Yes."

"You remind me of your father."

"Thank you," he said, surprised. "Have you worked here long?"

"Nine years," she said, lifting her chin. "You're not what I expected."

Alistair grinned, ruefully acknowledging her comment and the fact that in the past ten years he'd managed to avoid setting foot into the First Parish Bank and Trust. And he was sure his disappointed dad had called him a few choice names during that time. "No horns?"

She blushed. "No horns."

For the occasion, he'd pulled his thick shoulder-length silvery hair into a ponytail. He'd also purchased a navy blazer, gray slacks, and a fairly respectable tie. But he'd balked at squeezing his size twelve feet into dress shoes. It was just as well that Ms. New Accounts hadn't caught a glimpse of his

Birkenstock sandals. Even Alistair didn't have to be told that his casual footwear wasn't standard banker's garb.

"I can tell Mrs. Walling you're here," the bank employee said, "and perhaps you can wait in your brother's office."

Alistair nodded. He had a feeling if he left now he might not return. The bank building rose tall and sturdy within the confines of New Orleans's Central Business District, a mere ten blocks from his own successful, albeit unusual shop. But between the two sites ran Canal, the street that historically marked the divide between the French Quarter and the section of the city settled by the Americans who came in droves after the Louisiana Purchase of 1803.

That might seem like ancient history to most, but to Alistair, who'd lived all except four of his thirty-four years in this unique European–African–New World city, history walked side by side with the present. And in the present, Canal Street represented an even greater divide. He could sum up the differences succinctly.

In the Quarter, anything goes.

In the CBD, business rules.

"Mr. Alistair?" The New Accounts lady put down her telephone. "Mrs. Walling said you should go on back. Shall I show you the way?"

"No, thanks, that won't be necessary." Alistair smiled at her to thank her for her time and was rewarded by a hesitant return of his own gesture. He wondered what tales had been told about him within those walls. No doubt she'd heard the story of the last time he'd walked through the doors of his father's bank.

It was just as well that he wasn't given to worrying about what other people—other than his mother—thought. As Alistair headed across the vast marble floor of the lobby, he heard the murmur that rose in his wake. He passed the mahogany front of the tellers' windows. His great-grandfather had founded the bank, and Alistair could remember from his earliest years his own father speaking lovingly of the traditions and heritage of First Parish Bank and Trust.

No wonder it had broken his father's heart when Alistair, at the ripe age of twenty-four, had refused to take his place in the bank. He'd never regretted that decision, but he did regret the fight he'd had with his father.

Ten years. He'd expected the interior to look dim and musty and even older than it had in his youth. But today the dark mahogany didn't look anywhere as funereal as he remembered. It almost gleamed, as if it had been recently polished. The two massive chandeliers that hung in the three-story-high lobby glittered with rays of light as the prisms split and multiplied the sunlight streaming through the skylights. All in all, Alistair thought in surprise, the bank was beautiful.

He paused in front of the door that led to his father's suite of offices. Before he could turn the knob, the door opened.

"My, this is a surprise." Mrs. Walling, a widow who'd been his father's secretary for almost as many years as Alistair's mother had been his wife, stood on tiptoe as Alistair bent to have his cheek kissed. "A very pleasant one," she added in a low voice.

"You look terrific," Alistair said. The last time he'd seen her had been at his father's wake, and she had been crying softly in a heartbroken way that had alerted every one of Alistair's protective senses. He'd seen clearly then what most of his family chose to ignore. Whether reciprocated or not, Mrs. Walling had been in love with her boss for a long, long time.

"Thank you," she said. "And you look just like your father." She turned away, but not before he caught the look of loss in her eyes.

"A lot of people tell me that," he said, "but you and I both know Dad wasn't a ponytail kind of guy."

Mrs. Walling smiled. "Oh, you'd be surprised."

Alistair nodded and smiled in return. So his old man had shown a side of himself to Mrs. Walling he'd not shared with his family. It was a funny thought that made him feel equally protective of both this kindhearted woman and his mother. He wondered if his brother ever suspected and decided that was unlikely. Alistair was the perceptive one. His brother stuck to facts and figures and balance sheets. Alistair had often tried to lighten him up, to guide him gently to loosening the strictures he placed on himself, but to no avail. Despite their differences in lifestyle, though, the two of them got along fairly well.

But could they work together?

"You know, your brother is always in by now. I hope nothing has happened to him."

"Do him good if something did," Alistair said.

Mrs. Walling looked more thoughtful than shocked by his comment. "I'm surprised he's not here, because he had a meeting with a consultant at ten. And she's been waiting for half an hour."

"Do you want me to talk to her?"

"You?" Mrs. Walling's voice rose, then she recovered herself. "Well, if you'd like to keep her company, she's in the small conference room. I settled her in there with a cup of tea."

Alistair stretched his arms in front of him. "If I'm going to learn the banking business, I may as well get started."

The secretary's mouth dropped open. "But—but you never . . ."

He smiled, grimly. "Never say never, Mrs. Walling." Then he strode across the office and grasped the doorknob in one large hand.

The room was empty. He turned around and gazed inquiringly at Mrs. Walling. She pointed at the door on the other side of the hallway.

"Right," Alistair said, and flung open that door.

Two

"Hel-lo—" Alistair halted. The petite blonde with the softly curling pageboy didn't look like any of the bankers his father had brought home for dinner. His outlook brightened; banking in the twenty-first century might not prove to be such a bad business after all.

"Mr. Gotho?" Her voice marched across the table and up to his ears, the brisk tone at odds with his first impression of a woman all curves and softness.

Alistair nodded as he tried to place the accent. Faintly British? Or merely a Yankee strayed below the Mason-Dixon Line? "And you are?"

"Ms. Warren." She tapped the notebook computer positioned in front of her. "As you'd know if you had checked your appointment calendar. Speaking of which, we are thirty minutes behind schedule. So shall we get started."

Definitely no question mark at the end of that sentence, Alistair thought, catching his breath.

She lifted a pair of half glasses and perched them on the end of a pertly upturned nose. "Or don't you care that Warren and Associates bills by the hour?"

Alistair frowned. Oliver never wasted money. If anything, he kept a closer eye on the bank's finances than on his own tidy fortune. Something serious must have happened to keep him from this appointment. Letting his mind roll inward upon itself, Alistair visualized his brother; as attuned as he was to the unseen, he felt no indication of danger. Which meant Oliver had better have a darn good excuse for his absence.

Ms. Warren rustled some papers. "As requested, I've conducted a preliminary study of your bank's DDA system."

"DDA?" He drew out a chair and sat across from the consultant. He knew he should confess to being the wrong Mr. Gotho, but something about her competent air held him back.

Her brows lifted slightly. He noticed they were exactly the right shade of brown for her complexion. Too often blondes' brows were naturally too pale or artificially too darkened.

"Demand Deposit Accounting." She lifted a computer printout. "I couldn't help but notice right away that the system architecture is modeled on what's now considered an archaic—"

"Do you like banking?"

She blinked. "That's not a question I've ever been asked to answer before."

He grinned. Now he was on familiar turf. He'd always been good at the unexpected.

She sat back in her chair, a faint line tracing its way across her forehead. The jacket of her proper blue suit edged open, revealing a silky off-white blouse. "It's logical, adheres to structure, serves the needs of consumers, businesses, and the financial marketplace." She nodded, and Alistair could visualize her adding up the sum of her words within her mind. "So, yes, I guess you could say I like it." She toyed with a thin gold chain around her neck, the first personal gesture Alistair had observed. "And I've always been told I'm good at it."

He reached over and took the computer printout from her. "Thanks for answering the question," he said, staring at columns of numbers that might as well have been in Greek. Actually, if they had been, he'd at least have had a shot of interpreting them.

"No problem. The meter's running."

"So any question I want to ask is fair game as long as you're getting paid?"

She dropped her hands into her lap and straightened her already perfect posture. "Any question about banking."

"So how long have you been doing this kind of work?" If he could just keep her sidetracked, Oliver might show his face. Then Ms. Warren would never have to know that he had no idea what DDA was. Damn Oliver—why did he have to choose today of all days to be late for the first time in his punctual, well-ordered existence?

"Mr. Gotho, did you read the vita I sent you before we negotiated our contract?"

He threw her a grin, one of his really good ones that always worked, that usually got him more involved than he intended. "Just testing."

All he received for his effort was a faint shadow of a smile. "As I was saying, the system architecture is the first place to start in planning a revamping."

"New Orleans has some fine architecture."

She looked at him as if she was beginning to think he was a little bit touched in the head. Slowly, she removed the glasses from her face. After she did, her face took on a softer expression. Alistair was admiring the difference the change made in her demeanor as the door to the conference room burst open.

"Of all the places to find *you!*" His brother filled the doorway, hands on hips, breathing as if he'd just run the Crescent City Classic 5K.

Alistair smiled and turned his palms up as if to say, "What's so surprising about that?"

"I've been looking everywhere for you."

"And now you've found me." Alistair turned toward the banking consultant. "You've also found Ms.—" Pausing in mid-sentence, he stared at his brother's suit pants. Streaks of red, yellow, and purple smeared the front of what had to be a thousand-dollar suit. Though his brother, thrifty soul that he was, had no doubt purchased it on sale. "Oliver, what happened to you?"

Oliver advanced into the room, the expression on his face dazed. Or, Alistair thought in a flash of insight—love-struck.

"Warren," the consultant said. She extended a hand, and Oliver responded automatically. He spared her only a brief glance, which surprised Alistair. Five minutes ago he would have been willing to predict Oliver would have found Ms. Warren worth pursuing after business hours. They were, after all, two peas in a pod.

His brother pulled out a chair on the other side of the consultant and dropped his head into his hands. Alistair glanced over at the woman beside him, wondering what she must be thinking. Instead of staring, however, she'd busied herself with the keys of the laptop.

Slowly, Oliver lifted his head. "I met the most amazing woman this morning."

"Perhaps we should reschedule this meeting." Ms. Warren's voice hadn't dipped quite to frost, but it lacked its earlier warmth. She reached for the computer printout in front of Alistair.

Oliver snapped to. "Ms. Warren. Of Warren and Associates?"

She inclined her head.

"I completely forgot."

"Yes," she said. "I see that."

"I apologize." Oliver lifted one hand toward his head and smoothed his crew cut as if that gesture would calm him.

Alistair watched as a bright green feather drifted off the shoulder of his brother's usually impeccable jacket. He'd told himself he'd read no auras inside the confines of the First Parish Bank and Trust, but his senses flared to the strength of the color field now swirling about his brother. Waves of orange flashed, and Alistair forced his vision closed against the sight. To set Oliver's normally placid orange chakra aflame, the woman Oliver had met must be something quite spectacular.

"You will, of course"— Oliver grimaced as he continued but forged ahead with the words Alistair knew were coming—"bill the bank for your full time spent waiting for me."

"Certainly. But Mr. Gotho and I have already started to talk, so it's not a complete waste of your funds."

Oliver's response came out as a cross between a strangled laugh and a cough. "Well, it's good of him to keep you entertained, but my brother doesn't even work for First Parish Bank and Trust."

To Alistair's surprise, a smile played across her lips. "Well, he's quite at home for an outsider."

"You're sure you're Ms. Warren, of Warren and Associates fame? The firm the bank hired to redesign our DDA computer system?"

She nodded calmly.

"Then you're too nice. I'd be willing to bet you ten bucks my brother doesn't even know what DDA is."

She turned toward Alistair.

He smiled at her and this time received a much warmer response. Funny, but he was really starting to like this woman who wasn't at all his type. "Demand Deposit Accounting. Now pay the lady."

Oliver put a hand back to his head. Then he reached inside his pants pocket. His hand came out empty. He checked his other pockets rapidly, but produced no wallet. "Spot me ten?"

Hiding a grin, Alistair handed a bill to his brother, who passed it to Ms. Warren. She turned it so it lay just above her stack of papers, with Hamilton's image staring up at her.

Then his brother pushed back his chair and rose. "I think—" Oliver said slowly, still patting his empty pockets "—that today the world turned upside down."

"If I'd lost my wallet, I'd feel that way, too." Concern sounded in the consultant's voice, though she continued paging through the papers in front of her.

"It does seem as if I've lost it."

"Where were you?" Alistair was having difficulty reconciling the man who stood rifling his pockets with the younger brother who'd toilet trained himself at age eighteen months. "And what happened to your pants?"

"I've been in the Quarter. Looking for you."

As rarely as Alistair crossed into Oliver's world did his brother venture into his. "Is anything wrong?" He didn't add "with Mother," but that was understood.

Oliver shook his head. After one last pass at the pockets, he regained his chair. "No, but it's almost April 15, and I needed your signatures on Father's estate-tax forms." A shadow dimmed Oliver's features.

The sorrow mirrored itself in Alistair's heart. They'd both loved their father, and despite Alistair's adamant refusal to join the family banking business, his father had maintained a loving relationship with his elder son.

To Ms. Warren, Oliver said, "I don't like to rely on extensions."

"Oh, of course not."

Alistair suppressed a smile. Ms. Warren might be just what his brother needed, and not only to re-configure the bank's computer system. He'd been engaged to a woman for almost five years, never quite getting around to setting a date for the wedding. They'd broken off about six months ago, and Oliver hadn't acted as if he minded at all.

Yet Ms. Warren might have entered his life a day too late. This "amazing woman" seemed to have captivated Oliver.

"What's so amazing about this woman you met?"

Oliver closed his eyes briefly.

Alistair exchanged a glance with the consultant and, to his surprise, she was staring at his brother, her eyes bright, her lips slightly parted, hands stilled. Again, her look had shifted, as if an identical twin with a brighter aspect had swapped places with her. Most intriguing.

Oliver opened his eyes, and Ms. Warren snapped her attention back to whatever it was she was seeking in the documents.

"I'm not sure words can do her justice. Her body was perfection, her red hair a waterfall of fire. But more than that, she had this energy—a sense of excitement. Alistair, she made me feel as if I'd never been truly alive before I gazed into her eyes."

Not captivated.

Bewitched.

"You know I've never believed in coincidence. I've never believed in those magick spells of yours. I've lived my life based on facts and figures. Yet today, something led me to the Quarter. It was almost as if . . ." Oliver trailed off.

Alistair figured his realistic brother couldn't make himself say the words *as if it were meant to be*. Reaching over, he grasped his brother's hand and gave it a shake. "Don't fight something beautiful."

Oliver smiled. "Thanks, and it is beautiful. But this woman made me forget about an appointment. And the first thing I did after meeting her was to have my palm read. Me, Alistair, me! And I didn't even get her name!"

"Did she toss that paint on your suit?" Ms. Warren asked.

"Oh, no, I did that to myself," he said cheerfully. "I was so completely befuddled I backed into an artist at work."

"If you were coming to see me," Alistair said slowly, "why were you in Jackson Square?"

"How did you know that's where I was? Oh, I guess that's where the artists work." Oliver ran a hand over his close-cropped hair. "See what I mean? I went out of my way for no reason at all."

"Reason doesn't always rule," Alistair said, his eyes resting on Ms. Warren's as he pondered his own attraction to the consultant, a woman unlike any he'd ever been involved with.

Ms. Warren met his look, a puzzled expression in her eyes. She stopped sifting through the papers. Lifting one sheet, she said, "May I ask you to clarify which of you is Oliver and which is Alistair?"

Alistair exchanged glances with his brother, who then said, "Sure, I'm Oliver."

"And you are the president of First Parish Bank and Trust?"

"Yes."

"The man who hired me for this consulting contract?"

"Yes."

"I see."

"And what is it that you see?" Alistair had never been afraid to be inquisitive.

She adjusted her glasses and read from the paper in front of her. "First Parish Bank and Trust has been a family-run business for the past four generations. At present, I'm sorry to say, I am the only member of my family involved in the management, as my older brother spends his time dealing in fantasy rather than facts."

Oliver had the decency to blush.

Ms. Warren laid the letter and her glasses in front of her. "After this morning, I was just wondering if I had the two of you confused."

Alistair couldn't help but laugh out loud. "She got you, Oliver."

"I assure you, Ms. Warren," his brother said in a more controlled voice than he'd used yet, "that my behavior should in no way be judged by this morning. A most unusual day."

"I'm only here to analyze the DDA system," she said. "So there's no need to explain. I simply wanted to make sure I was answering to the right Mr. Gotho."

Alistair rose. "I'll make things simple. I've had enough of banking for one day, so I'll leave you two alone in the world of facts and figures."

"To return to fantasy?" She murmured the question, but not so softly that Alistair missed it.

He let the comment go. Most people either accepted or rejected the unknowable. What Alistair appreciated were those rare individuals who were willing to explore possibilities without needing to make a judgment.

"You never did tell me why you were here, Alistair."

"It can wait." He didn't feel like telling his brother he'd come to enter the world he'd walked away from. After hearing himself described pretty much as a flake in a letter to a complete stranger, something rankled within. Family was family, and he knew he'd be back to do whatever he could, but right now he needed some distance from his brother.

"Did you come for a job?" He asked the question lightly, but as if he knew the answer. At the same time, he turned his hand palm upward and stared down at it, frowning.

"Who told your fortune?"

Oliver looked up. "Sometimes I forget how perceptive you are. An old woman who called herself Sister Griswold." He fished a card out of his pocket and handed it over. "Do you know anything about her?"

"If she told you I've come to work for the bank, then she got at least one thing right."

Oliver shook his head. "You know you're welcome. Family is family. Besides, I can use the help, and it would free me up to do other things." He looked thoughtful, and then added, "But what ever will you do?"

Alistair shrugged. "I'm pretty handy at inventions. And perhaps Ms. Warren will have some suggestions."

The consultant glanced from one brother to the other, a look of fascination on her face. But in her businesslike voice, she said, "The meter's running. And as long as it is—"

"—You're happy to help." Oliver finished the sentence for her, then flashed his own patented version of the Gotho womanizing smile at her.

To Alistair's immense satisfaction, his brother got nothing more than a polite nod for his efforts.

Ten minutes later, after signing the tax forms, Alistair crossed Canal Street, striding into the Quarter on Royal, one block over from the perpetual party site of Bourbon Street. He began to whistle and shrugged out of his navy blazer. He stripped off his tie and loosed his hair from the ponytail. Fashioning a bandanna from the tie, he wound it around his head. Moving with ease, he made his way around clumps of tourists out for a stroll on the vivid spring day.

He told himself he'd walk through Jackson Square to the French Market to pick up some fruit before he returned to his shop. Even as the explanation crossed his mind, he knew it served as an excuse. He was headed to the Square to see if he could identify Oliver's "amazing woman."

No sibling rivalry here, he thought ruefully. He'd walked out and left Oliver alone with a pretty woman who'd caught his attention in a way that surprised him. Alistair had never once dated a woman as coolly competent as Ms. Warren. And now he was thinking it was about time he did.

Women loved him, and he loved women, but he had a track record of rescuing troubled souls, helping them rebuild their lives, and parting with nothing more to show for his efforts than a few fond memories and a dented heart. Well, to give his ex-girlfriends credit, they all stayed friends with him. He'd been to more weddings than a small town's only florist.

The times they are a-changing, Alistair sang in his head as he reached the edge of Jackson Square.

Today the city hovered on the brink of summer, yet held on to the ideal blend of sunshine, blue skies, and temperatures that stayed on the sweet side of eighty degrees. With the breeze coming off the Mississippi River in a particularly frolicsome way, this day outshone any of the others Alistair could remember.

He paused at the start of the flagstones that heralded Jackson Square, the open-air gathering place of the French Quarter. In a city that would soon swelter under an atmospheric mask of humidity, a day like today was to be especially savored.

Even the usually surly watercolor artist who held the spot nearest to the end of a row of painters displaying and producing their wares found a smile for Alistair.

"Nice day," Alistair responded. That proved too much jollity for the other man, who hunched a shoulder and turned back to his easel. Coming to life on the canvas was a painting of St. Louis Cathedral, the edifice that dominated one boundary of the Square and watched over the artists and many of the city's faithful. Alistair marveled that for all the darkness of the painter's attitude, his work was infused with a glowing quality that transformed what would otherwise be a mechanical product done for the cash-and-carry tourist trade.

"Hey, Mr. Alistair." The next artist, an older black man who specialized in vivid acrylics featuring jazz funeral scenes, had been painting in the Square for the ten years Alistair had lived above the Bayou Magick Shop on Bourbon Street.

"Hello, Saul. Lovely day."

"Yes, that it is." The older man lifted his face into the breeze. "Spring'll last about another two weeks, I'd say."

"So enjoy it while we have it?"

"Yes-suh, that's what I always say. And that's what I always do." He dipped his brush into a pot of brilliant red paint.

The color reminded Alistair of his brother's stained trousers. "Anyone new and interesting around the Square these days, Saul?"

The artist studied his painting, then dashed a stroke of red across the clarinet of the figure leading the funeral march across the canvas. "Can't say as if I've met anyone new."

"Do you know a Sister Griswold?"

The man snorted. "Sister? You mean one of those card readers?" He slapped his free hand against one thigh. "I've got no use for those phonies cluttering our space. We artists were here first, and that trash just brings down the neighborhood. Yes-suh, that's what I say and that's what I mean."

Alistair sighed. The tension between the fortune-tellers and the artists was an ongoing battle, much like the uneasy truce that existed between resident and tourist in the historic neighborhood flooded with holidaygoers and crowded with noise-driven bars and music clubs. His own business, the Bayou Magick Shop, benefited tremendously from the charge-card-wielding visitors, but many a night's sleep had been disturbed by the same people once revelry had overtaken common sense.

"What would you be wanting with one of those types?" The artist squinted at Alistair, then said, "There's nothing wrong with your life the right woman wouldn't cure." He chuckled and rinsed the red from his brush. "Yes-suh—"

"Good to see you, Saul. Catch you later."

Finishing his favorite refrain under his breath, Saul returned to his work in progress.

Alistair decided to cut through the park that graced the interior of the Square and try the other side, where a collection of tarot-card readers and fortune-tellers had carved out a bastion of sorts. He'd just reached the side of the massive statue of Andrew Jackson astride his rearing horse in the center of the park when the peace of the day was shattered by a bloodcurdling scream from the direction in which he was headed.

Picking up his pace, he headed straight for the commotion, racing out of the fence surrounding the central greenery. Whoever it was—and the high-pitched voice had to be female—she needed help.

He dashed onto the flagstones. Directly in front

of him, two police officers were talking heatedly with a slender redhead.

And what a redhead.

For her coloring, she had the creamy skin one would expect; also the vivid green eyes. Even a nun's habit wouldn't have hidden the lush curves of her figure; the flowing froth of her sleeveless dress accentuated them to the point of exclamation.

Alistair temporarily forgot about the screeching as he gazed appreciatively at the auburn-haired beauty.

As he watched, she didn't even stop for breath as she continued her debate with the officers, but, he realized, the screams continued from somewhere nearby. Scanning the surrounding area, Alistair's gaze lit upon a brightly colored bird sitting atop a card table, squawking to wake the dead.

Glancing back at the triad, Alistair put names to the officers' faces. They were Eighth District regulars and would be sure to remember the generous donations Alistair always made to the annual fund-raiser for the station that served and protected the Quarter.

'Course, that was only relevant if Alistair chose to get involved in this woman's plight. He edged closer.

"You can't take me to jail for not having a license when I had no idea I had to have a license."

Bernie, the older of the two cops, shook his head. "If you know what's good for you, you'll quit acting so know-it-all."

"Is that so?" Alistair heard the flash of temper in her voice. The woman couldn't be from New Orleans. Everyone knew arguing with a cop could only end in a trip to jail.

"And make that bird shut up." That was Curt, the rookie. "Before I wring its neck."

Those must have been fighting words for the redhead. She rounded on Curt and poked her finger into his paunch. "Don't you ever-ever-ever threaten to hurt an innocent animal."

"That does it," Curt said. "I'm taking you in for resisting arrest."

The woman laughed, a low gurgling sound that would have been more at home at a cocktail party than at this altercation. "How can you do that when you haven't even arrested me?"

Suddenly, the bird quit its screaming. Cocking its head to one side, it chewed on one gnarled toe, then said softly, "Buy low. Sell high." A bright feather drifted toward the flagstones below the card table, and Alistair experienced the dizzying image of a similar feather drifting off his brother's coat. Hair like a waterfall of fire. Oliver's description of his amazing woman echoed in his head.

"You bullies are scaring my parrot," the woman said, lowering her own voice. As she did, she raised her head and across the few feet that separated the two of them, her eyes found Alistair.

Something about the steadiness and intensity of her gaze created the feeling that she was spinning silken threads to join and gather him to her. He fought against the idea, reminding himself that only an hour ago he'd been contemplating the benefits of normalizing his life.

Nothing about this redhead fit under the heading of "normal."

The officers were conferring.

She parted her lips and smiled at him. He was never quite sure whether she mouthed the words *Help me please* or whether he imagined them.

Curt unsnapped his handcuffs from his leather gun belt.

Alistair sprang forward, cursing himself as he tumbled into the web.

Three

*I*f Barbara had stayed at the all-suite hotel located across the street from First Parish Bank and Trust as Mr. Gotho's secretary had arranged, her time in New Orleans would have been a lot like every consulting job she accepted. Every morning she would have eaten her usual breakfast of a dry English muffin, one-half grapefruit, and a cup of tea in her room as she reviewed her work for that day. Then she would have crossed the street, spent the day at the bank and the evening at the hotel.

Convenient and efficient.

And not very interesting, she conceded as she paid the cab driver who'd transported her to her godmother's house in a quaint residential section of the city.

"That's some purple," the driver said, pausing in his search for a receipt to gape at the house where they'd stopped. "Now, who paints a house that color anyway?"

Barbara had thought exactly the same thing herself, but she bristled at the driver's right to comment. "A most creative person."

"Either that or color-blind," the man said, handing her a slip of paper stained with a greasy thumbprint. "Or crazy, maybe."

Barbara crumpled the dollar tip in her hand and got out of the cab, which roared off and left her standing at the picket fence surrounding her godmother's home. At least the fence was white, though her godmother had murmured something the night before about finding the color a trifle ordinary.

Slipping the latch free, Barbara stepped through into a yard where the only spot not planted with greenery and flowers was the brickwork path leading to the house. She still hadn't figured out how her godmother, who she'd met only twice before, had convinced her to stay with her rather than at a hotel. Barbara rarely lost debates based on logic and practicality, but her mother's dearest childhood friend, Mrs. Maebelle Merlin, didn't deal on those terms. She'd simply launched a verbal tornado that didn't cease until Barbara said yes.

And she couldn't be rude to the woman who'd been so sweet at her parents' funeral and had remembered her birthday every year, shipping a traditional New Orleans king cake all the way to England, where Barbara had been raised.

"Yoo-hoo!"

Barbara jumped at the sound of her godmother's booming voice. For such a compact woman, she had a voice that could curl the wallpaper off the walls.

Mrs. Merlin bustled around the side of the house, dusting soil from her hands. Her orange-silver hair contrasted wildly with the flowing violet caftan she wore. Barbara remembered her mother fondly describing her childhood pal and recounting the pranks they'd pulled. Yet she found it impossible to reconcile her ride-to-the-hounds and do-good-works-between-charity-events mum with this dotty woman who lived in a purple house and talked to her cat as if the two of them were truly holding a conversation.

Barbara frowned. Darn, but she'd forgotten one of the reports she'd intended to work on that afternoon.

"Dear, are you ill?" Mrs. Merlin scurried forward. "If so, I have just the thing. I call it my magick tea. It always sets me right-to."

"Ill? Oh, no, I never get sick," Barbara said. "It's the bank president who wasn't . . . well, he wasn't quite his usual self." Apparently, nothing had been quite normal between the banking brothers that day. Barbara still found it curious that the supposedly weird one had been so together when the man she'd been corresponding with had appeared so scattered. And those paint stains; that expensive suit was ruined.

"So you have the day off?" Mrs. Merlin clapped her hands. "Lovely! Why don't you come grub in the garden with me? And later, remind me, and I'll make up some of my magick tea for you to take to him tomorrow."

Barbara felt it happening again. The next thing

she knew she'd find herself with dirt under her fingernails and a packet of tea tucked in her briefcase. "Thank you, but I'm not much of a green thumb," she said, easing toward the front porch.

"Oh, that doesn't matter." Mrs. Merlin spread her arms wide. "Why, look at me. When I first started gardening, this poor yard was nothing but plain lawn. And look at it now!"

"Let me go and change," Barbara said faintly. That could take quite a while.

"You do that, dear," Mrs. Merlin said. "I'll be in the back. I'm repotting some special herbs today."

No doubt some of her tea ingredients, Barbara thought, edging up the steps, across the porch, and into the house.

In the front room, she deposited her laptop and briefcase beside the table in front of the broad window that Mrs. Merlin had insisted she use as her "home office." She'd mumbled something about not needing an altar anymore, what with Alistair having put his foot down, a statement that had made no sense at all. But as the area served as combination living and dining room, Barbara had demurred. Only to be out-insisted, naturally.

Now she thought back on the exchange. Alistair was not a common name. Was it possible that her godmother was acquainted with the rather enchanting misfit member of the Gotho family?

Hoping against hope Mrs. Merlin would lose track of time while she puttered in the back garden, Barbara crossed the room to the fireplace. She'd noticed last night that the mantel was as crowded with framed photographs as the front yard was with horticultural offerings.

"Yoo-hoo! Are you coming?" Mrs. Merlin's voice wafted through the house.

"Not if I can help it," Barbara said under her breath, then called out, "In a minute."

She raised her eyes, planning to scan the photos from left to right. But a frame near the center of the fireplace arrested her attention. From within a neon pink frame, the image of her parents smiled at her. Well, technically, the two of them were smiling at each other, in that way they had of showing how smitten they were with each other even after years and years together. In the photo, as it had in their lives, that love reached out to embrace all within their view.

"Hello, Mummy," she whispered, reaching one finger to trace her mother's face. "And Tops," she said, using her favorite nickname for her father.

Her throat tightening, Barbara forced her gaze to the next photo over.

Pay dirt. Alistair Gotho, housed as only Mrs. Merlin would, inside a frame shaped like a rainbow, the image resting where one would picture the proverbial pot of gold.

Hmm.

It was a younger Alistair, with a mane of silvery brown hair flowing past his shoulders. He stood with one arm around Mrs. Merlin, in front of a narrow building front. Barbara could just make out the sign over their heads that read, BAYOU MAGICK SHOP.

His vividly patterned Hawaiian shirt and purple

shorts vied with her godmother's crimson caftan. Gone were the jacket and tie he'd worn in the bank. The sandals were the same, though, the look that Barbara associated with the outdated hippie style.

The man's image held her attention, even as he had today. Something about his eyes fascinated her. They were almost purple-blue, with a light she'd seldom seen in anyone's expression. He certainly didn't look like any of the bankers she'd done business with. Was it possible that today had been the first time he'd set foot in First Parish Bank and Trust?

Something brushed against her leg and Barbara jumped, just managing to stifle a yelp.

Mrs. Merlin's fat orange cat leapt onto the end table and glared at her, tail swishing.

"Sorry," Barbara managed to say, feeling extremely foolish speaking to a feline. "But you shouldn't creep up on me when I'm concentrating."

The cat lifted a front paw and gave her an insolent glance before turning its attention to washing its face. He was so fat he almost tipped over from the effort.

Barbara glanced back at the picture of Alistair Gotho. The spell had been broken, but she continued her study. His body was lean, compact, muscled. He towered over Mrs. Merlin, just as he had over Barbara in the conference room.

Looking down at her size five pumps and her short sticks of legs, Barbara sighed. That man had at least a foot on her. Oh, well, he was just some man her godmother knew. Besides, he was a business client, or at least his brother was, and that was one perfect reason for her to leave off wondering how she'd look walking by his side.

Besides, his brother was certainly more her type. Curious, Barbara scanned the length of the crowded mantel but found no picture of the bank president.

That wasn't too surprising. Oliver Gotho didn't strike her as a man who would have much in common with a woman who had painted her house purple.

Oliver reminded Barbara of all three of her previous boyfriends. Intelligent. Handsome. Confident. Successful.

"And dull as dishwater," she added aloud.

The cat leapt onto the back of the sofa and eyed a bird that had perched on a low-hanging limb on the other side of the glass.

"Can't catch it, can you, kitty?"

So near and yet so unobtainable.

Barbara sighed. That bird was just like her love life. The perfect prize, but beyond her reach. All the men she attracted were good souls, but just once she wished it could be the bad boy, the wild child, the reckless daredevil who would pursue her.

In truth, she was the one who was dull as dishwater, but she prayed to be saved from her own solitary, drearily conventional habits.

Just once.

She eyed Alistair Gotho's photograph and wondered how it would feel for a man like that to want *her*—brilliant but dull Barbara Warren.

* * *

"Whatever is keeping you?" Mrs. Merlin popped into the living room, then stopped when she saw her goddaughter standing at the fireplace, her trim blue suit still in place. "Why, you haven't even changed your clothes, and the sun is almost overhead."

"No, I haven't," Barbara replied, moving a scant foot from the fireplace.

She sure didn't seem in any hurry. "Well, if you'd rather watch, take off your jacket and come keep me company. Not everyone likes to grub in the ground. Mr. M., that's the second Mr. M., used to say not everyone was born a dirt farmer."

"A wise man, your second husband."

"I guess you could say that. *Lazy* is more the word that comes to my mind, but then, he's gone to greet the goddess, so it's not for me to judge."

Her goddaughter looked a little confused, but Mrs. Merlin didn't feel like launching into an explanation of her view of the order of the universe. The sunshine and breeze were calling her to the best form of communion she'd ever known, better even than the candle magick she so dearly wished she'd been able to perfect.

Barbara slowly slipped off her jacket. She did seem to have a mind of her own, but then Mrs. Merlin wouldn't have expected anything less from her childhood friend's daughter.

At least she was now walking toward the hallway that led past the house's two bedrooms and then through the kitchen to the backyard. Mrs. Merlin followed her reluctant guest, her mind skipping back and forth between the order in which she wanted to plant her circle of herbs and an even more pressing problem—how to liven up her goddaughter.

Outside, Barbara settled primly on the bottom step, her jacket placed over her knees. Mrs. Merlin reclaimed her trowel and glanced from the bed she'd dug earlier back to her goddaughter.

A strand of the young woman's pretty blond pageboy fluttered in the breeze, and she tucked it behind her ear. The same spring breeze had heightened the gentle pink of her cheeks and brought a sparkle to her solemn blue eyes.

Her godchild really was pretty. She just didn't play up her assets. And she had the money to do whatever she wanted. But in her efforts to succeed in business, she sold herself short on personal pleasures. A shame, really, Mrs. Merlin concluded, especially when Rusty and Gallagher, her parents, had been so alive and full of the possibilities of life's adventures.

"So you don't have any special man in your life?" Mrs. Merlin had already asked this question but saw no harm in returning to it. She tended to do that when working through a problem, until she'd settled on solutions in her mind.

Barbara shook her head.

"Sometimes you have to take chances in life." Mrs. Merlin folded her arms across the bib of her apron and mustered an encouraging smile.

Barbara nodded, politely enough, and said, "I've always said if the right man comes along, I'll know him when I meet him, and if that never happens, well, I have my career."

Mrs. Merlin sat back on her knees beside her seedlings of yarrow, penny royal, and cat's claw. She snatched at a mosquito buzzing around her nose. How could the child compare a career to a man? Mrs. Merlin had outlived three husbands and she had a good mind to find herself a fourth. A lock of her orange-and-silver hair fell in front of her eyes, and she puffed a breath to dislodge it.

"Oh, my, it's always something," she muttered, then wondered whether her mentor, Alistair Gotho, would frown on her if she performed a spell to help her godchild. What could it hurt? True, she had promised to leave candle magick to more proficient practitioners, but surely she'd be forgiven just the teeniest bit of meddling, given the good that could come of it. She closed her eyes and envisioned the delightful results of such a magickal assist to her twenty-nine-year-old godchild's loveless love life.

"Mrs. Merlin?" Barbara leaned forward. "Are you okay? You have a funny look on your face."

Mrs. Merlin opened her eyes wide and smiled lovingly. Selecting a different trowel from the assortment scattered beside the herb bed, she said, "Oh, I'm feeling better than I have in months."

"If you're sure," Barbara said, doubt clear in her voice.

Abandoning the trowel, Mrs. Merlin hopped up and slapped her hands together, scattering soil about. Barbara backed up a step, shielding her blue skirt and white blouse with her hands. Stripping off her gardening apron, Mrs. Merlin peered at this godchild she'd met only twice before, and said,

"How long did you say you'll be you in town, dear?"

"One month."

The apron fell to the brick pathway. Mrs. Merlin wondered if perhaps it wouldn't be better to simply ask Alistair to perform the spell. Then she'd still be helping but wouldn't break her promise to him. Absently, she said, "That's right, you explained how you're helping that banker fix his computers."

Barbara nodded.

"I've just remembered a very important errand," Mrs. Merlin said, pausing on the step beside her goddaughter and gazing across her back garden as if seeking guidance from the twining jasmine that rose on the fence behind her herb bed.

Barbara needed a man to rattle her sober little cage—someone to ignite the fire Mrs. Merlin just knew smoldered somewhere beneath that placid surface. She had Rusty's blood, after all.

Alistair himself was single, and quite sexy. But he wouldn't do at all. Mrs. Merlin didn't believe in opposites. They might attract, but they also either combusted or fizzled without the tiniest spark.

But Alistair was the very man to work some magick for Barbara. And he could take her out for coffee, get to know her, make her feel at home.

"Would you like me to go with you?" Her voice was polite, and Mrs. Merlin didn't get the feeling Barbara really wanted to accompany her. Just as well. It was probably best if she met Alistair somewhere other than at the Bayou Magick Shop.

Mrs. Merlin skipped up the steps. "Oh, no, that

won't be necessary. Just stay here and enjoy the day. I won't be long."

Mrs. Merlin whisked down the hallway to her bedroom and donned one of her favorite signature caftans, a deep blue ankle-length robe embroidered with pink and green cabbages. She'd done the needlework herself, right after she'd promised Alistair not to practice any more spells. Why, she had to do something with her hands once she'd given up candle magick.

As pretty as the cabbages were, sewing just didn't give her the same satisfaction as magick. When she thought of the people she'd helped—or tried to help—with her spells, her breast swelled with pride. Of course, there'd been times when those spells had caused a wee bit of trouble, like the time she'd accidentally shrunk herself to six and one-quarter inches.

Washing her hands at the kitchen sink, Mrs. Merlin shook her head at that memory. Thanks to Alistair, everything had come out right in the end, even in that close call!

Barbara was in the front room, her fingers hovering over the keys of her computer, when Mrs. Merlin paused by the front door. She grabbed the keys to her red 1965 Ford Galaxie and waved at Barbara.

In a hurry to put her rescue plan into effect, Mrs. Merlin backed her car out onto the street in front of another driver rude enough to honk at her. But in her motivated state, even that unfriendly gesture didn't ruffle her too much. It sure felt good to have a new person to rescue!

Four

The last thing Lauren Grace Stevens wanted was to be rescued.

Especially by some drop-dead gorgeous guy charging across the Square exactly at the moment she could most use a white knight.

"Perhaps I can be of some assistance?" The towering hunk with a wildly scattered mane of luscious silvery brown hair addressed his question to the two policemen giving her a hard time. To her he scarcely spared a glance.

"Well, if you want to know, you should ask me, not them," Lauren blurted out, running roughshod over the fact that that she had no wish for anyone to intervene on her behalf.

He turned toward her then, a flicker of amusement showing in his eyes.

That did it.

"I certainly don't need anyone's help," she said. "Please move on."

"Honey, if you're a friend of Alistair's, then we might be seeing things differently here," the cop with the potbelly said.

"Bernie, how ya been?" Silver-hair extended a hand and gave the cop a good old boy's handshake.

"He's no friend of mine," Lauren said, knowing even as the words crossed her lips she ought to chomp them back behind her teeth. What was wrong with her? She might be down to her last few dollars, but she wasn't desperate enough to seek lodging in jail, and that was surely where she was headed if these two bullies snapped the cuffs shut on her. And then what would happen to Buster?

"Buy low. Sell high." Her parrot switched from his excited squawking of a few minutes earlier back to his favorite phrase. Poor Buster. She'd risked life and limb to save him from the pound, and if she didn't get out of this scrape, he'd end up there despite her having fled the Plaisance house in such a hurry she'd left behind all the rest of her meager belongings.

"That true, Alistair?" The older man asked the question in a low voice, one hand toying with the key to the cuffs.

At least they hadn't locked them yet. Lauren had been in some bad spots before, but she'd never yet experienced a night in the hoosegow. "Ah, okay," she said, drawling out her words, "he's not my friend, but he is my . . . cousin." She raised her eyes, meeting the stranger's gaze head-on, daring him to deny her words. If he wanted to rescue her, well, darn it, let him do it.

But then she'd be off. She was determined, once and for all, to stay out of scrapes and to learn to live a more normal sort of life. Even her saintly father had warned her before she'd left for New Orleans that he was through bailing her out. But then he'd told her that before.

The man shrugged. "You know how it is, Curt," he said, drilling her with his eyes. "You can pick your friends, but you can't pick your family."

Off came the cuffs from her wrists.

"Well, missy, I don't know what history you've got between you and your cousin here, but he's a good man and well respected. So if you're going to spend much time here in the Quarter, why don't you be sensible and get yourself a license to perform."

Lauren suppressed a strong urge to tell the officer what he could do with his license. Why should anyone have to pay money to walk around on a city street with a bird on her shoulder? But a quick glance at the silver-haired man's expression froze her retort. She contented herself with a nod and kept her lips clamped shut. What with rescuing Buster and dealing with tourists who wanted to pet the parrot, who hated to be touched by strangers, she'd fought enough battles for one morning.

"Thanks, guys," the man called Alistair said, shaking hands with both of the officers. "Drop by the shop, and I'll take care of you."

"Hey, my wife really liked those red candles,"

Bernie said, a smile lighting his pudgy face. "You got any more of those?"

Alistair nodded. "I'll save you one."

The cops walked off, the potbellied one whistling. Lauren wondered what could be so special about a red candle. She studied the man before her, noting the deep-set eyes and the funny way he'd turned what looked like a pretty stuffy dress tie into a headband. His shirt was conventional; his gray slacks definitely on the boring side, as was the blue jacket he carried over his arm. Yet he wore Birkenstock sandals.

But he was also on a first-name basis with the cops.

It didn't compute.

Lauren smiled for the first time since the two policemen had so rudely accosted her.

"It's not funny," the man said. "Those officers were about to take you to Central Lockup. And that's no place for a . . ." He scanned her from head to toe and Lauren, much to her dismay, blushed.

"A what?"

He shook his head. "Never mind. Just be glad they let you go."

"And what? Be grateful to you for rescuing me?" No way was she going to "show" her gratitude to this man. She didn't care if he had the most violet-blue eyes she'd ever seen. She didn't care if he intrigued her with his blend of the dull and the different. She didn't care that he'd saved her from a night, or more, in jail.

She was through being rescued by men, and she was darn sure finished with showing them gratitude in the only currency they seemed to understand.

Alistair saw before him a woman with flowing red hair, sparkly green eyes, and pale skin so flawless and untouched by the sun she couldn't have been a street performer more than a day. He took in the frothy skirt that floated around her calves above strappy sandals and noted silver rings glinting on several of her toes. On one dainty earlobe paraded five studs and one dangling garnet.

But Alistair also read the defensive posture, the hurt of years flaming in her eyes. Her vivid hair accented the angry coloring that had leapt to her cheeks, a brightening that only enhanced her beauty. He admired, not just her appeal as a work of art in human form, but the fact that she hadn't traded on her "feminine wiles" to evade the police.

"I'm not looking for gratitude," he said, his voice gruff on purpose.

"You're not?" She relaxed her stance a trifle.

He shrugged. "What makes you think every guy you meet wants to hop into your pants?" It was crude, but if it took insulting her to make her feel safe, then he'd do what it took. He didn't want her to feel threatened. Why, the universe only knew. What he ought to do was hike back across the Square as fast as his sandals would take him. The lady was trouble.

"Well, I didn't actually consider it in those exact words, but if you're not, there's no need to discuss the subject." She lifted a lumpy paisley carpetbag off the flagstone and held out her hand to the parrot. The bird walked up her arm and took his post on her shoulder. "Thank you for your efforts."

"You're welcome." Alistair could see she was ready for flight. He had to stall her.

Had to?

Are you nuts?

For duty's sake, he assured himself, thinking fast, as she turned away from him and headed for the park in the center of the Square. If this was the woman his brother had been smitten by, didn't he owe Oliver the duty to get to know her, find out something about her? He pictured the bright green feather that had drifted to the floor of the bank's conference room.

The same hue as that of the parrot bobbing away from him.

His feet moved. It wasn't as if he were pursuing her for himself. Thinking of the calmly competent banking consultant, Alistair experienced a flash of relief. No way would he have to spend his life rescuing someone like that. Just as soon as he took care of this capricious beauty, he'd return to the bank, even though it meant slipping that noose of a tie back in place.

He caught up with her by the fountain rimmed with pink petunias.

"Have coffee with me?"

She turned. Her red hair contrasted sharply with the pink of the flowers, but Alistair found himself liking both colors better as a result. Something about this woman made him feel more vivid, too.

"Coffee?" She said the word as if she strongly suspected him of harboring nefarious intentions.

Solemnly, he said, "Only coffee. No gratitude."

She lifted one hand to Buster's tuft, stroked the feathers for a moment, then said, "So why are we standing here? Let's get that coffee."

Automatically, Alistair reached for her lumpy bag. She tugged, then relented. Without comment, he took off.

And the moment she fell into step beside him, Alistair regretted his invitation. He could have left well enough alone, could have let her walk out of his life. Chances were Oliver would never find her again and he'd return to his safer, saner pursuit of women who wore business suits, pumps, and pearls.

For someone who was supposed to possess mysterious insights into the secrets of the universe, he sure could make mistakes when it came to simple human interactions. He picked up his pace, rapidly clearing the flagstones of the Square and heading into the Quarter away from the river. They'd go to CC's on St. Philip. The corner shop had doorways that opened onto the sidewalk. They could sit there and the bird would technically be outside, keeping them safely from violation of any health codes.

Why was he worrying over the bird? Furious at himself for always falling into the role of caretaker, Alistair strode even faster.

"Hey!"

He kept going.

Lauren planted her hands on her hips and called again. "Hey, you!" He slowed, and she added, "You didn't tell me your name." Her words echoed vaguely in her head. Earlier that morning she'd said something similar to the blond fashion plate who'd been gaping at her. Earlier, she'd been mildly curious as to the man's response. At this moment, even though she'd heard the cops call him by name, she wanted to hear his name from his own lips.

At least the question brought him to a halt. He turned, and said, "Ah, I don't know yours, either."

Not the answer she expected, but at least he waited for her, a slight smile playing over his lips.

"Lauren," she said. "And this is Buster." The parrot obliged by extending one claw.

"Alistair."

"No last name?"

"Is Alistair enough for coffee?"

Lauren got the message. The man wasn't interested in her; the offer of refreshment had been made out of politeness. Just as well; she'd get a jolt of caffeine, and the guy would move on out of her life. Fine with her, he was pretty annoying. Bossy, too, and besides, he walked way too fast.

"Let's go," she said, forcing a shuffle step to keep up with his pace. "I'm craving the coffee." To herself, she added, "If not the company." But the sideways glance she stole to study this strangely angry, yet gentle silver-haired giant belied her own disclaimer.

Oliver Gotho lived his life in a manner calculated to bring little or no undue attention his way. He operated quietly, efficiently, and effectively, so quietly, efficiently, and effectively that he often shocked others by his appearance on the scene at exactly the right moment.

For example, his older brother's refusal to enter the banking business might have shocked his father, but not Oliver. The younger of the two Gotho sons had been preparing for years to step into the role their father envisioned for Alistair. During the summers of his college years, he'd worked as a teller, a credit checker, a customer service specialist, and a loan analysis clerk. He'd even learned how to operate the old-fashioned proof machine the bank had used to process the daily work until Oliver had eventually updated the equipment.

All this preparation he'd conducted in his neat, quiet way. Soon after Alistair had refused to do so, Oliver had settled behind the desk in the office of first vice president of First Parish Bank and Trust and the day after his father's funeral, he'd moved into his father's office.

The office of first vice president remained vacant still. In four generations, only a son of the president had occupied that office. But at the rate Oliver was moving in the matrimonial direction, it would be many a year before another Gotho sat in his old chair.

The screech of tires on blacktop and the blare of a horn shook Oliver from his internal world and forced his attention back to his surroundings.

It was the runaway mule that flung him to the ground.

Unable to breathe properly, he lay facedown on the street, the curb a pillow to his chin. The ignoble position reminded him of the folly of leaving the bank in the middle of the day. Had he stayed at his post, rather than venturing into the French Quarter for the second time that day, he'd at least be in one physical piece.

"Is he okay?"

"Somebody get an ambulance."

At those words, Oliver forced himself to raise his head and shoulders. His body wasn't hurt, just his pride. How could he have stepped from the curb without checking in both directions? "I am fine," he said, sitting back on his knees and dusting off the front of his once-fine cashmere jacket.

"Drunken tourist," someone muttered. "Ruining our city."

Oliver shot a glare at the passerby and rose to his feet. As he did, he saw a face he recognized in the small group that had gathered to watch his ignominy.

As he studied her, the old woman edged forward. "Looks like you could use the rest of that reading." The fringed edges of her shawl flapped in the breeze.

Oliver hesitated. Again, he simply was not himself today. Any other day of his life he would have brushed off her suggestion with aplomb. But ever since he'd spotted that auburn-haired sprite in the Square, things had been topsy-turvy. It was as if he'd caught a glimpse of a future so different from his present that the possibility had mesmerized him.

He frowned. *Topsy-turvy* wasn't even a word that normally appeared in his vocabulary. His life had no need for such a term.

It wasn't that he was boring. Or stuffy. He thought of himself as safe. Sane. And true—predictable.

The antithesis of topsy-turvy.

The old woman placed her hand on his elbow. The other curious souls scattered from the scene of the accident. She fixed a pair of dark, fathomless eyes on him, and Oliver sensed her trying to read into his mind.

He shifted and tried to free himself both from her gaze and her grasp. The idea not only made him uncomfortable, but it reminded him too much of his brother and his unusual and often unnerving talents.

"No, thank you," Oliver said at last. "I was actually looking for the woman with the parrot."

"Oh, *her*."

"Yes." The less said the better. Oliver knew the woman probably couldn't do anything so improbable as read his mind, but he saw no reason to take chances. Then he considered the woman. Perhaps it wasn't simply the redheaded beauty who had thrown him off his stride. Perhaps this crone's fortune-telling had rattled him more than he realized.

"Oh, if you want that silly girl, then come on. I'll walk you back. She was watching my things for me when I went to lunch." The fortune-teller started walking, and Oliver fell into step beside her.

They passed the next several blocks in silence. The spires of St. Louis Cathedral loomed larger. Try as he would, he couldn't keep his heart from beating faster. Sunlight gleamed on the statue of Andrew Jackson on horseback that graced the park in the center of the Square. Oliver breathed deeply, appreciating the velvety pink of the petunias planted in the urns inside the four gates of the center park.

It was funny, but that color, and the brisk spring breeze, were things he would have missed completely had he remained where duty demanded, at the helm of the bank.

He picked up his pace, eager to find the woman who'd wrought this change in his life.

"If you had these feet," the fortune-teller said, "you wouldn't race off like a horse heading for the barn."

"Sorry," Oliver murmured, and slowed.

"I guess I can't blame you for being in a hurry," Sister Griswold said. "She's not a bad sort of girl, and she's got one of those faces that makes men do crazy things. But I don't think she'll last long in the Square."

"I thought she said she was a regular."

Sister Griswold snorted. "I've been working this gig for eleven years. Now that's what anyone can call a regular." She tossed her head and her brassy earrings clanged. "She showed up this morning for the very first time, and if it hadn't been for me watching out for her, she'd be done in already."

"Done in?" A lot of people thought the French Quarter was a dangerous place. Oliver didn't agree with that point of view, but he did find it too dirty and noisy for his taste. Crossing the last street before heading into Jackson Square, Oliver skirted a pile of mule droppings.

"You've got to know how to work a mark to make it here." She winked at him.

"And how to charm twenty dollars out of an innocent such as myself?"

She nodded and grinned.

"So do you make up what you tell? Or do you really see things the rest of us don't?"

She wagged a finger at him. "No use trying to worm all my secrets out of me."

Despite himself, Oliver turned his right hand palm up and studied it. He noted lines and creases, some shallow, some so deeply entrenched they seemed to cast shadows. One line ran from the line of his wrist arcing up and around to just below the base of his index finger.

Nowhere did he see anything that would lead him to the message Sister Griswold has voiced to him that morning when she'd said, "In your hands you hold the answer to your dreams."

"If you think about it too hard," the fortune-teller said gently, "you'll just chase away the answer."

"Oh." Feeling foolish, Oliver stuck his hands into the pockets of his paint-splattered trousers.

"Well, there just aren't too many surprises in life anymore," Sister Griswold said, halting her slow forward progress and pointing to the area beside the card table bearing her name. "Some regular. Didn't even last a day." Then she frowned and muttered what Oliver thought sounded a lot like "damn little thief" under her breath.

Oliver scanned the area. No sight of the knockout redhead. "Maybe she's gone to lunch."

Sister Griswold settled herself behind her card table and spread her skirts. She tugged on a sparkly yet slightly dingy purple turban she fished from her handbag. With her practiced shuffle, she flashed the cards in front of Oliver. "If you want to know if she's coming back, I could find out." She laid one card face up on the table in front of her. "Mmm, that's interesting. For twenty dollars, I'll ask the cards."

Oliver shook his head. "Thanks anyway."

"Make your own path in life," she said, and bent her head over three cards she pulled from the middle of the deck.

Almost an hour later, Oliver dropped onto the curved bench inside the park and cradled his head in his hands. He'd asked every juggler, mime, balloon artist, and painter in the Square and not one of them recalled seeing the redhead with the parrot. He'd then resorted to offering Sister Griswold another twenty dollars, the price she demanded to reveal the mystery woman's name, only to remember he had no wallet. So he'd traded his sixty-dollar silk tie.

And then all he'd gotten was a first name.

Lauren.

He tasted the name on his tongue and played the sound of it in his mind.

He had to find her.

There were ways. He could hire someone. He began analyzing what to do first, then stopped as he heard Sister Griswold's voice in his mind. *If you think about it too hard, you'll just chase away the answer.*

That was a funny concept for Oliver to grasp. He spent his life analyzing, thinking hard, dealing in numbers and balance sheets and debits and credits. If he hadn't thought as hard as he had 365 days a year (minus most weekends) First Parish Bank and

Trust would be just another small bank gobbled up by the merger steamroller of the multistate banks.

But today was different.

Oliver rose and stretched his arms over his head, shrugged out of his suit jacket, and tossed it over one shoulder. Perhaps Sister Griswold possessed a kind of knowledge that didn't reveal itself in facts and figures and cost analysis.

If he thought too hard about how to find Lauren, he might never find her at all.

Walking with a surprisingly light step, Oliver strolled back across the Square, heading for the bank. As he walked, he saw things he'd never noticed before. Rather than the litter surrounding the trash can, he saw the bayou scene some enterprising artist had sketched on the side of the city property, cleverly designed to cover the name of the mayor.

Rather than frowns, he saw smiles on the faces of the passersby.

A street-corner juggler smiled at him without accosting him for a donation.

Oliver smiled back. He might be headed back into the Central Business District, but only to collect his car.

Oliver Gotho was about to take the rest of the day off.

Five

One step forward, two steps backward. That morning, Alistair had watched as his life shifted into a new direction, viewing himself almost like a character on a screen. But it had been Alistair Gotho inside the First Parish Bank and Trust. And it had been Alistair Gotho admiring the banking consultant, a woman unlike anyone with whom he'd ever been involved.

Now here he was, rescuing again.

He knew he shouldn't blame the woman skip-hopping along to keep pace with him. *He* was the one who'd stepped in to rescue her from the brave warriors of the Eighth District police. *He* had invited her for coffee of his own volition. And no one else but *he* had insisted when she'd demurred.

"You walk really fast even when you're trying to slow down," she said. A faint whisper of perspiration dotted the fair skin above her wide mouth.

Alistair's hand itched as he pictured himself reaching over and dabbing it away with his thumb. Or better yet, his lips. "Thank you," he said, rather curtly, but then it was his own wayward thoughts he was trying to rein in.

"That wasn't a compliment." She halted and he pulled up.

"I have a pebble in my shoe," she said, a tiny pucker creasing her forehead. She tugged at her sandal, trying to free it. She made a wobbling attempt to keep her balance.

Alistair waited, wishing she wouldn't bend so far forward in her efforts. The skimpy top of her dress was giving him a beautiful shot of cleavage that was making him forget all about how he wasn't getting involved in this woman's troubles. And if she weren't careful, the way she was tugging at that shoe, she'd topple right—

"Whoa!" Alistair caught her by the waist as she tumbled forward. The parrot dropped to the ground in a flutter of wings. For his troubles, Alistair got a jolt of heat flowing through him as his hands spanned her narrow waist. One slight shift of his hands and her breasts would fill his palms.

She quit moving.

He told his hands to remove themselves from her body.

Those fine instruments that had seen him through four winning seasons of college basketball refused to yield their treasure. Instead of letting go, he gave in to the temptation to graze the heavy weight of one breast with one finger. Foolish; he only wanted more.

But given her reluctance to accept the coffee, he counted himself lucky she hadn't slapped him yet. Oh so slowly, he began to let go.

Lauren was close. Too close. She peeked through her lashes and caught a full-on view of Alistair's chin. If she lifted her head, she'd bump smack into it.

Or maybe his mouth.

She nibbled on her lips. Lips. He probably wanted her to do something predictably silly like kiss him. Most men wanted her to kiss them. But she was so tired of doing what most men expected of her. And the reward was so slight. Men were always swooning over her, just like the blond hunk that morning.

Lauren had yet to figure out what all the fuss over sex was about. No matter how excited her partner got, she never knew any particular satisfaction that made it worth all the fuss. Men inevitably said things like, Was it as good for you as it was for me, not really caring what her answer was. Some asked her if she'd come. She always sighed and smiled and said, Oh, yes.

Five years ago, on her birthday, Lauren had sworn off sex. It was all just too much bother. 'Course, she kept her options open, just in case some miracle happened. But Lauren wasn't holding her breath. She figured there was more chance of her finishing her dissertation than there was of her meeting the man who could help her unravel the secrets of sexual satisfaction.

Now she sighed and as she did, she realized just how closely he held her. She opened her mouth to protest, but all she could think of was that she actually, for the most fleeting of seconds, wanted to kiss this man. And not because he expected it, but because she wondered what his lips would feel like tasting her own.

The heat of his hands around her ribs intensified. She caught her breath as a tingling built in her breasts. Staring at his hands, still not daring to look at his face, she watched, fascinated, as her nipples puckered and swelled. Yet his hands didn't seem to be moving at all.

With a sigh of anticipation, she parted her lips and tilted her head for his kiss. Quite impossibly, she wanted to kiss him.

"Hey, get a room!" The booming call of a passerby bounced off her head. Lauren jerked free at the same moment he dropped his hands. Buster reacted in a flapping of wings.

Without a word, Alistair scooped up her shoe, dumped the pebble, and handed it to her. So silent. And so stern. Not at all like a man she'd been about to kiss.

Hmm. She positioned Buster back on her shoulder and walked beside him, fascinated by the almost angry look on the man's face. Why anger? The way he'd held her communicated desire. Frustration maybe? Lauren noted the way his brows drew together over his finely carved nose. Perhaps. Goodness knew she felt a little bit frustrated, and she didn't even like kissing.

Usually.

But she suspected that nothing about the way this man kissed would ever be usual.

He halted abruptly and jerked his thumb toward a table half sticking through a doorway of a corner shop. "CC's okay?"

She nodded. Anywhere with food and drink—and Alistair—was fine with her. He'd make even McDonald's seem fine.

"Sit here, and that bird won't get you in trouble again." He pulled out a chair on the sidewalk side of the table.

"Buster didn't cause the problem," she said, seating herself and letting the bird perch on the back of her chair.

Alistair deposited her bag at her feet. "Oh?" He didn't sound as if he believed her.

"I caused the problem all by myself. Like I always manage to do."

He stepped back. "Don't tell me. Things just happen to you. Complications. Turmoil. Disasters!" His voice rose with each word.

Lauren folded her hands together on top of the table and smiled at him. He caught on fast. Smart. And kissable. A dangerous combination. Her hands danced free of the control she'd tried to exert over them, and she fidgeted with a placard advertising a tour of haunted cemeteries. This man could end up haunting her if she weren't careful.

"I'll get the coffee," he said. "Au lait okay?"

She nodded. She'd learned to like the dark coffee mixed with steamed milk. She practically licked her lips just thinking of the sweet warmth, and suddenly a vision of the hot drink with whipped cream mounded on top filled her mind. "With whipped cream on top?" The request slipped out before she could stop it. But she was so very, very hungry, and the vision had filled her mind instantaneously and forced the words from her mouth. With Lauren, that happened a lot. Think something; say it.

"Whipped cream it is," he said, his expression unreadable.

After he'd moved over to the counter, Lauren lifted her bag onto her lap and searched through it. Somewhere she'd stashed a bag of seeds for Buster. She pulled out a small sketchpad, a book of Shakespeare's sonnets, three hair clips, an empty bottle of spring water, and a wallet.

A wallet?

Lauren stared at the rich chestnut leather. Where had it come from? Casting a glance over her shoulder, she saw Alistair was next in line to order. Fearful, almost as if she'd discover something she'd rather not know, she eased open the wallet. From a Louisiana driver's license, the face of a serious-eyed blond man stared at her.

Not just any man—the man she'd met that morning.

Lauren blinked. She might be troubled, but she'd never experienced a blackout. She couldn't have taken this man's wallet, so how had it gotten into her bag?

"Buy low. Sell high."

"Buster?"

Lauren peered into the wallet's bill compartment and gasped when she counted four one-hundred dollar bills and two fifties.

"No," she said aloud, thinking of the less than ten dollars she had to her name. "No way."

She checked the name and address on the license. Oliver Gotho, 1212 Philip Street. She repeated the address to herself. She'd ask Alistair where it was.

As if thrusting the idea of all that cash from her mind, she pushed the wallet into the bottom of her bag, found the seeds, and offered some to Buster. Softly, she said, "So where did it come from?"

He fixed her with a steady eye and for a fleeting moment, she would have sworn he was trying to tell her something.

"Café au lait with whipped cream." Alistair said, then stared. "What happened to the table?"

Lauren swept the contents of her bag back from where they'd come.

Alistair set a large mug of coffee in front of her. "You carry all that stuff around with you?"

"Sure. Well, maybe right now I have more than usual, what with having to leave ..." Lauren let that sentence finish itself. He'd already seen her about to be arrested. He had reason enough to think her a complete ditz without revealing how she'd fled her former employer's home in order to rescue Buster from the animal shelter pickup crew.

"Having to leave?" Alistair prompted this adorably irritating woman, more curious than he ought to be as to what she'd been about to say. That she was hiding something he was certain. In trouble, quite probable. Unemployed, most definitely.

He set down the other coffee, then moved back to the counter. Anyone as skinny as Lauren who asked for whipped cream on a café au lait was either starving or a sugar-fat junkie. He'd bet on the former. He collected the plate piled with croissants and assorted muffins and wound his way through the other tables.

As he walked, he watched her dip one finger into the cream, pop it into her mouth, and suck. The expression of ecstasy on her face set his pulse racing.

It also set up a beating of desire in him he had no business feeling. Having reached the table, he plopped the plate down and took his seat quickly.

Her eyes widened. She slipped her finger from her mouth and glanced at him half-guiltily. But she didn't reach for any of the food.

Alistair spread two napkins, the first in front of her, then his own. Pointing to the pastries, he said, "Dive in."

"You didn't have to feed me," she said, gazing at the almond croissant like a child counting her presents on Christmas morning.

"I hate to eat alone," he said, slicing open a harvest nut muffin.

She snatched a croissant from the plate and broke off a piece. A flurry of buttery flakes littered the table in front of her. "Is that true? Or did you say that to make me feel better?"

She was quick. Messy, too, he couldn't help but notice. "Actually, I'm quite comfortable alone, so you did catch me on that."

"You spend a lot of time by yourself?" Some nuts from a muffin joined the croissant flakes. Buster eyed the table. Lauren broke off a piece of the bread and handed it to the parrot, who cradled it in his claw, eyeing it rather than eating it.

"Yes, I suppose I do."

"Are you married?"

"No. That's an unusual follow-up question, isn't it?"

She shook her head. "Not necessarily. Do you have a girlfriend?"

"Not at the moment."

She took another bite. He wasn't sure whether she asked another question or not, but then she said, "Trouble."

"Trouble?"

"I imagine girlfriends are a lot of trouble. Always needing you to smush a spider or change a light-bulb or put the angel on the Christmas tree . . ." She trailed off, a wistful expression on her face that both surprised and touched Alistair.

"Is that what boyfriends do?"

"The useful ones." She licked some crumbs off her thumb. "Not that I've ever had one of those. All guys want with me is—"

She cut off her stream of words and gulped her café au lait. When she lowered her cup, a dot of whipped cream accented her nose.

Alistair lifted a hand. Her eyes widened as he reached across the table. Gently, he blotted the cream and turned his hand so she could she what he'd done. "Don't worry," he said in a low voice, "you're safe with me."

"I am?"

To Alistair's mixed relief and annoyance, she sounded disappointed. Oh, no, he wasn't falling for this minx of mishaps with her bag of troubles.

"Yep." He wiped the cream from his finger on his napkin. "I've sworn off slaying dragons and savaging fair maidens."

"Oh." She blushed. Then she fixed him with her deep green eyes. Alistair wished she wouldn't do that. When she looked at him that way, he could almost lose himself.

Almost.

"I haven't met many men who've sworn off sex with women," she said.

Alistair sat up. That wasn't exactly what he'd said and it sure wasn't what he'd meant.

"Maybe sometime," she added, "you could tell me more about that decision. It's something I can relate to."

He was torn between a laugh and a groan. He hadn't meant his statement literally!

She pointed to the last croissant. "Do you mind if I take that with me?"

"All yours." He pushed the plate closer to her. "Are you leaving?"

"Oh, yes, but thank you so much for your hospitality." She fumbled in her bag, peered at something in its mysterious depths, then said, "I have a, um, errand I must do. Can you tell me where 1212 Philip Street is?"

"What's the number?"

"Twelve-twelve."

"Are you sure?"

"Well, I often get my numbers wrong, but yes,

I'm pretty sure." Again she checked inside the bag, then nodded.

Twelve-twelve Philip Street had been in the Gotho family for three generations. Oliver lived there now, on the lower edge of the Garden District, conveniently close to the bank's CBD address.

Why did Lauren want to go there? He narrowed his eyes. No wonder Oliver hadn't been himself. An assignation with this bombshell could rattle the most controlled and rational man.

Oliver must have worked fast that morning. Alistair frowned.

Lauren paused in her wrapping of the croissant. "Did you change your mind? Do you want it?"

Did he want it? Alistair gazed at the woman, not the pastry. "No," he said, shortly. "Don't confuse it with St. Philip here in the Quarter. "Take the streetcar. Get off at First Street and walk back one block. Go toward the river."

She nodded, but looked a little bit confused.

"Just ask the driver," Alistair said, unwilling to help her too much in her rush into his brother's arms. He wasn't going to take her hand and lead her there. Though why the thought bothered him he couldn't quantify. She was nothing but trouble. And he'd sworn off troubling women, even ones as adorably delicious as this one.

He scraped back his chair.

Oliver was welcome to her.

He said a quick good-bye and left her sitting there, still gathering her bag and her bird, and covered the two blocks to his shop in swift strides. He'd had enough of both moving into life's mainstream and of rescuing for one day. Pushing open the door to the Bayou Magick Shop, Alistair inhaled the incense-scented air and let his eyes adjust to the dim interior.

A knot of tourists gazed at the story of Marie Laveau and her voodoo magick framed on one wall of the small shop. Toward the back of the store, an older man stood alone, engrossed in one of the books on candle magick. Alistair had run this business for the past decade and he'd known from the earliest moment which customers came to gawk, and which ones came seeking knowledge—knowledge Alistair had been born with, like it or not.

He relieved his assistant at the register, knowing how Kara hated to be cooped up on a beautiful spring day. With a wave, she ran out for a smoothie. She was good with the customers and fairly dependable, a combination not always easy to find in the employment pool in the French Quarter.

He'd interviewed many more applicants who reminded him of the nutty redhead he'd just left. When he found himself wondering if she'd found her way to the streetcar and what she would do when the driver wouldn't let her take the parrot on board, Alistair shook his head and turned to his next customer.

Let his brother worry about her.

He was ringing up 121 dollars of voodoo dolls and candles for one of the tourists when the belled horse collar on the door jangled. A gust of April wind whipped its way into the shop. Alistair glanced up. Too soon for it to be Kara.

The door stood open, and only the breeze entered. Then, waving like a flag, appeared the vivid robes of the last person Alistair expected—or wanted—to see. He handed the VISA card back to the woman from Cincinnati and bit back a groan. Trust Mrs. Merlin to materialize just when he was meditating on normalizing his life.

"Ooh, Alistair!" Mrs. Merlin called his name so loudly everyone in the shop except for the serious man at the back turned to stare. Not that he could blame them, for Mrs. Merlin wore one of her more outrageous caftans. The wind had formed spikes of her orange-and-silver hair, and, with the dark glasses she had propped on her nose, Mrs. Merlin could well have been a member of a rather radical band.

"Mrs. Merlin," Alistair acknowledged, and waited to see the purpose of her visit. Whither went Mrs. Maebelle Merlin, complications were sure to follow.

"Do let me shut the door," she said, turning to force it shut with a bang. The Sally Mae shopping bag she carried rattled as she advanced on the register. From the bag, she produced a box of pralines, which she presented to him with a flourish. "I was in the neighborhood," she said with a straight face Alistair couldn't help but admire, "and I remembered how you love pralines."

He nodded and rang up one more sale. She eyed the box, then opened it and plucked one piece of the sweet confection and popped it whole into her mouth.

Alistair smiled at the departing group of shoppers, then said in a stern voice, "Mrs. Merlin, are you in trouble?" He refrained from adding "again" to his question, but both of them knew she rarely set foot in the Bayou Magick Shop unless she was indeed in what she called a "bit of a pickle."

Around her mouthful, she said, "No spells. But"— she looked up at him with that gamine expression that had fooled him into helping her more than once before—"that is why I'm here."

Kara returned just then, bearing a take-out cup and smiling. "It's such a beautiful—oh, excuse me," she said, staring at Mrs. Merlin.

Mrs. Merlin returned her look, no doubt taking in the lime green streaks in Kara's purple hair and the three silver nose rings.

Kara swapped places with Alistair behind the register, all the while staring at Mrs. Merlin.

"We'll be in the back," Alistair said.

Mrs. Merlin snatched the box of pralines off the counter and followed him. She paused beside the man who stood reading and stretched around him on her tiptoes to see what book he held.

The man just kept reading.

Mrs. Merlin muttered something under her breath, and followed Alistair into the storeroom that doubled as his office. He dumped a stack of engineering design journals off his chair, and Mrs. Merlin sat down, still clutching the box of pralines.

He leaned against a filing cabinet and folded his arms over his chest. A small sigh must have escaped his lips, because she said, "Don't be sad, dear, I've kept my word not to practice any candle magick. That's why I'm here, to ask you to work a spell for me."

"It's for you?"

The third-to-the-last praline in the box seemed to

take all of Mrs. Merlin's interest. At last, she said, "Not exactly."

Alistair shook his head, then realized she was still studying the box. Gently, he said, "I don't think that would be a good idea."

"It's not meddling," Mrs. Merlin said, "it's helping." She licked her fingers, and said, "There's such a difference between the two."

He couldn't help but grin at that. "The time you turned that attorney into a cat—that was helping or meddling?"

"Helping, of course. And everything turned out just fine. Do you know she and her detective are having a baby? And I ask you, would that have happened if I hadn't been trying to help my friend with that tax problem and simply gotten my magick just a little mixed up?"

Alistair couldn't answer that question.

And Mrs. Merlin knew that.

She looked at him, triumphant.

"Who do you want to help this time?" He uncrossed his arms.

"My goddaughter. She's in town and staying with me. She's a lovely girl, and bright, too. But she's twenty-nine and never been in love."

"You know I don't believe in love spells."

"Piffle!" Mrs. Merlin waved one hand and, with the other, caused the next-to-last praline to disappear into her mouth.

"If it were something else," Alistair said, "perhaps I could help. But not a love spell. Those are always trouble. Love is the most unpredictable, uncontrollable force."

Alistair smiled, and thought of his intentions to get to know Ms. Warren. He pictured her, calm and competent, seated at the conference table. But as he did, her face blurred and wavered and the vision of a green-eyed redhead took over. As his mind filled with Lauren's image, the neat stack of journals toppled to the floor.

A sharp snapping of fingers brought Alistair out of his vision-turned-nightmare. Mrs. Merlin had risen and was leaning toward him, waving a hand. "I don't know where you went, Alistair," she said, "but it wasn't a good place."

"What do you mean?"

"Your aura went from normal to muddy, and then flashed like a neon rainbow."

"Impossible." Alistair stared at her. "I was merely thinking of the improvements I'm making to my life."

Mrs. Merlin sniffed. "What's wrong with your life the way it is?"

"I'm resigning from magick and joining my family's bank."

Mrs. Merlin sat back on the chair with a thump. "In all my living days I never thought I'd hear those words. Why, you'd better do a love spell for yourself. If you found the right woman, you'd never do such a harum-scarum thing."

Alistair shook his head. Mrs. Merlin had it backward.

"And as long as you're at it," she went on, "see if you can't just throw one in for my goddaughter at the same time." She shuffled in her shopping bag and produced a delicate linen handkerchief. "Her name is Barbara, and I borrowed this from her suit-case."

Alistair didn't reach for the token. Instead, he said, "What's wrong with joining the bank?"

Mrs. Merlin cocked her head to one side, obviously giving his question serious consideration. Then she said, "For another man it would be fine. A good, solid, dependable paycheck. But if doing that means turning your back on the gifts the goddess has given you, then it's a bad idea. A very bad idea." She looked at him, then down at the last praline. "Besides, it would be giving up who you are."

"A career doesn't define a man." He heard the stubborn note in his voice.

"Maybe you have a touch of the flu," Mrs. Merlin said, sliding the last praline into her mouth. Talking around it, she said, "I've heard of it going around, despite the spring weather. So don't make any rash decisions. Sleep on it. If you still plan on doing this thing, then why not make the love spell for Barbara your last good deed?" She licked her lips. "Think of it as the price you're paying for turning your back on the goddess."

"Wow, you're tough," Alistair murmured, turning over Mrs. Merlin's words in his mind.

The older woman nodded, seeming quite satisfied with his comment.

"Alistair?" Kara's voice drifted back. "Can you come help me?"

Mulling over Mrs. Merlin's words, Alistair called, "Coming," and headed up front. Over his shoulder, he said, "I'm sorry, but I really can't assist you this time."

Mrs. Merlin dabbed her mouth daintily with the sleeve of her caftan. "Since you can't do the spell, will you at least have lunch with Barbara? She doesn't know anyone else in town."

Twenty-nine and never been in love? Alistair tried not to imagine what this goddaughter must be like. He'd washed his hands of rescuing women, but it was the least he could do. Mrs. Merlin was taking his "no" with such good grace. "Of course," he said, then excused himself to tend to Kara.

Left alone in the storeroom, Mrs. Merlin eyed the floor-to-ceiling shelves. Alistair really ought to check his aura. He was definitely not focused today. Why, leaving Mrs. Merlin in his storeroom was something he would never ordinarily do!

And for good reason, Mrs. Merlin thought, as she snatched a cherry red passion candle from the back of a row. She tucked it down the neck of her caftan, then tossed two green essence-of-life candles into the shopping bag. As she turned to leave the room, she spotted a vial made of smoky blue glass. The container curved in and out, forming a shape similar to a curvaceous female form. The lettering on the front read, "Essence of Infatuation."

The vial joined the candle in her caftan, and Mrs. Merlin whirled around just as Alistair approached from the front of the store.

"It's not that I don't trust you, Mrs. Merlin," he said, "but I'm afraid I'll have to check your bag before you leave."

"Oh, dear," Mrs. Merlin said, holding forth the Sally Mae bag with a penitent sigh. "I'm afraid you've busted me."

Six

$\mathcal{A}$ degree or two of sanity had begun to set in to Oliver's heated mind by the time he returned to his house. After leaving Sister Griswold, he'd been almost back to the parking garage at the bank when he'd decided to leave his car and return on foot to search for the redhead.

He'd walked the streets between Jackson Square and the river, seeking the auburn-haired Lorelei who'd cast her spell on him. The farther away he went from the Quarter along the riverfront, the more the neighborhood deteriorated, and finally his rational mind reared itself and he reversed his direction. At last he headed back to the bank to collect his Volvo from the parking garage and drive the short distance to his house, still determined to take the day off.

The rambling structure on the edge of the Garden

District had been his residence for almost a decade, but he realized as he approached it that he still referred to it as his "house."

Not home.

For the house to become a home, Oliver instinctively knew he would have to share it with a woman who held his heart in her hands.

And that was a woman he'd despaired of ever finding.

Until that morning.

"Buy low. Sell high!"

Oliver was halfway up his front steps when he heard the phrase that set his heart racing. Could it be?

Lost in his thoughts, he hadn't seen the woman curled in one of two white rockers on his porch.

He stumbled and slammed his shin against the top step. A muffled oath escaped his lips, and he grabbed for his injured leg.

"Oh, you poor thing!" The woman of his dreams floated from the rocker to the top of the stairs. Oliver blinked and tried to clear his mind as she knelt beside him. Her hair brushed his thigh, and he groaned.

"You're hurt. Here, sit down." She put her hands on his waist and guided him toward one of the rockers.

"It's nothing." If she left her hands on him another minute, he'd take her in his arms and kiss her right there on the porch. And he knew without a doubt that Miz Columbina, his housekeeper who had been his childhood nurse, was spying on them from behind the front-parlor draperies.

Freeing himself gently, he moved to one of the rockers and pointed to its twin. "Please, have a seat."

She did, tucking her feet under her in the rocker. In a swirl of soft fabric, her floral skirt covered her legs. "I bet you're surprised to see me," she said, talking fast and almost tripping over her words.

He nodded, wondering what miracle had brought her to his house. Too late, he realized he should have said, "Surprised, but pleased." Why was it he could never get the small talk right? He never had that problem in business. He could catalog the personal information he knew about his employees. Marriages, births, graduations, hobbies, vacations— all these Oliver learned of in conversations. Not for him his father's formal style of the boss keeping to himself.

She was rummaging in an oversize bag, done in yet another floral print. "I have it here, or at least I thought I did, but now I can't seem to find it." She furrowed her brow, and Oliver was hit by an overwhelming desire to kiss the tiny line.

"Would you like some lemonade?" He blurted out the words before he could consider just how unsophisticated they sounded.

She glanced up, her eyes shining. "That would be wonderful. I did get awfully thirsty on my way over."

"Did you drive?" Oliver hadn't seen any unfamiliar cars on the street.

"Oh, no, we took the streetcar."

He was in the process of rising, careful to keep his weight off the still-stinging shin. "We?"

"Buster and I."

Oliver stared at her, both astonished and impressed. "They allow birds on the streetcar?"

"Oh, I'm sure they don't, but since I've already had one brush today with the po—" She clamped her lips shut and turned back to her bag shuffling.

Oliver knew as sure as the Mississippi flowed upstream less than a mile from his house that she'd been about to say "police." Yesterday, the idea of becoming involved with a woman who strayed into the path of the law would have been laughable. Looking down at her gleaming auburn hair and her dainty toes peeking out from beneath the folds of her skirt, he couldn't think of one thing wrong with the concept. Whatever had happened, she'd been innocent. He couldn't imagine it otherwise. Of course, he'd never thought that toe rings could be charming, but the ones sparkling on Lauren's toes proved him wrong.

"I'll go see about that lemonade," he said. "Would you like to come inside?"

A shadow seemed to cross her face. Speaking more to the bag in her lap than to him, she said, "It's so lovely today, why don't we sit out here?"

He nodded, wondering whether his rampant passion for her was emblazoned on his face or whether she was just normally cautious. She didn't strike him as the shrinking-violet sort, but he hadn't imagined that look. A sense of protectiveness welled within him. Someone must have hurt her, but he never, ever would.

Just then the front door opened and Miz Columbina popped out, holding forth a loaded tray.

Lauren looked up from her search for Oliver's wallet when the front door opened. A slender black woman with silver-white hair walked out laden with a refreshment tray. Lauren gaped at the woman. "Gosh, did you read his mind?"

"There's nothing that a glass of fresh-squeezed lemonade won't make better." She smiled and cast a slow wink at Oliver. "No matter how good it might be already."

To Lauren's surprise, the man laughed in an embarrassed way. Someone as gorgeous as this hunk, who possessed a house this elegant and wore such expensive clothing, surely had no need to blush at being found with a woman. Why, no doubt Oliver Gotho was a lady's man of the first resort. He'd certainly been obvious enough about his interest in her.

"Thank you, Columbina," Oliver said.

She settled the tray on a low table beside the rockers and stood back, crossing her arms over the crisp white apron she wore over a black dress. "You could have asked your friend in, you know."

"Oh, that's okay," Lauren said, her mouth watering at the sight of the plate of cookies. "He did, but I love being out-of-doors. It's so healthy, the fresh air and all." Jeez, why did she always have to rattle on and on and on. "My name's Lauren."

Oliver filled the two glasses with lemonade. "And this is Miz Columbina. She runs my house and the Gotho family."

The woman smiled at Oliver with what Lauren read as genuine affection. "It must be nice to have someone to take care of everyone," she said.

"It is," Oliver said, offering the plate of cookies to Lauren.

She took one.

"These are Columbina's famous oatmeal cookies," he said, biting into one.

The housekeeper waved one hand nonchalantly. "One of these days you're going to find out I really unpack them from an Archway box," she said with a chuckle. "I'll leave you two, but if you need anything, I'll be right inside."

"Nice to meet you," Lauren said.

The woman smiled and disappeared back into the house.

"She's nice," Lauren said, looking around. "Did you ring a bell?"

He grinned, and she thought how much more relaxed he looked. "Oh, no, she's perfected watching through the window."

Lauren peered around the back of the rocker just in time to see the edge of a drape fall back into place. Rather than bothering her, that knowledge made her feel much more comfortable. She sipped her lemonade.

Oliver seated himself again. "So how did you find me?"

Lauren nibbled on a cookie. That gave her another minute. She'd worried all the way over whether he would think she'd stolen his wallet, then changed her mind in a fit of guilt. But if she'd done that, she certainly wouldn't have had reason to seek him out to return it.

"Your wallet."

"You found my wallet?" He looked really excited. "I lost it today."

She nodded and pointed to her bag. "It was in here, only I have no idea how it got there. You do believe me, don't you?"

He started to nod, then her heart dropped as she read the hesitation on his face. He wanted to believe her, but why had she mentioned the police? "I didn't take it, if that's what you're thinking," she said. "I may cause trouble wherever I go, but I'm as honest as the day is long."

"Of course I don't think you stole it." He blurted the words and rose from his chair, crossing to her.

Before she knew what was happening, he'd taken her glass of lemonade from her and clasped her hands in his. Gazing down at her, he said, "You're too perfect to ever do a thing like that."

"How do you know?" She left her hands in his, but it did feel a little funny. "I mean, you don't even know me."

"You're here, aren't you?"

"Yes."

"Need I say more?" He was looking at her with an intensity that made her nose itch. She always wanted to sneeze when someone wanted to kiss her. It helped ward off a guy.

Only, she realized, she hadn't wanted to sneeze at all when Alistair had held her close.

"Ah-ah-ah-chooh!" There, she'd sneezed. She tugged her hands free and patted at her nose. Oliver pulled a monogrammed handkerchief from his pocket, handed it to her, and backed away a polite step.

Still, he kept on looking at her. His blue eyes had darkened almost to the color of midnight. Lauren made a show of using the handkerchief, then reached over and dumped her bag onto the porch, tucking the hanky out of sight beneath her rocker. If she took it with her, she'd feel duty-bound to launder it and that implied finding Oliver again. Right now, she needed to return the wallet and make her exit.

"You actually carry all of those things around with you?"

Lauren glanced up at Oliver. Rather than repulsed by her magpie collection, as the man she'd had coffee with had been, Oliver seemed fascinated.

"You never know what you might need." Lauren fished out the bag of seeds and fed some to Buster, who'd been surprisingly silent during their visit.

"Women's purses are mysterious things," Oliver murmured.

"It's not exactly a purse," Lauren said. "I just packed in a hurry."

"You're moving?" The curiosity was clear.

Darn. Why had she said that about packing? The less this man knew about her, the better. Lauren instinctively knew he'd pursue her. And the last thing she needed was a man. Well, actually, the closer the day got to evening and she still had no roof over her head, she needed her father to bail her out just this one last time, but after that, she'd stand on her own feet. No more scrapes. 'Course, her dad had sworn that if she went off to New Orleans with Mrs. Plaisance rather than buckling down to finish her dissertation, he'd be blind and deaf to her next appeal for funds. But her dad always bailed her out and had done so ever since her mother's untimely death.

"You could say that," Lauren finally answered. There, under a tube of ocher and a bottle of Cover Girl, she spotted Oliver's wallet. "Here," she said, holding it out to him. "I don't know how it got in my bag, but it's safely back to you now."

"Buy low. Sell high!"

Lauren checked the parrot's expression. Once again, she could swear he was trying to communicate with her. But that was impossible. Wasn't it?

Oliver accepted the wallet and slipped it into his back pocket.

"Aren't you going to check it?"

"That's a very good question," he said slowly, regaining his seat in the matching rocker. "Any other day of my life, I would have verified the contents immediately. I know exactly what I carry in my wallet." He smiled, almost sadly, and added, "I'm a banker, you see."

"Ah," Lauren said, not seeing at all. Her dad was a doctor, and he couldn't even yank a Band-Aid off himself without creating a fuss.

"But today is different." He smiled, not at all sad this time. "You've changed things."

"Me?" Her voice rose. She didn't want to change anyone's life. Why, she couldn't even navigate her own. She held the record at Primalia University for the student who'd gone the most number of years and failed to complete a dissertation in art history, or a dissertation in any other field, for that matter. Things distracted her. Causes. Animals. Friends in need of help. Guys who were all wrong for her. Printed texts that danced before her eyes and sent her off to lie down with a cool cloth draped across her forehead.

She sat up in the rocker, dropping her feet to the floor of the porch. "How can you say I've done anything? I've already reminded you that you don't even know me."

He was shaking his head. "It doesn't matter. It's almost as if I've been bewitched."

"Well, not by me." Lauren started shoveling the contents of her bag back where they belonged. The next thing she knew this man would be declaring his undying love for her and penning sonnets limned with tributes to her red hair and green eyes. Oh, it had happened to her before, and when she was younger and stupider, she'd fallen for it, and always at her expense. "Look, I've got to be going."

"Please, don't rush off." He half rose from his chair. Lifting the plate of cookies, he said, "Have another?"

Lauren scooped up two and wrapped them in one of the paper napkins printed with pink and orange begonias. "Thanks," she said.

"At least let me thank you for returning my wallet," he said, replacing the platter on the table.

She eyed him warily. A reward? Now that she could use. "Well, it's nothing any decent person wouldn't have done."

"But you brought it all the way over here to my house. You could have called me to come get it. My business cards are in my wallet."

Gee. How obvious. Lauren shook her head. She

tended to pick the difficult way to do things. Her school counselors had called it thinking outside the lines, but she really wasn't sure that kind of talk helped her.

"Let me take you to dinner." He looked so eager, so pleased with himself for asking, that Lauren almost said yes.

"We could go to Delmonico's."

Even McDonald's was more than she could afford. Lauren hesitated, but the anticipation on his face scared her. First there would be dinner, then drinks, then he'd invite her back to his house, then . . .

"Thank you, but I really have to go." She turned, lifted Buster onto her shoulder, and held out her hand. "It's very kind of you, but there's no need to reward me. Please thank Miss Columbina and tell her the cookies are fabulous." She rescued her hand from his grasp and tried not to meet his eyes. Given an inch, he'd try again. Men always did.

"Can I call you?"

She was down the steps and halfway to the front gate when he called out the question. "Sure," she shot back over her shoulder. "I'm in the book."

Not waiting till the streetcar carried her back to the French Quarter, Lauren jumped off across from a Wendy's and raced over to the outdoor pay phone. She opened her carryall and let Buster sidle out as she lifted the receiver.

Lauren called collect, as she always did.

She'd just walked away from not only a free dinner, but from what she knew was a meal ticket to a life as easy as she could imagine. Oliver was clearly smitten with her, and he wasn't a bad sort of man at all, but she'd known she had to get away in order to be free.

Her dad had to be home. He ran the night shift at the emergency room, so the afternoons were always the best time to find him in.

The phone rang and rang, and finally the operator broke in to advise her to try her call again later. Lauren gripped the black-plastic handset even more tightly, feeling as if there were no such thing as later for her. She had no money and nowhere to go.

Reluctantly, she returned the phone to the cradle. She still had ten dollars. She could go into the fast-food restaurant, buy a soda, and wait to try again. The sunshine of the afternoon had waned far more quickly than she'd realized as she'd whiled away the time on Oliver's comfortable front porch and a rather seedy-looking group of guys had gathered at the phone booth next to where she stood.

She walked slowly toward Wendy's, coaxing Buster back into her bag, and pushed open the door. She'd order a Coke and nibble on Miss Columbina's oatmeal cookies.

Mrs. Merlin did not understand what she was asking of him, that much was clear. Alistair sank into his favorite chair in his spacious apartment above the Bayou Magick Shop and propped his feet on a hassock.

Love spells were nothing but trouble.

Unbidden, the image of the redhead he'd rescued from Bernie and Curt swam into his mind. Nothing but trouble. In all the years he'd been practicing candle magick, he'd never once performed a love spell. And finding the perfect match for another person was an almost impossible task. Alistair often marveled when he met men and women who'd managed to achieve such an accomplishment. And magick, more than any other quality, in his opinion, had less to do with this achievement than sheer luck and stick-to-itiveness.

Take his parents, for example. They'd been married, happily, Alistair would have sworn, for thirty-five plus years when his father had passed away. Yet, here was Mrs. Walling, who had obviously been in love with his father. And Alistair believed in his gut now that those feelings hadn't been one-sided, no matter how perfect his parents' relationship had seemed.

"Go figure," he muttered, and reached for his television remote control. A couple hours of sports would annihilate all these thoughts from his mind. But the irony that on the very day he'd decided to rejoin the mainstream of humanity, Mrs. Merlin had blown in, intent on destroying his path to normalcy, did not escape him.

He could simply ignore her.

True.

He'd done so before.

But it was the question she'd raised that he couldn't let go of.

Was there such a thing as a perfect match love spell?

And if so, could he conjure it? And not, he admitted somewhat guiltily, only for her goddaughter, but for himself as well. And, thinking to escape the sin of greed, he added his brother to the picture, too. If he were to perform such a spell, perhaps doing it for someone else would salve the karmic price of asking the outcome for himself.

Because there was a price.

What many people failed to realize was that tinkering with the natural and random order of the universe always carried a price. He'd been fortunate in his magickal practices; he'd normally intervened only when someone had been in dire need. He hadn't asked to be born with the gifts of the unknown and unknowable. When he had at last, after a raucous four years of college at LSU, come to grips with the fact that his powers weren't going to go away, even if induced to do so by an alcoholic haze, he'd reluctantly accepted the gifts.

Reluctantly.

True, he made a lot of money off his Bayou Magick Shop, but he'd inherited the business from his mentor, a wise old man who'd possessed more knowledge of magick than Alistair could have ever garnered. And truly, Alistair had earned most of his considerable wealth from his inventions of a technical, engineering nature. He loved puzzles, and he prospered from them.

But he was determined, as he neared what felt like a major threshold in his life, to join the bank, turn his back on his youthful frolics, and reach out to others who flourished in the mainstream of life.

He yearned, he acknowledged, for a more normal existence.

And the banking consultant represented that possibility to him. Even though he'd met her only briefly, Alistair had glimpsed in her a measure of stability he coveted.

He rose from his chair and walked across the length of his front parlor. He had only to turn the knob, open the door, and descend the stairs. Two floors below him lay the pieces of the perfect match spell.

Almost as if in slow motion, he lifted his hand. He grasped the antique brass knob and, staring at his hand, he turned it.

As he did, the telephone shrilled.

Alistair stared from his hand to some point over his shoulder. The sensing part of his inner self called out that he should heed the interruption and answer the phone.

The part that desperately sought the answers to the questions he could only half articulate in his life bade him to ignore the ringing of the bell.

Seven

*L*auren waited inside the fast-food restaurant for as long as Buster would keep still and quiet within the confines of her carryall. Almost an hour after she'd drained her Coke and crunched the last remaining pellet of ice, she hoisted her bag, propped open for Buster to breathe, and ventured back out to the phone booth.

It wasn't even a real booth, the kind where she could shut the door against the world. Only the scarred Plexiglas shields surrounding the telephone box stood between her and the passing cars and loitering men, several of whom looked in dire need of a drug fix.

Please be home.

"Dr. Stevens."

At the sound of her father's voice, Lauren almost sobbed with relief. But she had to be calm, had to make him think nothing was amiss with her life. "Hi, Daddy," she said, "It's me."

"Lauren, how are you?"

The words were familiar, but something in her father's cadence and tone unnerved her. She'd never heard him speak to her—his baby—in such a formal tone.

"I'm fine," she said, far more brightly than she felt or had intended to indicate.

"And where are you these days?"

Lauren kicked her toe against the pedestal of the phone. What was wrong with her dad? He knew where she was. "New Orleans."

"Ah, yes," he said. "And how is Mrs. Plaisance?"

That question took her by surprise. Why pretend he didn't know where she was and then remember her employer's name? Her *deceased* employer. At that thought, all her defenses crumpled. "Oh, Daddy, she's dead! And I had to run out of the house and leave all my painting things and my notes and research and I don't have any—"

"Lauren, stop."

"What?" She caught her words even as she tried to catch her breath. She couldn't remember her father ever speaking to her so abruptly.

"Do you remember the discussion we had after you met Mrs. Plaisance at the Art Institute and decided to go to New Orleans?"

She nodded, a sniffle escaping from her.

"I'll take that as a yes." He said it gently, but every hair on Lauren's arms stood at attention. Something terrible was about to happen.

"This is probably harder on me than it is on you,

but I've been in counseling, and I've come to accept that you have to take control of your own life on your own terms." He spoke pretty fast, almost as if he had to get out the whole terrible thing before she could interrupt him.

Lauren tried, opening her mouth to shout, "Stop it!" But no sound came out.

Her father kept on talking. "I told you when you left for New Orleans that that was the last time I'd be here to rescue you. You've been running away from responsibility for your life and until you take the reins, well"—his voice broke—"there's no more I can do. I'm only hurting by helping you."

Hurting her? Lauren glanced at a scary guy with a scar on his cheek waiting none too patiently for the phone. She had managed to get as far as the dissertation part of her doctoral degree, but she felt no compulsion to complete it. Why did it matter so much to her dad to have a Ph.D. for a daughter? He'd never answered that question, not to her satisfaction, anyway.

"I don't need a lot of help," she said, finding her voice at last. "I just need some cash to tide me over till I can get a job."

"Lauren, we've talked this over—"

"What do you mean 'we'?"

A long silence followed.

Behind her, the uptown-bound streetcar rumbled by. Lauren wished herself on it, wished herself anywhere but where she stood, both physically and in her misbegotten life.

"Mrs. Bristol and I. That's who I mean by *we*. She's become very important in my life."

"Your *therapist*?" Lauren's voice screeched almost as harshly as Buster in a bad moment. The parrot even lifted his head from the depths of her carryall and fixed her with a questioning eye.

A rustle and murmur sounded in the near background, as if her father were talking to someone else. Lauren strained to hear, but with the din of the traffic behind her and scarface, who'd started strolling back and forth beside her booth and snapping his fingers, she couldn't make out any more.

"Actually, Mrs. Bristol hasn't been my therapist for well over a year. She's much more than my therapist. This is probably not the best time to tell you this, but Bonita has agreed to become my wife."

Lauren dropped the receiver. She didn't even try to catch it as it banged against the metal pole holding up the booth.

Marry Mrs. Bristol! Lauren's mother had died when Lauren was thirteen, but she could still remember her soft brown hair and loving smile. No one could take her mother's place. Especially not some scheming counselor who called herself a therapist and undoubtedly only wanted to keep her father's money safe for her to spend. Even as she thought those horrid things, she realized how unfair she was being. Her father deserved someone in his life. But why now?

From the dangling receiver, her father's voice called to her in a tinny, echoing way. She heard him repeating her name as she grabbed her carryall and backed away from the booth. The loitering man leered at her, and said something she couldn't understand, but she figured that was just as well.

Crossing the tarmac lot of the fast-food place as quickly as she could, she made her way to the other side of St. Charles Avenue. Grasping the pole of the streetcar stop sign with both hands, she tried to catch her breath. Her father's news had been a body blow to her.

It wasn't that she begrudged him happiness. But in the past sixteen years, he'd never remarried. His life had revolved around her, his only child, and the hospital. Her dad was a great doctor, and the whole town of Arbordale admired him. He deserved all things that were good. But what was going to happen to her now?

A metallic shriek drew her attention. Two blocks away, the streetcar halted to pick up and discharge passengers. Lauren rummaged in one of her skirt pockets for the fare, then stilled her hand. From her bag, Buster croaked, "Buy low. Sell high."

What was she going to do?

Where was she going to go?

Where would she sleep?

"Oh my goodness," she said aloud. What had she done to herself? She should have at least stayed on the line, congratulated her dad, cajoled him into sending her money one "last" time. She'd done that before more times than she could count. It wasn't her fault things always got screwy, that she couldn't keep a job. She tried. She really did, and once she finished her dissertation, she'd find a nice teaching post and stay out of trouble, once and for all.

The streetcar stopped in front of her. The doors slid open, and the driver glanced her way. Slowly, she shook her head. She needed every dollar she had. It wasn't dark yet. She'd walk back to the Quarter.

In the end, Alistair had answered the phone.

And now, two hours later, on his knees in one of the two slave quarter apartments tucked in the courtyard behind his shop, surrounded by a clutter of candles, lamp oil, tissue paper, and packing noodles, he was glad he had.

Oliver needed him.

Oliver needed help.

Perhaps those two were one and the same. Alistair wasn't sure about that truth quite yet, but he'd known his brother needed him to be there for him. And despite some of their differences over the years, and his practical brother's skepticism over Alistair's alternative gifts, the blood ran strong.

Oliver had raved for fifteen minutes about letting the woman of his dreams walk away, and how he had to find her. All he'd done was serve her lemonade and ask her to dinner, and she'd taken off like a bullet shot from a .22. His brother's voice rang in his head still.

"Dinner, Alistair! It's not as if I asked her to spend the night with me. I simply offered to buy her a meal for returning my wallet."

Alistair paused in his sorting and packing and considered his brother's rather naive statement. Oliver wasn't a hard-core womanizer, but if he could get a pretty woman in bed, he wasn't one to turn down the opportunity. Given what Lauren had told him en route to coffee about her celibate state, all her sensors must have been on alert. Small wonder she hadn't accepted his brother's invitation.

Lauren knew how the game was played, knew that for guys like Oliver dinner was an opening gambit.

And what about guys like you, Alistair? Lauren's allure was palpable, yet he'd walked away and left her sitting there at CC's.

From a group of four candles, Alistair lifted a luminous pillar candle that shifted from cherry red to deep violet in the play of the lamplight. Cherry red was the magickal color of passion; violet symbolized the enduring spirit of the soul.

Admiring the candle, he tried to put his conversation with Oliver to rest. Before getting off the phone with his brother, he had assured him that if he was meant to find the mysterious redheaded Lauren, he would. Then he'd walked downstairs, through the shop where Kara was closing for the night, and let himself into the apartment.

The building dated from the early 1800s, constructed in an era when the slave quarters had been used for the purpose their name implied. Now Alistair kept one apartment for friends who wanted to stay either long- or short-term in the playground of New Orleans. At present the plumber had done a good job of rendering that one unusable. The other apartment he used as a retreat for his magickal undertakings.

The rooms were outfitted for occupancy, but at present much of the floor space was covered in the tools of his magick. He'd been at work off and on for several weeks, sorting items to dispose of, sell, or give away.

On a low table in front of the room's daybed sat the items Alistair had once used when called to perform a spell. He'd last burned the powerful candles almost six months ago, and he'd begun to feel with the passing of time that his gift had begun to fade.

Or perhaps he faced a crossroads. Either he delved further into magick or rejoined the rest of the world. He didn't think he could continue to live with one foot in each of the realities. But given that he'd agreed to help his brother, that choice would have to wait for another day.

Any spell wrought by candle magick required the construction of a special altar. Alistair had always used the low table for this purpose, changing the pieces displayed on the tabletop as the spell dictated.

An altar also required compass points to mark the four ends of the earth. Where earth ended and spirit took over gave life to the magick Alistair was able to summon, and he always paid special attention to the items he used to commemorate the four points of the compass.

Still on his knees amidst the clusters of tissue paper and packing materials, Alistair closed his eyes and sought an image to lead him to the vision of love in all its perfection.

He'd loved many women in his life, always finding the best in every one. But so far, no one had returned his feelings as deeply as he knew he needed.

To Alistair, love consisted of mind and heart and

sex and soul. Opening his eyes, he reached, unbidden, toward the velvet-lined box of mementos he'd gathered for altar building. His fingers closed around two pieces that lay in the front of the box beneath the altar.

A silver pin in the shape of a question mark represented the mind.

A rose-colored stone in the shape of a heart joined the question mark.

Mind and heart, he breathed to himself.

For sex—his mind wavered. His fingers had touched a test tube, and, with a smile, Alistair placed it on the east compass point. Sexual chemistry, how fitting.

For soul, he lifted his hands to his head and plucked out one long strand of silver hair. Curling it into a circle, he added it to the altar. He and Oliver were the same blood, and to represent soul, the object needed to possess life force.

Within the circle of the compass points, Alistair placed the four cherry-violet candles.

Normally he performed a spell with a single candle, but for a perfect match love spell, the extra numbers called out to him.

He couldn't say why, but if forced to the point, he'd have to admit that he knew in his heart this spell wasn't just for his brother or for Mrs. Merlin's mysterious goddaughter.

This spell was for him.

Egoism.

The hairs on his forearms lifted, and Alistair drew back from the altar. He could not perform this spell unless he could approach the altar with a pure heart.

Perhaps he should remove all but one candle and intercede for Oliver alone. He did so, then paused.

He rocked back on his heels and stared at the altar he'd built.

He didn't move for a very long time, and when he did, his feet tingled and his ankles creaked. He rose, more slowly than a man in his prime physical shape should move, and backed from the room.

Tomorrow he'd dismantle the altar and pack up the rest of his supplies. He'd let the broker list his shop for sale. He'd call Mrs. Merlin's goddaughter and take her out for coffee.

And then, all his chores completed, he'd be ready to get on with his life.

The steadier, saner life of banking—and a prim and proper blond-haired, blue-eyed consultant—beckoned to him.

If only.

Lauren's shoulders sagged from the physical burden of carrying her heavy bag, and her spirits drooped even more with each repetition of that terrible phrase.

If only Buster hadn't gotten them kicked out of the hotel lobby where she'd tucked herself away. In a dark corner, sheltered by the high back of a Queen Anne chair and a shading palm, Lauren had held high hopes of spending the night.

But at precisely 2:00 A.M., Buster had demanded she buy low and sell high. And the night manager had demanded they both depart his premises.

If only . . .

Lauren had kept to Bourbon Street, the best lit of the French Quarter streets, but as the hour grew later, the people lurching about in the street closed to traffic made her rethink her strategy. She'd just passed a hotel and was considering trying yet another lobby when the wink of a flame on an upper balcony caught her eye.

At least there was another person around, perhaps someone who would call the police if anyone accosted her. She caught a whiff of cigar smoke and decided to rest for a few minutes.

This block was less raucous, with businesses outnumbering the bars. She set her bag down for a moment and fed one of the last seeds to Buster. He took it, held it in his claw, then cracked it open. The noise sounded as loud as a rifle shot to Lauren's nervous ears.

If only, she thought, sinking down in a crouch to stretch her lower back, she hadn't rushed out of the Plaisance house. The family surely would have paid her the last month's wages she was due. And she probably could have talked them out of calling the animal shelter by simply offering to care for the bird herself.

She sighed and reached for the last of Miss Columbina's oatmeal cookies. Thank goodness for the two snacks she'd had, courtesy of the two men she'd met that morning.

Such different men, too. Lauren's mind started to drift, and then she jerked it back. This was no time to get distracted. She had to survive the night. To-morrow, she'd get a job.

Getting a job was never a problem for her.

Keeping one was.

She sighed, and thought of the dinner she could have had with Oliver Gotho. She'd passed by Del-monico's on the streetcar ride to his house and trudged past it on her walk back to the Quarter. Judging by the stuffy look to the place, and the snap-to-it attitude of the valets, she knew the ex-perience would have been a culinary delight. New Orleanians took their food seriously.

Thinking of Oliver Gotho started a new train of thought in her mind. She was like that, always jumping from one thought to another. That was one of the reasons her dad always wanted her to settle down and focus on the task at hand.

Help, why, he ought to seek help. Marrying Mrs. Bristol!

Lauren quit chewing her cookie, the thought of losing her father too much to bear.

And suddenly she knew what she had to do.

She had to marry, too.

Eight

$\mathcal{A}$listair enjoyed a good cigar, especially when he experienced mild insomnia. He never smoked for long, but the ritual of the preparation pleased him and served to still his mind and ready him for sleep.

Quite often, he'd wake in the early-morning hours and stroll from his bedroom, arranged in the back of the third-floor apartment to spare him the rowdy street noise, through to the front, and raise the sliding door/window that opened onto the street-facing balcony.

There, perched above his city, he'd settle into the swing and savor the quiet time with a cigar.

Tonight he'd slept three hours, then awakened, his mind alert. Gone was the restlessness he'd experienced earlier in the evening. He felt ready, but for what he couldn't say.

Cigar and lighter in hand, he looked across the

balcony and said aloud, "Okay, life, show me what's out there waiting for me." Then he put the flame to the end of the cigar.

A short time later, a faint pop, much like a cracking sound, disturbed the street below.

Aware of the dangers of late-night crime, Alistair leaned forward and peered past the baskets of petunias and ferns his housekeeper kept in beautiful bloom and condition.

As he did, he felt a soft brushing of fur against his calves and knew his cat, Midnight, had come to join him in his nocturnal smoke break.

At first he saw nothing to catch his attention, certainly no evidence of anyone in trouble.

And then, as his eyes sharpened, he made out the shape of a woman crouched on the sidewalk, half propped against the storefront opposite to the Bayou Magick Shop.

"Tell me it's not so," he breathed.

Midnight's damp nose nudged Alistair's left ankle as Alistair stared at the woman.

Long hair spilled over her shoulders. She sat forward, as if stretching her back as she crouched. The parrot perched at her feet.

In the light of the streetlamp, she was mostly in shadow, but Alistair knew beyond any doubt, that the quirky, undeniably pretty, but most definitely pesky Lauren of-no-last-name had crossed his path again.

What had he said to his brother? *If she's meant to be in your life, she'll show up again without you having to search for her.* Well, perhaps his brother was right to be smitten by her.

But God help him, Alistair thought, reflecting on the havoc she wrought in such small fragments of time. Just remembering all the junk she'd dumped onto the table at the coffeehouse made him shudder. Alistair had never thought of himself as particularly fastidious, but he did appreciate a sense of order. He certainly didn't thrive on chaos, at least not the type Lauren seemed to accept as customary.

He watched as she reached into that suitcase she called a purse and popped something into her mouth.

Poor child. She must be starving. And bone-weary, judging by the way she leaned forward, stretching her arms in front of her, then reaching back with one hand to rub her lower back.

Poor child? "Oh, no," Alistair said, once again talking out loud to himself. Don't start thinking that way.

Midnight lifted his nose to the faint breeze, all that was left of the brisk winds of the day before. His whiskers quivered, and he mewed expectantly.

"No parrot steak for you, fella," Alistair said, and sat back on the swing, forcing himself to gaze at the glowing tip of his cigar rather than down to the street below.

Was she out there alone? No one else had been in sight.

He took a long slow swallow of the pungent smoke, but the effect wasn't nearly as satisfying as it had been a few minutes earlier. How could he sit there fat, happy, and content, knowing a woman as prone to trouble as that redhead was alone and friendless—except for the bird—on Bourbon Street at three in the morning?

Not to mention that his brother would wring his neck if he found out he let her slip away.

Midnight had already headed inside. As usual his cat, the empathic feline with the silver eyes he'd found in a trash can and nursed to health from kittenhood, was one step ahead.

Alistair tamped his cigar in the ashtray and replaced it in the case he kept handy. He rationed his smokes, making one cigar last quite a few evenings. While slipping into his Birkenstock sandals, he drew a faded LSU T-shirt over his head and padded downstairs. To his cat's disgust, he left Midnight inside. As Alistair headed down the passageway that ran from the courtyard beneath his apartment toward the street, he heard Midnight loudly expressing his opinion at being left out of the fun.

He unlocked the door, then stepped outside, careful to lock the door behind him with the single key he carried. Alistair enjoyed the bohemian freedom offered by the French Quarter's easy-come easy-go attitude, but he was realistic about the need for security. As he'd been to known to say more than once, the universe helped those who saw to the details themselves.

When he walked out onto the street, Lauren had disappeared.

Alistair checked left and right and then paused, smiling faintly as he considered the resemblance between himself and Midnight sniffing the breeze for a scent. Maybe he should have let his cat come out to assist him.

He paced to the quieter end of the street, away from the rowdier bar scene that ruled in the other direction. Checking the side streets, he saw no sign of a woman and a parrot. Yet in the brief time it had taken him to throw on his T-shirt and sandals, she couldn't have gotten far.

Perhaps she'd opted for the safety of numbers and gone toward the activity in the opposite direction. Alistair reversed and moved up the street.

He moved quickly, driven by a sense of urgency, alerted to a danger he didn't quite understand. But Alistair knew his instincts were usually accurate, and for that reason, he knew he had to find her, and find her quickly.

So focused was he on his search that he looked only in front of him and never once behind him. At the end of his block, he checked both directions at the cross street, but though there were other people, he saw no sign of Lauren. He halted to consider the situation.

"Don't move or I'll blow you away."

Alistair froze. He'd always figured that was pretty much a cliché, but once he heard those words, he didn't even blink.

The voice came from behind him.

He'd been looking for danger ahead, never once watching his back.

The thought caused him to shake his head at his own folly.

"I said don't move!"

"You got it," Alistair said.

"Shut up and give me your wallet."

Now that presented a problem. Alistair had left

his apartment with only the single key he carried when he went jogging. No identification, no money.

"You're welcome to pat me down," he said slowly, "and you'll see I don't have one."

"An old man like you, you've got to have some flash."

Alistair smiled to himself. It must be his gray hair that had caused his assailant to think he was old. Perhaps that could help him. The thug wouldn't be expecting someone of Alistair's strength to whip around and kick the gun from his hand. 'Course right then that gun was too firmly wedged in the back of his ribs to tempt Alistair into any heroics.

"No flash, no cash."

The gun didn't budge, but Alistair felt one hand move roughly against his back and the sides of his hips. The single key to his place was tucked in a tiny pocket in the front waistband of his running shorts, and the robber didn't even check there.

"Man, how come you don't have any money? I go to all this trouble, and you got nothing to give me."

"Sorry," Alistair said.

"Shut up and give me your shoes."

Alistair started to step out of his Birkenstocks.

"Whoa, you call them shoes?"

The disgust in his assailant's voice concerned Alistair. He found himself wishing he'd worn his two-hundred-dollar basketball shoes. With those he could have bargained his way out of this predicament. He smiled briefly, thinking this was exactly the sort of situation Mrs. Merlin would refer to as a "pickle."

That thought cleared his mind. As Mrs. Merlin liked to say, there was always some solution made for every pickle. If nothing else, some of the people farther down the block would surely stroll his way, and that would scare the thug away.

"Turn around with your hands up," the man behind him ordered.

More slowly than he could remember ever moving, Alistair inched around. Given one clear opportunity, he'd have the guy's gun.

The gun was pointed straight between Alistair's eyes. "I don't like your shoes, and I don't like you."

"Oh migod, look at those sandals!" A female voice, ending in a sound between a giggle and a shriek, accosted Alistair's ears. "I've been looking everywhere for a pair of those."

The gunman swung toward the woman who'd materialized beside them. "Shut up," he said, "and raise your hands."

Alistair stared at the redhead who'd appeared out of nowhere. Lauren. He tried shaking his head and glaring at her to get her to shut up.

"I'll pay you for those shoes," she was rattling on, her hands clutching the straps of the bag draped over her shoulder. "I've been trying to find a pair for my dad, and I know they're worth at least two hundred dollars."

"Those things? Are you crazy, lady?" The assailant let his gun drop slightly, but it remained pointed at Lauren, who just couldn't seem to stop talking.

"They happen to be Italian," she said.

The man sniffed. "Wop shoes."

"Say what you will, but they're definitely worth stealing. Why, if you don't want them, I'm going to buy them from this guy."

"Says who?"

The nutty redhead said, "Go ahead and steal them, and I'll buy them from you." She lowered her bag to the ground and bent toward it.

"Hey, get up!" The man jerked the gun nervously.

Alistair rolled onto the balls of his feet. If he could just catch the guy off guard and if he would just take the gun off Lauren, he could make his move. But Alistair couldn't risk him shooting Lauren.

She'd opened the top of the bag. Alistair saw the feathered top of Buster's head and groaned to himself. Now he had the bird at risk, too, and somehow he knew that creature ranked high enough with Lauren that if he got it caught in any cross fire, there'd be hell to pay.

Voices grew closer from down the street.

The man pointed with his gun to the sandals. "Give me the shoes—and the bag."

"There's no need to be greedy." Lauren put her hands on her hips. "I offered to pay you for the shoes."

This time Alistair groaned out loud.

"Who you calling greedy?" Indignant, the robber lowered the gun to a point between Alistair and Lauren. Lauren moved her foot, wedging the bag open a bit more.

The gunman lowered his body toward the bag. When he did, Buster leapt at him in a flutter of wings and a flash of swinging beak.

Alistair leapt at the man and chopped at the

man's wrist. The gun clattered to the ground.

"Motherf—" the robber screamed, shielding his face and trying to run.

Alistair toppled him easily to the ground and pinned his arms behind him.

"Not bad for an old man," he said.

"I'm blinded!" the robber said. "I'm gonna sue you."

Alistair shook his head and turned to check on Lauren.

She was standing stock-still, staring from him and the downed assailant back to Buster. Suddenly, she started to scream.

And the woman who'd cleverly and calmly rescued him from what could have been death by gunshot didn't stop screaming until the police arrived ten minutes later.

Several hours later, Lauren followed Alistair through the passageway next to the shop he said he managed. He'd been such a rock of comfort during the ordeal of the aftermath of the holdup, sticking by her side at the police station, disappearing only once to return with a slice of gooey cheese and pepperoni pizza from some mysterious late-night source.

He was the one who'd been mugged, and technically she should have been comforting him, but somehow he'd turned those tables on her. He called her his hero and said she'd been so brave and clever she deserved to fall apart.

That praise warmed Lauren's heart, and when

he'd offered her a place to crash, she'd not hesitated to accept his invitation.

At the foot of an outdoor staircase at the front of an interior courtyard, Alistair halted. "Want a snack before you sleep?"

Lauren felt her face perk up. "It is almost time for breakfast."

"Buy low. Sell high." Riding on her shoulder, Buster preened.

"I think the winged hero is hungry, too," Alistair said, glancing at the bird.

Lauren liked the smile she saw on his face. She'd thought him a real grouch earlier in the day—was that only yesterday? But he was starting to grow on her. His silky long hair had long ago slipped free of the casual ponytail, and she liked the way it flowed over his shoulders. She'd never known any guys with long hair, and Alistair's fairly fascinated her.

He pointed up the stairs. "Come on up and I'll make us an omelet. Then I'll bring you back down here. There's a spare apartment where you can crash."

"Thanks," Lauren said, still appreciating his hair as she walked behind him up the stairs. "This is a big place. Is it all yours?"

He didn't answer right away, and when he did, he said, "Oh, I guess you could call me the caretaker."

"Well, whoever owns this must be rich."

"Why do you say that?"

"It's so big, and I know property in the Quarter is expensive."

He nodded, and she watched the back of his head and the power in his broad shoulders and the way his muscled legs propelled him effortlessly up the stairs and forgot all about the size of the building and its commercial value.

In the back of her mind she remembered that she'd decided earlier that night she had to marry, and of course that meant marrying someone with enough money to take care of her when she found herself unable to do so. It was too bad Alistair was only the caretaker; when he wasn't grouching at her, he was nice. Plus he'd sworn off women, so he wouldn't be trying to jump her body.

Lauren sighed. Somehow that last thought wasn't the consolation she'd expected it to be.

Alistair unlocked a door at the top of the stairs. "*Mi casa es su casa*," he said, beckoning her in.

Nine

Later, much later, Alistair attributed his behavior to the relief of being alive after the confrontation with the armed robber.

Certainly when he'd crossed the threshold of his apartment he'd had no intention of seducing Lauren.

"So what do you like in your omelets?" He flicked on a lamp in the front room.

His rescuer-guest glanced around the room rather than responding. She seemed to approve of the casual pairing of art deco and French Empire, the latter donated after one of his mother's redecorating spurts. Alistair found it a bit jarring, but as one of the items included the perfect thinking chair and footstool, he'd taken the lot off his mother's hands.

Finally, still clinging to her carryall, she said, "What do you have?"

"Come on back, and I'll check." He took the heavy bag from her and set it beside a love seat covered in striped satin. He'd been meaning to get rid of that piece, but somehow with Lauren standing next to it the furniture seemed just right.

From his perch on Lauren's left shoulder Buster craned his neck around and checked out his new surroundings. Alistair stepped into the hallway that ran to the rest of the apartment, namely the kitchen, bedroom, and attached bathroom.

He stopped abruptly and when he did, Lauren bumped into him. Alistair felt the brush of feathers against his neck.

Midnight sat in the hall, staring past Alistair, his eyes fastened on Buster. He wasn't quite licking his chops, but Alistair could see that the cat shared their plans for an early-morning snack.

"What's wrong?" Lauren whispered into his ear, after the adventures of the evening no doubt expecting another armed and dangerous criminal.

"My cat."

"He doesn't like birds?"

"I think he likes them a little bit too much."

"Oh, you mean they won't get along. But I've known cats and birds that do. Why sometimes, if you train them right—"

He cut off Lauren's stream of words by turning around and placing a finger lightly over her lips.

She blinked, surprise clear in her eyes.

"Let's not take any chances," Alistair said, slowing removing his hand.

"Of course not," she said, her eyes wide. She touched her lips together where his finger had been.

His body reacted to the sensual gesture.

Big-time.

Swinging back around, he said, "Come on, Midnight, into the bedroom." Yeah, but it wasn't the cat he wanted to scoop up in his arms and deliver straight to the four-poster bed. Nonetheless, he did just that, Midnight meowing piteously as if his every pleasure had been taken from him.

Alistair empathized.

Why did the redhead have such an impact on him? She was a ditz, a very brave, but maybe also very foolish one, to rescue him the way she had, but still, she was exactly the kind of trouble Alistair had sworn to avoid. Yet she spoke to his body more directly than a dedicated phone line.

"I am hungry," she was saying, as he returned from closing the bedroom door against Midnight's protests.

Now why didn't that surprise him? Alistair grinned and flipped on the lights in the kitchen, and indicated a stool beside the counter. The space was compact but efficiently arranged.

He opened the refrigerator door and hid his lower body behind the rows of bottles, letting the containers of relish, catsup, stir-fry sauces, marinades, and mayonnaise protect his body from betraying his aroused condition. The cool air would help, too.

"I like mushrooms," she said, playing with the salt and pepper shakers on the counter. She skimmed them along the countertop as if they were line dancers stepping to a tune only she could hear.

"Mushrooms we have," Alistair said.

"And red peppers." The shakers executed a pirouette at the end of the counter and headed back in the other direction. Buster hopped off Lauren's shoulder and onto Alistair's immaculate countertop.

Alistair reminded himself that the parrot had attacked the mugger. He turned back to the refrigerator. "What about bell peppers?"

She shook her head, then stopped. "I guess beggars shouldn't be choosers."

"You're no beggar," he said. "You saved my life."

"All I did was distract the guy," she said. "And I'm really good at distractions. I mean, they come to me like second nature."

Watching the dancing salt and pepper shakers, Alistair understood what she meant. "How about cheese and mushroom?"

"Great. Do you want me to help?"

He shook his head, then stepped from behind the refrigerator door. As long as he didn't touch her, he'd be safe. It was the touch, he decided, something electrically charged about the feel of her skin, any part of it, connecting with his own body that put him so out of control. Small wonder that Oliver had been so dazed by her.

She shimmied off the barstool and held out a hand. "Give me the eggs, and I'll crack them," she said.

He stared from her open palm to the egg carton he held. Holding it by one end, he extended it to her.

She took it, then said, "A bowl?"

"Ah, a bowl." Alistair pointed to a glass-fronted cabinet over the stovetop.

She rose on tiptoe, and he moved in one swift step to reach over her and hand the bowl down to her.

As he did, the front of his body brushed against her back.

"Don't touch," he said.

"What?" She paused, the bowl held out in front of her, arms extended. "Did I do something wrong already? I'm always making a mess in the kitchen."

"You're fine," Alistair said, stepping back, out of range. He was the one who wasn't coping here. She seemed completely unaffected by his presence. Which, if he could stop and think rationally for a moment, was a really, really good thing.

"But you're my guest," he said, "so why don't you sit back down and let me whip up the omelet."

Hearing the command in his tone, Lauren sighed, but she couldn't blame him for not trusting her in his kitchen. From the gleaming countertops to the glass-fronted cabinets, the room was immaculate. A few minutes with her wielding an eggbeater in one hand and a spatula in the other and Alistair wouldn't recognize his own home. She handed over the bowl and the egg carton and climbed onto the stool beside the counter that separated the kitchen from the front room. She wondered how he knew it wasn't safe to let her loose in the kitchen. Teasingly, she said, "Are you psychic?"

His head whipped around from where he was slicing mushrooms. "Why do you ask that?"

Intrigued by his reaction, she said, "Just a good guess?"

"Not exactly," he murmured.

She waited for more, but he kept his attention on those mushrooms. He'd tied his hair back with a length of cord, and she took a moment to admire the sight of such a masculine kind of guy making breakfast for her as the sky warmed from gray to pale pink outside the windows.

Buster hopped back onto her shoulder, and Lauren scratched the top of his head. "You're the real rescuer."

Alistair glanced around. "What does he eat?"

"Seeds. Nuts. Fruit."

Her host produced a bowl of grapes and a bag of pecans.

Lauren fed a few grapes to Buster as Alistair frothed the eggs, blended the omelet, and produced thick slices of toast, all without spilling a drop or creating a crumb.

Lauren's tummy growled and her mouth watered as Alistair presented two plates laden with breakfast for her inspection. "Wow," she said. "I bet you never got kicked out of home ec."

He grinned. "I never got in the door to that class." Then his smile faded. "I usually eat at the counter."

"Great, that's fancy enough for me."

He just stood there.

Finally, she realized he was staring straight at Buster, already enjoying his snack on the counter.

"Don't mind Buster," she said, "he's quite clean."

"Ah. Humor me?"

Lauren started to object, but she was staying on kindness here. "Okay," she said, depositing Buster on top of the refrigerator along with a handful of grapes.

Between bites, she said, "Where did you learn to cook?"

"My mother."

Funny, but he'd taken only one bite to her every three. He kept watching her instead of paying attention to his own plate. She cut a dainty portion of the hot, fluffy concoction dripping with melted Swiss cheese. "Is your mother still alive?"

He looked surprised, then thoughtful. "She lives here in the city, just off St. Charles Avenue."

St. Charles was the street where she'd taken the streetcar to return that wallet. Funny, but she might have traveled past this man's mother.

"When did you lose your mother?"

Lauren jumped at the gently delivered question. Her fork clattered to the floor, smearing a gooey strand of Swiss cheese in its wake. "Sorry," she said, slipping off the stool to recover the utensil and dab at the mess with her napkin.

"Here," Alistair said, handing her another fork. "We'll worry about that later."

She accepted the fork, feeling strangely shy. His eyes, far too wise and knowing, were fastened on her face in a way that made her feel as if he could read every thought inside her head. "I thought you said you weren't psychic."

"It was the way you asked the question about my mother," he answered, holding her stool out for her.

She climbed back on, but suddenly she wasn't hungry anymore.

"Had enough?"

"There you go again," she said softly.

He collected their plates and dumped them in the

sink without scraping them. Lauren would have been willing to bet that wasn't something he did very often.

"You're a funny kind of guy," she said, as usual speaking what came into her mind without thinking what it might sound like.

"Oh?" He turned and leaned against the sink, his arms folded across his chest.

"You take me in, feed me, actually *listen* to me"—she stressed the verb—"and you haven't even made a pass at me. 'Course, you did say you'd sworn off women."

He coughed and made a strangling noise. Lauren leapt off her stool, and as she did, her right calf muscle cramped. "Ow!" Hurling herself toward Alistair, who was still coughing, she pounded him on the back with one hand and grabbed at her leg with the other.

Finally, he caught her flailing hand in his. "I'm okay," he said. "But what's wrong with your leg?"

"Cramp." She bent with both hands to nurse the aching muscles. "I walked around a lot today."

"Mmm."

Mmm? Was that all he could say? "Do you have any Myoflex?"

"I'm afraid not," he said. "But I do have some eucalyptus cream."

She rolled her eyes. Her father swore by Myoflex. Right then, though, she'd take anything.

"It's in the bedroom," Alistair said, sounding hesitant.

"Take me to it," she said, truly feeling as if her leg would split in two.

Alistair reached out and placed his arm around Lauren's shoulders, knowing he shouldn't touch her. He should leave her right there in the kitchen, writhing in agony, and go in search of the aroma-therapy cream he kept for sore muscles. The last thing he needed right now was Lauren in his bedroom.

"Lean on me," he said.

She clutched his waist, and Alistair forgot all about what he should do.

He inched open the bedroom door, careful not to let Midnight escape, then helped Lauren inside before closing the door behind them. "Have to protect Buster," he murmured, as he felt her stiffen at the sound of the door clicking shut.

"You're so thoughtful," she said, a tear inching its way down her cheek. "I've never walked so many miles in my life before in one day, and I guess it was just too much for my body."

He eased her down on the side of his bed. "Let me see that leg," he said, trying to sound professional, like a doctor at work.

She was a lot of help, throwing back her head and shoulders and heaving in a dramatic fashion that sent her breasts rising and falling in a way that made Alistair's body react in only one direction. Upward.

He stifled a groan and reached into a drawer in the bedside table where he kept massage oil. He'd use that and find the sore muscle cream later. Spilling several drops into the palm of one hand, he said, "You'll feel lots better soon."

"Ah! Oh! Oh, God!" She kept writhing and

throwing her head back, every bit like a woman in the throes of orgasm. Alistair remembered her telling him she'd sworn off sex and wondered whether she'd been pulling his leg. But when he placed his hands on her calf and felt the muscles in the grip of spasm, he understood her actions.

"Just let me have it," he murmured, applying slow and steady strokes from the base of her ankle upward to just below her knee. As he worked, her contortions eased, as did the muscle. He felt her knotted calf go completely limp, and he smiled, somewhat grimly. Now if only he could manage the same miracle on his own body!

She'd calmed down and was lying back on the bed, her foot cradled in his lap. "That was amazing," she said. "Did your mother teach you that, too?"

He shook his head, then lifted her other foot and slipped off that sandal. He began massaging her toes and working his way up her calf muscle.

"That one doesn't have a cramp," she said, but didn't rise from the bed.

"It's important to keep your body in balance," Alistair said, knowing that what he said was true but also realizing how much it sounded like any guy's excuse to touch her incredible body.

"You're very wise," she said, her voice slowing.

Right at the moment, he couldn't agree with that statement. Wise would be to get up and leave his own apartment and run at least a 5K. Wise would be never to have gotten involved with this redheaded siren who seemed to have no idea of the effect she had on him.

Wise certainly wouldn't be to rise and say softly, "Turn over."

She didn't even blink, just rolled over on the bed and scooted up closer to the pillows. Alistair eased a few more drops of massage oil onto his hands and caressed the back of both of her legs.

"That feels so good," she said. "I can't believe what a nice person you are. Most men—"

"Don't remind me," Alistair said. She didn't seem to realize he was "most men." And that innocent trust held him back. "I hope you don't make it a habit of letting strange men massage you."

"Of course not," she said. "I never feel safe enough."

"And you feel safe with me?"

She nodded, a gentle smile on her lips.

Alistair stifled another groan and prepared to sacrifice himself to the cause of her trust in him. Judging by the feel of her legs, she could seriously use some body-balancing massage. "If you want me to do your back, I'll give you a robe to put on."

Lauren sat up and turned around.

"You would really do that? I mean, and only do massage?"

He fought a brief battle with the desire she sparked in him, but the awe and trust in her gaze won the victory. "Friendly massage—only."

She smiled, her eyes alight, then ran one hand up her leg, marveling at how good it felt after the intense pain of the muscle cramp. "I haven't had a massage in so long," she said, "I think I've forgotten what it feels like."

Alistair rose from the bed, crossed the room, and

returned with a silky robe. He handed it to her, and Lauren took it and in one swift move, she tugged her dress over her head.

She heard a noise that sounded a lot like that choking cough Alistair had made in the kitchen, and from behind her clothing she said, "Are you all right?"

"Sure, sure," he answered.

Lauren realized most women would probably have turned their backs and most women would probably be wearing both bra and panties, but she'd left the Plaisance house in such a hurry, she hadn't had time to worry about niceties like proper underwear. She'd grabbed a pair of bikini underwear that barely qualified for the name.

Growing up in a medical household, she'd developed a fairly blasé attitude about nudity, to the point she often forgot other people reacted to such things. She'd also done so much sketching of nudes she scarcely gave flesh a second thought. She hoped Alistair wasn't as fussy about naked bodies as he was about birds eating alongside humans. She was starting to like him.

Alistair forced himself to do the decent, honorable thing and turn around.

But the image he'd gotten of her body in that single moment burned on the backs of his eyelids. Lush breasts with rosy nipples, a gently rounded tummy, and a thatch of dark hair scarcely covered by a scrap of pink satin. No bra. If he'd known all along how little she wore beneath that frothy dress, she certainly wouldn't still be saying he wasn't like other guys.

"I'm ready," she said.

So was Alistair.

He edged around and saw that she'd nestled in the middle of his king-size bed, the silk robe loosely arranged over her back.

Her face was turned toward him, and she was smiling, a sleepy dreamy sort of smile. "I just want to thank you," she said.

"For?" He gripped the bottle of massage oil and realized he shouldn't touch her. One more feel of her warm skin and he'd ruin the angelic reputation he'd achieved with her.

"For being nice enough to trust." She rose up on her elbows and the robe skittered halfway down her back. She hadn't even put her arms into the sleeves. "I've never met any man I trusted, and I guess some people would say I'm naive to be here with you when I don't know you, but somehow I feel as if I do know you." She frowned in a puzzled way, then added, "Did that make sense?"

Alistair nodded. It made too much sense. It also meant he couldn't touch her, at least not in the way he was dying to touch her. "I understand," he said. "Now how about that back rub?"

She lay down and with her voice muffled against his comforter, said, "G'night."

Kneeling beside her on the bed, he lifted the robe to the side of her body and turned the bottle to spill a few drops onto the creamy skin of her back. Starting above her cheeks, he worked his hands up her back in long, slow brushing movements. He made sure not even his kneecaps brushed her body. Any more contact than absolutely necessary and he'd be lost.

What kind of a fool gets into a situation like this? He asked himself the question, then decided to let it go. Lauren wasn't the woman he needed in his life, which meant she wasn't a woman he needed to take to bed. His body might scream otherwise, but he had to let his head rule on this one.

She sighed and moistened her lips. "So good," she murmured. Her fanny wiggled slightly, and her legs, relaxed now, opened farther.

His gut tightened, and he forgot all about being good.

"Lauren?"

No answer.

Leaning over her, he whispered, "Lauren, about not being like other guys?"

Her only answer was a tiny soft snore.

Ten

Maebelle Merlin could never remember the Latin for "seize the day," but she did follow the motto in her own selective fashion. Housecleaning chores, particularly windows or floors, could always be put off to the morrow.

But taking care of friends and family required immediate attention.

That's why she presented herself at the First Parish Bank and Trust promptly at a quarter of noon the day after her visit to the Bayou Magick Shop. Alistair had put his foot down so hard on her request for a spell for Barbara that he could have created yet another New Orleans pothole. So she had no choice but to take matters into her own hands.

And since she had promised to forgo magick, here she was, trying her best to meddle the old-fashioned way.

Once inside the bank, she presented herself at the New Accounts desk. A person with that duty should know pretty much everything there was to know.

The woman didn't disappoint her.

"Ms. Warren? You mean the consultant who's here from Philadelphia working with Mr. Oliver?"

Mrs. Merlin gave her a thumbs-up. She didn't know who Mr. Oliver was, but he might be the bank president Barbara had mentioned. Probably seventy if he was a day and no doubt equipped with a wife. Tugging at the spikes of her orange-silver hair to spruce them up a bit, she asked the way.

The woman pointed to the end of the lobby. "Would you like to hear about our new account special while you're here?"

"Mustn't be late for Barbara," Mrs. Merlin said, but since the lady had been so helpful, she added, "but I'll take a brochure."

Not that she'd read it. She kept all her money in Claussen pickle jars, having been saving the containers since she'd discovered the world's best pickle over a decade ago. Her mouth started watering as she thought of the crunchy chilled delight. She enjoyed one daily. The only days she'd missed were the one time she'd had a root canal and that brief period of time during which she'd accidentally shrunk herself to six and a quarter inches.

Crossing the lobby, she frowned as she thought of Alistair turning his back on candle magick to come to work in this mausoleum. It did have rich, dark wood and impressive chandeliers, and the karma didn't feel negative the way she'd expected, but why spend his days indoors with cash and numbers and doubtlessly demanding customers when he could surround himself with marvels of the universe few were privileged to experience?

With a sigh, she pushed opened the door marked EXECUTIVE OFFICE. Hoity-toity president. She sniffed, and said to the silver-haired woman behind a large desk, "I've come for Barbara."

A faintly puzzled look crossed the woman's face, then she said, "Of course. You're Ms. Warren's god-mother. She mentioned the two of you were having lunch."

"Three. The three of us."

"Oh?" She didn't say it in a challenging way, just vaguely questioning as if filling in the blanks of the conversation.

"Alistair is going, too."

The lady's face brightened. "That will be nice. He's such a special young man."

Mrs. Merlin warmed to the woman. "Too special for banking, if you ask me. I mean, what's he do here, anyway?"

"I'm sure he could do anything he wanted to," the woman said, "but he's not here. He's only been inside this building once in the last ten years. And that was yesterday."

"Really? Well . . ." Mrs. Merlin considered the possibility that Alistair had been playing a not-very-funny joke on her. She certainly hoped so, 'cause this was one she'd gladly forgive him. "He did tell me he was working here."

"We haven't seen him today, and I don't think Oliver has heard from him."

Mrs. Merlin smiled broadly just as one of the doors behind the woman's desk opened and Barbara appeared. To the lady behind the desk, she said, "We'll just go meet him at home." Holding out her hand to her goddaughter, she said, "Ready, my dear?"

Barbara froze, wishing she could retreat into the conference room and spend the next sixty minutes buried in computer reports. The last thing she was ready for was her meddling godmother, no matter how well intentioned she meant to be.

But rather than cause a scene of the sort she despised, Barbara summoned a polite smile and let her godmother clasp her hand for a brief moment, then tucked it firmly onto the strap of her shoulder bag. "I'll only be an hour," she said to Oliver's secretary.

"Don't start the time clock yet," her irrepressible godmother said, wagging a finger at the secretary.

Barbara suppressed a sigh and followed her hostess/captor from the bank. Outside, the day reminded her very much of the day before, except that the wind had died down to nothing stronger than a scurry every so often. Pausing beside Mrs. Merlin, Barbara glanced back at the front of the bank building and admired the solid lines of the facade. That morning she'd learned some of the bank's history from Oliver as they had worked side by side, and the business had taken on a life of its own within her mind.

She wasn't a woman given to imagination, but

she'd been moved by Oliver's references to his father's and grandfather's struggles to hold the bank together. She'd been touched by his tales of how they had funded loans for local families who might otherwise be denied their dreams of home ownership, and most recently, fended off the overtures of one national megabank intent on gobbling up much of the local competition.

The building itself exuded a sense of sturdy security, and Barbara realized, as Mrs. Merlin pointed toward an ancient red car parked beside a fire hydrant, that Oliver possessed that same quality.

At least he struck her that way this morning, composed and immaculate in a beautifully tailored navy summer wool suit. Gone was the crazed soul of the day before who'd appeared splattered in paint and not been able to focus on the work at hand.

Barbara didn't know what had happened, and she certainly didn't ask. Perhaps it had to do with the absence of the bank president's unpredictable but supposedly eccentric brother. Maybe his presence the day before had thrown his brother off in some way.

Whatever the reasons, Barbara had found herself enjoying the morning's work in a way she could scarcely remember experiencing. For every question she asked, Oliver had the answer. Sometimes she'd trail off in mid-thought as she met the president's gaze and seemed to read the answer from his mind. It was truly an amazing compatibility and both of them, Barbara knew, had sensed it. If she weren't careful, given their efficient teamwork, she'd be

done with this job much earlier than she had antic-
ipated.

Mrs. Merlin said, "Let's go, dear," and swung
open the passenger door of her ancient and bright
red car. Barbara glanced at the squared shape and
the long length of the car and guessed its vintage
as mid-sixties. Carefully, she seated herself and
reached for the length of seat belt. She hoped Mrs.
Merlin drove more carefully with a passenger in
place than she did as the sole occupant of the vehicle. Mrs. Merlin had caused quite a commotion
just backing out of her driveway the other day.

"We're just scooting over into the Quarter," Mrs.
Merlin said, settling behind the wheel, "but I don't
think my feet can take the walk. Or the parking
ticket," she said, waving cheerfully at the meter
maid who'd started to write out a citation, no doubt
for the car being parked by the hydrant in a clearly
posted TOW AWAY ZONE.

Barbara clung to the armrests as they sped
through a yellow light blurring to red at Canal
Street. Mrs. Merlin slowed slightly as they bumped
into the crowded streets of the French Quarter and
kept on going, block after block.

She thought it was worth one more try to dis-
suade her hostess from introducing her to her
friends. The last thing in the world Barbara wanted
was to be set up with someone who would be stuck
entertaining her. She'd far rather spend her nights
curled up in the hotel room, if she ever got there,
with an Agatha Christie or Georgette Heyer novel
that she'd read five times before than pretending to

be entranced by something some stranger said to her.

"I really appreciate—" Barbara's words were cut off as Mrs. Merlin screeched the car to a halt.

"Piffle!" Mrs. Merlin had managed to kill the engine. She restarted the car then proceeded more slowly. "The stop signs used to face the other way," she muttered, seemingly by way of explanation.

"Oh," Barbara said, relaxing her grip not one bit on the armrest. "As I was saying, I really appreciate your efforts to entertain me, but you really don't have to introduce me to—"

"A space!" Mrs. Merlin brought the car to a dead halt and the truck behind them swerved and missed them by less than an inch. "Do you know how hard it is to find a parking space on this street in the middle of the day?" She backed the car in, quite neatly, and said, "The goddess is clearly with us today. Let's go."

Barbara reminded herself that this woman had been her mother's dearest childhood friend. Not once, but twice she repeated that statement in her mind. Then she climbed slowly out of the car, smoothed the skirt of her sensible navy blue suit, and said, "Lead the way."

"That's a dear," Mrs. Merlin said. "You won't be disappointed. Mind you, he's not the man for you, but he'll know who is. And that's worth almost as much."

Not the man for her? Barbara bristled. How did Mrs. Merlin presume to know who was and who wasn't the right kind of man for her? Why, she'd be the judge of that.

Her godmother paused in front of a shop that seemed oddly familiar to Barbara, although she knew she'd never set foot in there before in her life. Pushing open the front door, Mrs. Merlin beckoned to Barbara to follow.

A bell fastened to the door jangled loudly. A young girl with oddly dyed hair greeted Mrs. Merlin from behind the register. Engrossed in the decidedly odd contents of the shop, Barbara didn't overhear the conversation. But she did see Mrs. Merlin point toward the back of the shop and head in that direction, beckoning her to follow.

Through a maze of mysterious objects that she guessed had to do with voodoo and various oddball cults, Barbara shadowed Mrs. Merlin. The image of the photograph on Mrs. Merlin's mantel flitted through her mind, but she dismissed it as too coincidental.

"We'll just pop upstairs and see what's keeping him," Mrs. Merlin said, taking to the staircase in the courtyard at the back of the shop as if she were thirty years younger than her birth certificate claimed.

Almost as if mesmerized, Barbara followed. What else could she do? Slip off on her own and find a nice quiet place to enjoy her favorite lunch, a chef salad with blue cheese dressing on the side? On the side, of course, because she couldn't quite let herself indulge in the richness, but she also couldn't prevent herself from enjoying the simple pleasures of life.

Right now, though, following Mrs. Merlin up two fairly steep flights of stairs, she'd settle for a salad with limp lettuce and a smattering of vegetables. Her life hadn't been her own since she'd landed in New Orleans.

When the door to the apartment opened and she found herself face-to-face with the other Mr. Gotho, the intriguing and whimsical brother of the sensible bank president, she wished heartily that she'd retreated sooner.

She should never have let Mrs. Merlin talk her into this visit. Who could have predicted this outcome?

What, afraid, Barbara?

What of?

Too much man for you?

She swallowed, hard, and managed a "good morning," as if he were in the bank's conference room wearing a suit and tie.

Rather than clad only in a scanty pair of purple running shorts. He stood quite at ease in the living room of what had to be his apartment, naked except for those exceptionally short shorts. Dark hair tipped with silver matted his chest.

He ran a hand over his eyes and yawned and when he stretched his sinewy arms over his head, Barbara saw more hair under his armpits. Normally that sort of image did not do much for her. Right at that moment, she thought she'd never seen a sexier sight.

"Good morning," he said to Mrs. Merlin, then turned toward her. "And who is ..." his voice trailed off, and he turned swiftly around and grabbed something off the couch.

"Noon and you're not dressed," Mrs. Merlin said,

a note of approval in her voice. "Couldn't do that if you worked for that silly bank."

Alistair pulled the shirt over his head. "True," he said. "Won't you have a seat?" He pulled an afghan off the sofa and pointed to it.

Barbara sat, not knowing what else to say or do.

"Tell me," Alistair said to her godmother. "Were you in the neighborhood again today?"

He certainly didn't sound very pleased. Barbara wished herself away, far away, to any place other than where she was. No man would be interested in anyone who had to be foisted on him like a twenty-minute special offering on Home Shopping Club. And she couldn't blame him for being annoyed by Mrs. Merlin's visit. Barbara hated it when anyone dropped in on her unannounced or unplanned. Not that anyone did, of course.

She was out of town more than she was at home, so it was no wonder that her friends never "dropped by." Barbara squirmed slightly on the sofa as she thought of how she had drifted from her college and MBA school friends. She liked people; she really ought to make more of an effort to keep in touch. But that didn't change her empathetic reaction to Alistair's annoyance.

"Of course we were in the neighborhood," Mrs. Merlin said, perched on the arm of the sofa. "Let me introduce my goddaughter, Barbara Warren. She's in town for such a short time I didn't want to waste a moment introducing her to my most significant friends."

Alistair glanced from Barbara to Mrs. Merlin. Barbara wondered, for the most fleeting of moments, if he wanted to let her think they hadn't met. She paused, waiting for his lead.

He moved over, extended his hand, and said, "Pleased to meet you, Ms. Warren. Any friend of Mrs. Merlin's is a friend of mine."

In a funny way, she was glad she hadn't blurted out that they'd met the day before. She wanted to please this magnetic hunk of a man in a way she couldn't recall ever wanting to please anyone, not even her mother or father when she'd been the model child.

Mrs. Merlin clapped her hands together. "I knew the two of you would hit it off. I'll just toddle off. I have a few things to pick up. As long as I'm in the neighborhood," she added.

"Nothing from downstairs?" Alistair said, fixing her with a look that would have made Barbara confess even if she had nothing to be guilty of.

"Oh, don't be silly," Mrs. Merlin said. "You know I've given up all that."

Alistair nodded. He walked Mrs. Merlin to the door, waved her off, and then turned. "Well."

Well, indeed. All of a sudden, Barbara wished she'd followed Mrs. Merlin out the door. This man had no wish to be stuck with her.

"Small world, isn't it?" Barbara could have hit herself over the head for saying such a stupid thing.

But Alistair only grinned, and said, "I couldn't have said it better myself. Let me put some clothes on and we'll get some lunch. Is that okay by you?"

She nodded, feeling not only grateful, but also very pleased. Maybe Mrs. Merlin knew a thing or two. Only she had pronounced that Alistair wasn't the man for Barbara. Barbara crossed one leg over the other, letting her foot swing gently. Her skirt inched upward and it did her heart good when she saw Alistair glance at her legs before he turned around.

As he started to cross the room, the door that closed the room from the rest of the apartment opened. Did he have a roommate? One check of Alistair's expression alerted Barbara. He was staring at the doorway, glaring as if he dared the door to open the rest of the way.

Which it did.

Barbara had seen a lot of beautiful women. Her parents had moved easily in their socialite crowd, and from her youngest years, Barbara had known some of Britain's loveliest beauties.

This woman with long auburn hair, perfect pale skin, and huge green eyes topped them all. She blinked and stretched her arms lazily. As she did, the oversized T-shirt she wore, which looked exactly like the one Alistair had snatched from the couch, rose to her upper thighs.

"Oh," she said, finally seeming to focus. "I didn't know you had company."

Barbara managed a faint smile. Clearly Alistair hadn't been expecting any, either. She started to rise, to make her excuses, but none of her muscles would obey her mind. Instead, she uncrossed and recrossed her legs to let her skirt compete with this woman's T-shirt.

"Buy low. Sell high." A bird hopped up to the redhead, and she bent to let him walk up her arm to her shoulder. "Buster's hungry," she said.

"And I suppose you are, too." Alistair spoke at last.

Barbara thought it an odd greeting and wondered why he didn't seem at all flustered. Most men caught between a blonde on the sofa and a redhead in the bedroom would probably react with at least a degree of guilt.

Not that he had anything to feel guilty about, she acknowledged. Maybe this was his roommate. That thought cheered her, and she said to the woman, "Hi, I'm Barbara."

The other woman smiled and walked forward. "Lauren," she said. "This is Buster. I'm always hungry."

"Are you?" Barbara observed the woman's slender legs and the way the T-shirt showed her feminine perfection in all the right places. "You must have a great metabolism."

"I suspect it's because I rarely get to eat."

At that Alistair did show a reaction. He grabbed his head in his hands, and said, "Okay, okay, you can come to lunch with us. That's what you want, isn't it?"

The redhead smiled, and said to Barbara, "Alistair is so nice. He isn't like other men at all. Let me tell you what he did last night."

Barbara hated to admit it, but she leaned forward, interested in exactly what this man had done the night before. Mrs. Merlin might say he wasn't the man for her, but as she wasn't picking up any signals to indicate these two were a couple, she wanted to know more. Much more.

Lauren dropped to the couch beside Barbara, apparently settling in for a cozy chat. Alistair retreated from the room.

Pulling her long hair back from her face and twisting it into a makeshift knot that she held with one hand, Lauren said, "Have you ever been held up at gunpoint?"

Barbara shook her head.

"Well, Alistair was, and he says I saved his life. That's why he was so grateful and was so good to me last night."

Just how good had he been to her? A flare of jealousy she had no right to feel erupted in Barbara, and she wasn't sure if she wanted to hear any more of this woman's story.

"Meow!"

A blur of black streaked from the far end of the sofa, headed straight for the bird perched on Lauren's shoulder.

Lauren jumped up, screaming. The cat missed its prey by a scarce inch, and landed on the floor, twitching its tail, its huge silver eyes fixed on the bird.

Barbara had leapt up, too, not sure of what was attacking. Alistair burst into the room, calling out, "Midnight! Get in here."

Both women turned to stare at Alistair. He wore only a pair of white briefs that revealed more than they covered. Barbara felt like the cat anticipating the taste of the bird. A glance at the intimate way Lauren was studying Alistair's body confirmed what she suspected—whatever had happened last night, Lauren wanted Alistair as much as Barbara did.

Eleven

Alistair could have kicked himself for inviting Lauren to join him and Barbara for lunch. Mrs. Merlin had dropped the banking consultant into his lap, and he'd blown a perfect opportunity to get to know her outside of the confines of First Parish Bank and Trust.

Meaning, he was honest enough to admit, away from his brother. Barbara reminded him of several of Oliver's past girlfriends, and if he had any hope of stealing a march on his brother while he was infatuated with his "mystery woman," he had to work quickly.

As quickly as his cat had hunted Buster, Alistair scooped up Midnight. The cat struggled against his chest, his fur tickling Alistair's bare chest. The sensation brought Alistair back to the rest of his senses.

He'd rushed out of the bedroom wearing only his skivvies.

"Excuse me," he said, beating a quick retreat, squirming feline in hand.

Not that Lauren would object to his seminude state. The image of her slipping that dress over her head and revealing her lusciously bare body filled his mind. As it did, his body stirred in remembered reaction. But it wasn't Lauren he was concerned with; he didn't want to chase Barbara away. And so far, he couldn't have made much of an impression on the competent, attractive consultant.

He yanked on a pair of comfortably faded jeans and a T-shirt, then frowned as he met his reflection in the mirror. Barbara, dressed for business as she was, would be embarrassed to be seen with such a slouch.

He'd never in his life felt a need to change himself to please a woman, but now he stripped off the T-shirt, folded it, and took a starched dress shirt from a hanger. He tucked it into his jeans, folded back the cuffs neatly, and then stepped into his Birkenstocks. He smiled slightly, thinking of how Lauren had saved them—not to mention him—from the robber.

Lauren still had to get ready. That would give him time alone with Barbara.

When he stepped back into the front room, Lauren was performing a pirouette between a coffee table holding a Baccarat decanter and a curio cabinet that housed his collection of miniature wizards, warlocks, and witches. He caught his breath, praying that she'd not cause her usual calamity.

Barbara watched from the sofa, Buster now seated on her shoulder.

"Oh!" Lauren whirled around, the T-shirt she'd cribbed from his closet scarcely covering what Alistair knew was a bare fanny. "I was just showing Barbara what happened to us last night."

The thought of the bare fanny reminded Alistair of what had not happened between the two of them. His body surged with a sexual hunger brought on by the lack of release. "Why don't you get dressed, and I'll tell Barbara how you saved my life."

"Sure. Do you two mind watching Buster?" Without waiting for an answer, she sped from the room.

"Not at all," Barbara said to her departing back.

Alistair crossed to the kitchen area, located a clean tea towel, and lifted Buster to arrange the towel on Barbara's shoulder. "To save your suit," he said.

"Thanks." She uncrossed her legs at the knees. Alistair admired the shape. Barbara had a neat body, perfectly proportioned. He wondered what she did for exercise. Someone who worked as much as she seemed to must find some form of physical release. He started to ask her, but found himself uttering an incredibly stupid question instead.

"So how's business at the bank?" *What a stupid thing to say.* Asking about banking wouldn't show him to any advantage.

"Oliver and I accomplished quite a lot this morning."

Alistair didn't like the way she paired herself with his brother. It sounded too proprietary to suit him. "Oh? I'll be there tomorrow."

"Really?"

She didn't have to look so surprised.

"Really."

"Oliver said he rarely works on Saturdays."

"Tomorrow's Saturday?"

She nodded and edged her head away from where Buster was trying to capture her hair in one of his curved claws. "If you want me to come in, I certainly don't mind."

Alistair could think of many interesting things the two of them could do on a Saturday, especially on a beautiful weekend in April that found the French Quarter enjoying its annual locals' celebration known as French Quarter Fest. Certainly, poring over computer reports that made his vision blur appeared nowhere on the list.

"Why don't we—"

"I'm back!" Lauren materialized, looking fresher than ever, despite wearing the same dress she'd worn the day before. She'd piled her hair atop her head, and a few wispy curls escaped down her neck.

Alistair cut off his invitation for Barbara to spend the next day with him in mid-sentence. He'd wait until they were alone to ask her, or he had a hunch he'd find himself escorting a threesome to the French Quarter Fest. For now, he'd take them to lunch at the Quarter Scene, a locals' hangout, and make the best of the chance to get to know Barbara.

It went against Lauren's better judgment, but she let Alistair talk her into leaving Buster behind in his apartment. Midnight was locked out of reach in the bedroom, but she still felt bad leaving the parrot behind.

Two thoughts consoled her. She had nowhere to go and no money, and at some point she'd have to return to Alistair's place to collect Buster. To Lauren, that meant if she spent the day wisely, and didn't return till late, she'd probably have a roof over her head one more night. The other consolation was Alistair's promise to stop at a pet store to purchase some seed. As soon as her life was right-way up again, she'd paint him a picture to thank him for his kindness.

Speaking of kind, he certainly was being nice to Barbara. Lauren tripped along, silent for once, listening to Alistair describe bits of Quarter lore and architectural highlights to the blonde, who obviously wasn't from New Orleans.

Lauren felt superior, being in full possession of the history of the only parochial school within the nine-by-thirteen block area of the Vieux Carré, or French Quarter. They were passing the school where children, most of them fairly neat and tidy in their uniforms, were romping around the small play yard. Watching, she wanted to kick off her sandals and join them. Being a child had been so much fun. Except for school, where the only subjects she'd enjoyed were art and recess.

She glanced sideways at Barbara. She'd probably been a straight-A student. Lauren had made a few A's, too, but she'd also scored quite a few F's, something she'd be willing to bet this woman had never done. Barbara said something that made Alistair smile in that slow, sleepy way he had that Lauren loved to see, and she bristled. What was this woman who looked like an MBA recruiting poster doing with her ponytailed hero?

Don't be ridiculous, she told herself. Alistair wasn't her hero any more than he was Barbara's. Why, he barely suffered her to remain in his presence. She still remembered the expression on his face when he'd seen the contents of her bag scattered over the table at the coffeehouse. Despite his beatnik appearance, he was a neatnik. The two of them would never rub along together. He was nice to her today because she'd saved his life last night. Once that thrill wore off, he'd be right back to remembering he didn't care for her, her scattered ways, or her bird.

She sighed and wondered whether her blood sugar had hit bottom. That would explain her suddenly depressed feelings. "Are you sure there's a restaurant around here?" She interrupted Alistair in mid-sentence. "This block looks purely residential."

Even as she asked the question, they were crossing a street. Alistair pointed at the doorway set into the corner of the building right in front of them. Lifting her eyes, Lauren read aloud, "Quarter Scene Restaurant. Closed Tuesdays.

"Well," she said, feeling like an idiot let out for a field trip, a feeling not at all unknown to her, "it's a good thing it's not Tuesday."

Barbara smiled politely, but at least Alistair chuckled as he held the door open for them.

"What a cute place," Lauren said as she bounced in and took in the vivid wall murals depicting scenes of society life in the past century.

"Quaint," Barbara said. "I hope they do salads." She glanced around and said, "Those murals remind me of Seurat."

"You mean Delacroix," Lauren said.

"Do I?" She had the grace to look a little uncertain, and Lauren pounced on that. She might be incapable of finishing her dissertation, but French Impressionists she had locked up.

"Sure, this mural is even modeled on one of Delacroix's paintings. Seurat was the creator of pointillism. Someone even wrote a play, silly though it was, inspired by one of his paintings, *Sunday in the Park with George*." Lauren made a face. Her father had taken her to see it on Broadway, and she remembered thinking he'd wasted his money on the tickets. A day spent at the Metropolitan would have been more sustaining.

But her dad had meant well.

Then. Back when it had been just Lauren and her father, long before Mrs. Bristol had come on the scene.

She stiffened and pushed the thought of his rejection from her mind. "Well," she said, "so much for our little art lesson. I'm starved."

A waiter with a scrawny ponytail pointed nonchalantly to a vacant table in front of one window. Alistair pulled out a chair for Barbara, and one for Lauren on the opposite side of the table, then seated himself next to the blonde.

Lauren wrinkled her nose and studied the menu. As used as she was to men going gaga over her, she couldn't decide if she found Alistair's cavalier treatment of her annoying or refreshing.

Barbara seemed to be eating up the attention, though.

Oh, well, who cared as long as she enjoyed a good meal? Lauren hated to be that mercenary about it, but when all was said and done, she was really up the creek. She ought to be out looking for a job rather than lunching like the idle rich.

Alistair was leaning over and pointing to something on Barbara's menu. Lauren stretched her neck. "What do you recommend?"

"They do a mean shrimp po-boy," Alistair said.

Now it was Barbara's turn to wrinkle her nose. "Deep fried?"

Alistair nodded. "The only way to fix shrimp for a po-boy."

Barbara turned back to the menu.

Lauren closed hers. "Sounds great," she said.

The waiter unfolded himself from the latticework wall where he'd been lounging and strolled over. "Hey," he said, "I almost didn't recognize you."

Alistair glanced down at his starched shirt. "Did I overdress?" He said it almost seriously, yet Lauren knew he had to be teasing. She smiled and so did the waiter. Barbara was still studying the menu, no doubt in search of some food that contained no fat, no sugar, and no flavor.

"Two shrimp po-boys, dressed, and—" He turned to Barbara.

"I'll have the chef salad, but only Swiss cheese, and hold the black olives."

The waiter studied a man walking by in front of the broad window. "Dressing?"

"Blue cheese, but on the side, please."

"Uh-huh," he said, whether in response to Barbara's particular order or to the hunk passing in front of his view, Lauren couldn't be sure. Whatever the stimulus, he faded away, disappearing into the kitchen.

Silence fell over the threesome, and Lauren fidgeted with the salt and pepper shakers. Any minute now someone would say something stupid and strained, the way strangers had such a habit of doing to one another. Oddly enough, alone with Alistair, she hadn't experienced that constraint. But triads, she knew, always changed things. Again, the thought of Mrs. Bristol filled her mind, and she clenched the saltshaker.

"So," Barbara asked, "are you a student of art?"

Lauren relaxed her death grip on the saltshaker and exchanged it for her knife. Dancing the utensil on its end, she said, "I guess you could say that."

"Does that mean you're in school?" Alistair was looking at her as if he really cared about her answer. "Are you at Tulane?"

Shaking her head, Lauren said, "No, but that would be great. I'm actually A.B.D. at Primalia."

"Is that some sort of parole status?" Alistair smiled as he said it, and the kindness in his look overrode his words.

"It might as well be," Lauren said. "I feel like I'm serving a life sentence."

"A.B.D." Barbara said thoughtfully. "That's when you've finished your studies but not your dissertation."

"Yep." Her knife danced even faster on the tabletop. Boy, did she hate these discussions.

"What's your topic?" Barbara actually sounded interested.

"Uh, it's kind of complicated." Lauren held the twitching knife between both her hands, wishing she didn't feel the need to keep moving.

"I think dissertations are supposed to be." That was Alistair, actually giving her encouragement.

She smiled briefly at him, lowered her head, and said to the tablecloth, "It's convoluted, but I've been working on a theory about Freudian analysis and Mary Cassatt. I mean, just why did she paint all those women in white? What was with her anyway?"

Barbara looked quite blank. So did Alistair. Lauren noticed their expressions as soon as she lifted her head. "Let's not talk about me," she said so quickly she tripped over her words. "What do you do, Barbara?"

"Banking computer consultant. Not very exciting, I suppose," she said.

"But sensible," Lauren added. "You should be glad you have such a responsible job. Even if it is dull," she added, unable to stop the thought in her head from reaching her tongue.

"Really?" Barbara was clearly taken aback. "And what's dull about it?"

"Numbers. Logic. Everything balancing all neat and tidy." Lauren made a face just as the waiter delivered their plates, wishing she didn't always say what was in her mind.

"Not complaining already, are you?" the waiter joked as he settled their po-boys, mammoth pieces of French bread heaped with deep-fried shrimp, shredded lettuce, and tomato in front of Alistair and Lauren, and a large salad plate of greens and pale strips of cheese for Barbara.

"Did you go to graduate school, Barbara?" Alistair asked the question, almost as if he felt he had to step in between the two of them. Lauren felt no real need to argue; she simply couldn't fathom doing anything as boring as banking. And, too, it called for precision, definitely not one of her strong suits.

"I have an MBA."

Lauren stared as the banking consultant cut her lettuce with a knife and fork. She was watching her so intently she failed to notice a huge shrimp slipping from her own sandwich. It plopped onto her lap, smearing her dress with mayonnaise. She lifted her gaze from the mess to find Alistair staring at her. Jeez, no wonder he acted as if Barbara were a queen; next to Lauren, she could be Emily Post reincarnated.

"And I bet you went to Harvard." Lauren said the words before she could clamp her mouth shut. She had no need to be jealous; Alistair meant nothing to her—other than representing a place to spend the night before she faced the inevitable question of how to rescue herself from the mess she'd made.

Barbara dabbed a piece of lettuce in the side dish of dressing and nodded. "Guilty," she said.

Lauren took a very big bite of her sandwich. That ought to keep her foot out of her mouth for a few minutes.

"What about you, Alistair?" Barbara cut a teensy piece of cheese and tasted it.

Lauren wondered whether she'd learned her style of eating at Harvard, too. Lauren's father had spent a fortune educating her, but cocktail-party manners had never been included in the curriculum. Or perhaps she had skipped those classes.

"LSU." He, too, took a big bite of his sandwich.

"Louisiana State University," Lauren said. "Home of Pete Maravich and Shaquille O'Neal."

Alistair kept chewing but nodded. After a long moment, he said, "I'm impressed. Do you like basketball?"

Lauren didn't like it, but she did know a lot about it. Checking Barbara's fairly dismayed expression, she widened her eyes, and said, "Crazy about it. Did you play for LSU?"

"Yep."

Lauren sized him up from across the table. "Forward?"

"You're good," he said.

Her heart swelled at the unexpected praise. Her dad had loved it when she'd swapped stats and scores and high points of games with him. She'd often thought his one release from the rigors of his practice and hospital schedule was his enjoyment of basketball, baseball, and football. College and professional, he followed them all.

"What did you study?"

Lauren and Alistair both looked at Barbara as if she'd asked a very funny question.

"He went to LSU," Lauren said, as if that explained everything.

The banker continued to look puzzled. Alistair popped the last shrimp from his sandwich into his mouth and took his time chewing it. Lauren considered him, and decided he was smarter than he tried to act. Had he been a nerd and played ball to hide the fact? Or had he skimmed through a general studies program by the skin of his teeth? Or was he a closet accountant who liked those numbers Barbara went for? She sure hoped not.

Alistair took a sip from his water glass, then said, "Engineering."

"Nice," Barbara said.

He might as well have said accounting. Lauren licked a spot of mayonnaise from her fingers.

"You and Oliver are both numbers men," Barbara said.

Lauren's ears perked up. Oliver. That was the name of the blond hunk whose wallet she'd returned.

Alistair smiled, and said, "I'm afraid my brother holds all the cards when it comes to banking."

"He's very good at what he does," Barbara said, wiping her mouth neatly with her napkin before taking a drink of her iced tea.

Lauren wished the other woman weren't quite so neat. Alistair probably thought he'd landed in heaven, seated next to someone who didn't scatter crumbs or let her parrot eat at the same table.

"Though I will say I was a bit concerned yesterday."

"Oh?" Alistair eyed a few crumbs of French bread on his plate, but Lauren was willing to bet he wouldn't go for them with his fingers.

"When he showed up with that paint all over his suit," she said, "I thought he was the other brother."

Alistair grinned. "Ah, you mean the slightly nutty one."

A faint smile on her face, she nodded.

Lauren stopped, one hand suspended over her plate. Oliver. Paint on his suit.

"Oh, brother," she said.

Twelve

*F*or the second time in two days, Oliver ventured into the Quarter in search of his brother. He and Barbara had spent a productive afternoon meeting with the bank's programmers, and he felt as if he could accomplish anything. He even offered to entertain Barbara the next day, but she surprised him by saying Alistair was taking her to the French Quarter Festival.

Spurred on by the thought that his brother was making progress with Barbara while he still hadn't located the divine redhead, Oliver crossed Canal and headed down Bourbon Street. He'd always been fairly skeptical of his brother's skill with the magickal arts; never before had he called on him for help.

But he had to find Lauren.

Why was it so important?

To the fury of a beer-truck driver, Oliver stepped in front of the vehicle. That very action, he realized, explained his sense of urgency. Ever since he'd first sighted the redhead yesterday, he hadn't been himself.

And Oliver found that refreshing.

He liked his life just fine, but he wanted to break out. He wanted to walk on the wild side. Not forever, of course, but he'd been so responsible for so long, taking over the bank, stepping into his father's shoes. He'd been so intent on pleasing his father and forestalling the storm he knew would come when Alistair refused to enter the bank that he'd lived his life for everyone but himself.

Somehow the mysterious woman represented a turning point in his life, the possibility that he might still find something he hadn't realized had been lacking until that moment.

Another delivery truck honked at him, and this time Oliver paused on the corner. Late afternoon showed Bourbon Street at its most unappealing. The faded signs advertising total nudity and bottomless and topless delights failed to stir the least bit of anticipation in passersby. With signs that sad and worn, what must the "delights" look like? Bourbon Street thrived at night, when the neon, rhythmic music, and usually inebriated state of the tourists served as a collective magic wand to turn the street into one big happy playground.

Oliver stepped around a pile of trash and wondered why his brother, who could afford to live anywhere, remained in the Quarter. Oliver never had understood his brother, though, despite his affection for him. It was funny, how well they got along despite their different outlooks and lifestyles.

A few more blocks found Oliver in front of the Bayou Magick Shop. A man in a suit and tie walked out the door, followed by Alistair, who shook his hand, then started to turn back into the store.

He paused, and Oliver raised his hand in a wave as he crossed the street.

Alistair shook his head, as if shaking off a thought, then smiled. "What's up, bro?"

"Not much." Oliver followed his brother into the shop, jumping as the massive bell tied to the door clanged. A girl with neon hair looked up from the counter, then, when she saw the two guys, returned to the newspaper she was reading.

"Come in the back with me for a minute," Alistair said.

Oliver followed him past his ghoulish collection of merchandise. As his brother's banker, he appreciated just how much money that junk brought in, but he failed to appreciate the appeal.

Alistair walked to the desk in his office/storeroom and jotted a few notes. Oliver glanced around, studying the multitude of candles. They were arranged by color and size. Alistair always did have a penchant for neatness. "Not changing bankers, are you?"

"What?" His brother glanced up. "Oh, you mean who was the man in the suit?"

Oliver nodded as he touched one finger to the iridescent surface of a purple-and-silver candle.

"He was a real-estate broker, and I wouldn't touch that candle if I were you."

Oliver jerked his hand back. "Buying or selling?"

Alistair grinned. "Buy low. Sell high."

Oliver's heart skipped. "What did you just say?"

The grin faded from his brother's face. "Oh, shit."

Oliver covered the space between them in one step. "Are you holding out on me? Do you know where Lauren is?"

"I'm not sure she's the woman for you, Oliver."

"Who are you to judge that?" For the first time since they'd been boys, Oliver wanted to punch his brother's face.

Alistair lifted his hands in a gesture of surrender. "You're right. It's none of my business."

"Damn right. I was desperate enough to beg you to do one of your silly spells to find her for me, and all along, you know who she is and where she is!"

"Well, I wouldn't go that far."

Oliver stepped back. Without realizing it, he gripped the purple-and-silver candle. Stroking it, he said, "She's not for me, is she? And don't touch this candle. Hey, I'm not your kid brother anymore, got that?"

"I'm sorry, Oliver."

Oliver put the candle down. His brother did look contrite. "Take me to her, and I'll forget about it."

"I don't know where she is."

"Swear on your roomful of candles that's true."

"I swear."

"Then do the spell for me."

Alistair shook his head. "I started to, but I had to stop. I'm sorry, Oliver, but I just can't perform a love spell. You're the second person to ask it of me in two days, and I can't do it for either one of you."

"Was Lauren the other one?" He knew he sounded hopeful, and even as he said it knew how silly it sounded.

"Nope. Coincidentally, it was Ms. Warren's godmother, Mrs. Merlin."

"That funny old lady friend of yours is Barbara's godmother?" Oliver had never met Mrs. Merlin, but he recalled a fantastical story Alistair had related. He hadn't believed all of it. No one could accidentally shrink oneself; it wasn't consistent with nature.

"I think of her as ageless, and she's concerned about her godchild."

Oliver smiled. "She needn't be. I've never met anyone as together as Ms. Warren. Anyway, don't try to protect me, okay?"

Alistair nodded. "I can tell you Lauren will be back here at some point."

"And how do you know that?"

"She left her bird in my apartment."

"Alistair, tell me you two didn't . . ." Oliver almost didn't want to hear his brother's answer. The sad truth was Lauren was much more his brother's type than she was Oliver's. And women fell for his devil-may-care looks and that long hair.

"Nothing like that." An unreadable expression on his face, Alistair said, "I bumped into her on the street. It was late, she had no place to go, so I let her sleep at my place."

"Sleep?"

Alistair lifted his hands in a gesture of surrender. "Innocent."

"You never could turn away a person in need,"

Oliver said. "Do you mind if I wait it out at your place until she returns?"

"Be my guest. The door's unlocked."

Oliver turned to the door. "What are you doing with a broker?"

"I'm putting the building up for sale."

Oliver was shocked. The property on Bourbon Street had to be worth half a million, at least. "Why not lease it out?"

A sorrowful smile drifted across his brother's face. "When you're making a change, Oliver, it's best not to go halfway. That's more than likely to cause trouble."

"You're selling so once you join the bank you can't change your mind."

Alistair nodded.

For once, Oliver felt like the wiser of the brothers. "If you have to force yourself, maybe it's a mistake."

They looked at each other, silent.

Then the ringing of Oliver's cell phone broke the moment.

Alistair watched from behind his battered and scarred desk as his brother's face took on a look of annoyance. Impressed by Oliver's insightful comment, he stared down at the agreement to list the building for sale with the broker. Why was he forcing himself to act? And why hadn't he called Oliver that morning and told him he could find Lauren at his place?

Oliver snapped his phone off. "Mrs. Walling," he said, "has just reminded me that I'm due at the

Sheraton for a fund-raiser and that I have a date for it."

"Who's the lucky woman?"

"Daffodil Landry."

Alistair whistled. "Sounds like a great night."

His brother frowned. "The only woman I'm interested in I can't seem to be within the same square block of. Besides, Daffy is like a sister to me."

Taking pity on him, Alistair said, "Look, I'll help you out here. Barbara is going to the Fest with me tomorrow. When Lauren comes back, I'll let her stay in the downstairs apartment and ask her to join us tomorrow. You can show up and take it from there."

The smile on his brother's face was so grateful it was almost pathetic. Alistair instantly regretted his offer. Any man that infatuated shouldn't be encouraged. Why, Alistair was acting quite calm and collected in his pursuit of Barbara.

"You're a prince," Oliver said, and dashed out the door.

"I don't know about that," Alistair said to his brother's back. He moved around his desk and picked up the purple-and-silver candle his brother had been touching. Heat shimmered on its surface, and Alistair collected the warmth in his hands. The right amount of heat from this candle charged one's touch with a powerful magnetism.

His palms tingled and his mind filled with the image of Lauren naked on the bed, his hands massaging the creamy skin of her back and buttocks. He knew, through the way he had of seeing, that his brother had been having similar thoughts while he had held the candle.

The only difference was, Alistair had felt her body beneath his hands, while at this point, Oliver only dreamed of it.

Alistair couldn't say why, because by all rights it was Barbara's naked body he should be thinking of, but he felt pretty strongly that Oliver should just keep those thoughts in a dream state.

"And so should you," Alistair said.

He put the candle down.

Even though he stored a lot of magick supplies in the lower apartment, it was better to have Lauren spend the night there. Upstairs, anywhere near his bed, he didn't know how long he'd continue to prove himself unlike those other men Lauren liked to reference.

Five minutes before the ten o'clock closing time, Lauren pushed open the door of the Bayou Magick Shop. She had a brand-new blister on the little toe of her right foot, another cramp forming in her calf, and total dejection in her heart.

She'd been turned down for jobs she couldn't believe she'd actually applied for. Waitress, dishwasher, shop assistant at a candy store, checker at a corner market. And she'd already gotten fired from the one place that had offered her a job on the spot as a cocktail waitress.

It didn't take long for her to discover that pawing the help was acceptable; slapping the customers was not. Furious with the manager of the hole-in-the-wall bar for yelling at her for giving the lecherous customer what he deserved, Lauren had torn off her apron, wadded it into a ball, and thrown it at the man. It had landed atop a candle guttering in a beer bottle and burst into flames.

The fire department had been on its way when Lauren ran out the back door, the manager shouting after her, "You're fired!"

She might be desperate, but she still had her pride.

"Can I help you?" The girl behind the register glanced at Lauren, then pointedly at her wristwatch.

"I'm looking for Alistair."

"Who isn't? Is he expecting you?"

With Buster still upstairs, he'd better be. Lauren nodded. Funny how she had trusted him enough to leave the parrot for the day. But then, he wasn't like most men.

The girl picked up the phone and dialed, said a few words, then hung up. "He'll be right down."

Relief washed over her. Edging her right foot out of her sandal, she looked around. This was the first time she'd been inside the shop. Behind the counter she noted a stack of the stylishly lettered purple-and-silver bags she'd admired on the street only yesterday. "Nice bags," she said to the register girl.

"Would you like one?"

"Oh, yes." She answered without considering how odd she'd look carrying one of Alistair's empty bags from his store. She admired it, she wanted it, so she took it, folding it carefully before tucking it under her arm.

"Alistair did the design," the girl said.

"Wow."

"Yeah, it's pretty good. For commercial art." The adjective definitely carried a stigma with the girl.

"Are you an artist?" Lauren asked.

The girl pulled up one of her long black sleeves, revealing a rose with black thorns trailing up her arm. "Tattoo," she said with pride.

Lauren squeezed her eyes shut. "Ooh," she said. She couldn't stand tattoos. A thought struck her, and she opened her eyes. Thankfully the girl had pushed her sleeve down. If this self-mutilator with the green-and-purple hair had gotten hired, maybe Alistair could get Lauren a job. He'd said he was the caretaker, so he might have some influence with the owner. "Do you like working here?"

The girl nodded, then moved from behind the counter toward the door, where she shook her head at a couple about to enter. "Closed," she said, and turned the sign to prove her point.

Why, Lauren would have let them in to shop. What harm would it have done?

That proved it. She'd be a great voodoo-shop employee. And what she didn't know about the merchandise she could invent. The tiers of voodoo dolls, incense, magick books, silver crosses, replicas of Marie Laveau, who was practically the New Orleans saint of voodoo practitioners—why, all those items begged for tales of invention.

Cocktailing held no lure for the truly creative.

"You want to work here?" The girl opened the cash register and started counting bills. "Is that why you're looking for Alistair?"

"Not exactly." Lauren's hopes died as quickly as they'd been born as she watched the girl competently count the cash, not even losing track as she continued her conversation.

"I'll tell Alistair about you if you want me to."

"Tell Alistair what about whom?"

Lauren jerked around from her fascinated study of the cash-drawer operation. He'd appeared as silently as his cat had moved when stalking Buster.

"Hey, Alistair," the girl said. "I need a vacation, and she's willing to cover for me. Any problem with that?"

"You've only worked here two months."

"My point exactly."

Alistair didn't look at all thrilled by the idea. His reluctance spurred Lauren to embrace the idea she'd been about to nix. "I'm great with people," she said. "Your customers will love me."

Alistair tugged on a strand of his long silvery brown hair. Lauren felt her mouth watering just watching him, and willed away her reaction.

"And I'm a quick learner," she added. If he went for the notion, he'd soon find she wrote her numbers in reverse, which meant she had a lot of trouble adding figures, but if she handled the customers, surely he could count out the cash drawer and do any necessary sums.

"I'll work for minimum wage." She added a smile and a tiny flutter of her eyelashes. And to herself, she said, "Plus room and board."

Alistair knew better than to say yes. He stood there, watching her huge green eyes and the hopeful curve to her ruby red lips. She was leaning forward in anticipation of his response, and her dress dipped enough to reveal cleavage he had no business fixing his gaze on. Say no, he commanded his tongue.

Kara stacked the bills and charge slips tidily in the bank bag, and said, "Aw, come on, Alistair. Don't make me invent a sick auntie. I really want to get out of town and catch some beach rays."

Alistair thought of his date with Barbara. He'd planned to spend all day Saturday with her, sharing the flavors and sounds of the city he loved, making an impression on the woman he'd decided to court.

"All right, but you have to work tomorrow and train her."

"Cool." She picked up her purse and was halfway to the door when Alistair realized his brother would have his head on a platter if he followed through with that plan.

"Wait!" He considered his options. "You work tomorrow, and I'll train Lauren on Sunday." Talk about karmic payback. If he'd called his brother first thing that morning and told him where he could find his precious redhead, Alistair would be well rid of this complicating, pesky female. He certainly wouldn't be putting her up for the night or getting ready to fill out a W-2 form for her as his employee.

"Whatever you say." Kara put away the cash and bounded out the door.

Alistair locked it behind her and turned to face Lauren.

She was looking at him with those huge eyes of hers, very much the way Midnight had looked up at him the day he'd found the tiny, helpless kitten.

He'd rescued him and taken him home to be bottle-fed.

Alistair sighed, and said, "I suppose you're hungry again."

Thirteen

*L*auren offered another seed to Buster and tucked her feet under her on the sofa in what Alistair had referred to as the "guest apartment." Alistair was with her, seated in a chair opposite the sofa, not saying much as they waited for the pizza delivery he'd phoned in.

"Why a magick shop?" she asked, thinking she'd like to know more about this unusual man and she might as well learn about the job she—or rather the other girl—had talked into existence.

"It's a good business," Alistair answered. "Especially in a tourist-oriented city like New Orleans."

"So is ice cream," Lauren said. "Or gumbo."

He grinned, almost reluctantly. "Touché."

She smiled in return. "So why magick?"

"I actually inherited the business from an old man who befriended me while I was in college."

"What was his name?" Lauren handed yet another seed to Buster. The poor thing was starving, just as she was!

"Olin Desque."

"What an odd name."

He shrugged. "Olin was a man unto himself."

"How did you meet him?"

A faraway look stole over Alistair's face, and Lauren snuggled against the cushions where she rested, settling in for a good story.

"He found me, I suppose."

"During college?"

He nodded. "He'd come to the basketball games and sit near the center of the court. During tip-off, I would see him watching me. I didn't know whether he was a fan or simply a lonely old man with nothing else to do, but I was glad someone was watching the games."

"Your father didn't go?"

He shook his head. "Working, you know. And it's about an hour and a half drive from here to Baton Rouge, where I went to school."

Lauren nodded. She'd spent many an hour following her father's favorite teams, but there had been more than one art showing when no one had been there for her. But she'd understood; her dad was a doctor, and his time was not his own. But a banker? Surely Alistair's father could have attended some of his games.

"One night, after a championship game in which I'd been high scorer, Olin came up to me." Alistair shifted on his chair. "He said he'd been watching me, and I said I knew that. He nodded, and told me I had choices to make and that the course of my life would depend on which path I claimed as my own."

"Ooh," Lauren said, for the second time that night. Goose bumps rose on her arms.

Alistair shrugged again. "That's true for any of us, you know. I didn't pay much attention to it, but later, I remembered every word of what he'd said to me."

"And when was later?"

"I was twenty-four. My father appeared and took me to lunch. He said he wanted me to come into the business because he'd been told his heart was weak and he might not live a long time. I didn't believe him; I thought he was just trying to play my emotions." Alistair rose from his chair and crossed to the door. He opened it, and listened, then shut it. "I refused to join the bank. My brother stepped in. My dad died last year."

"I'm sorry," she said softly.

He nodded. "When my dad came to ask me, I was already working at Olin's place, the Bayou Magick Shop. I threw myself into studying magick. He taught me more than anyone else could ever teach me."

Lauren wondered about that statement, but she let it go. "Do you really deal in magick?"

Again he nodded. "On different levels, yes. To some people who wander in and buy souvenirs, I sell them the possibility of magick. To others, who believe in their hearts there is more than only the pragmatic, the everyday universe, I sell them the bridge to that reality."

As much trouble as she got into, Lauren still considered herself grounded on planet earth. "What do you mean by that?"

"It happens on different levels," he said. "For instance, I remember one woman who came into my shop and bought five voodoo dolls. They were silly items on the surface, bits of straw and fabric with gashes of purple and red and orange across their voodoo doll faces. But she chose each one with particular care, then later came back and told me she'd named each of the dolls for attributes each of her friends needed to own and conquer, and given them as gifts with the explanations. I shivered at the power of what I'd sold to her."

"Wow," Lauren said, hugging her arms around her knees. "That is heavy. But when you spoke of magic I thought you meant spells and trances and poof, now you see it, now you don't."

"The power of the mind is often all the magick one needs." He placed one hand on the doorknob. "Your pizza should be here. I'm going out front to collect it."

Arms still wrapped around her legs, Lauren nodded and considered what Alistair had shared with her. The revelations made him seem even more special, and even more unlike any other man she'd ever known. An image of her and Alistair curled up on a magick carpet drifted to her mind.

She blinked and then focused on the coffee table in front of the daybed. A sturdy cherry red candle sat amidst four trinkets. She eyed the setup, then cleared the space to the side of it. Alistair would soon be back with the pizza and she didn't want to be sitting there daydreaming when he returned.

She was curious about what he could accomplish with magick. She didn't think there was much hope of changing her penchant for problems, but if he could wave a wand and help her get a handle on her life, she'd be more than grateful.

Buster cracked a seed loudly enough to wake the dead. She looked at him, and said, "You got something to say?"

Holding the seed aloft in one claw, he fixed her with that piercing stare of his, and she could have sworn he was trying to talk to her. Buster was like that, and that had been one of the reasons she couldn't bear to leave him to the fates the Plaisance family had in mind for him. Lauren might be pretty much a mess in many ways, but she understood the parrot; Buster was too special to be left with someone who did not.

He waved the seed, then slipped it into his beak.

"Yes, yes," she said, "you wouldn't be eating that delicious seed if it weren't for Alistair." She smiled. No need to rely on Alistair's magickal powers. Why, without any supernatural aid at all, he'd given her a job and a place to stay, at least temporarily. And he had talked to her just now as if he enjoyed sharing his ideas and thoughts with her. Today had already improved a hundred percent over the day before.

The door opened, and a pizza box appeared, hovering waist high, followed by Alistair. "Double pepperoni with the works," he said, placing the box on the space she'd cleared. "Enjoy. Then get a good night's sleep."

"Aren't you hungry?" She'd been looking forward to his company more than she realized.

He looked torn, but he shook his head. "I've already had dinner."

"Sit with me?" She lifted the lid of the pizza box and inhaled the pungent aroma. The rounds of pepperoni sat in oily pools that would have sent Barbara, Ms. Dressing-on-the-side, screaming. Lauren smiled. She could eat anything and never gain a pound.

"Better not." He mumbled his response, but Lauren was sure she'd heard him correctly.

"I won't cause any trouble," she said, lifting a slice of pizza.

Buster sidled over to the box and peered in. "Oh," Lauren said, halting with the pizza halfway to her lips. "It's Buster. You don't like that he's by the food. I'll put him on the floor."

"That's okay," Alistair said. "I really have eaten." He stood there, though, not leaving and not staying, gazing down, looking almost as hungry as she felt. "I guess I should have told you this sooner, but I invited Barbara and my brother Oliver to spend the day with us tomorrow. That's why you can't start in the shop until Sunday."

"Are they dating each other?" Lauren still held the slice of pizza in her hand. If Barbara and Oliver were involved, that would certainly throw a monkey wrench into her own plans. Taking a huge bite of the pizza, she contemplated the situation. To be honest, she didn't feel much like marrying for money at the moment. If only Alistair would let her stay there. She would earn her keep and finish her dissertation.

Lauren chewed in silence as Alistair studied a spot on the floor between his feet and the coffee table. He was frowning, but Lauren couldn't figure out why. She hadn't done or said anything wrong in some time now.

Then she realized, mulling over her situation, that she should have thanked Alistair for rescuing her. It was thanks to him and his generosity that she was tucked in this apartment, warm and cozy. Out of deference to his neatness, she chewed her pizza completely, then swallowed and patted her mouth with a napkin before she said, "Is there some way I can thank you for all you've done for me?"

He coughed and choked slightly, which only made him choke again. She leapt up, tackled his arms from behind, and prepared to execute a Heimlich maneuver on him. She wasn't a doctor's daughter for nothing.

"I'm fine. I'm fine." Alistair forced his cough to stop. How did she get such reactions out of him? But it was too much, her sitting there on the floor by the coffee table, barefooted, long hair flowing like a river over her shoulders, with her mouth closing in on that pizza in a way that made him think of only one thing. And why in this world or any other hadn't he corrected himself and clarified that Barbara was *his* date?

Now her body was wrapped around his, her breasts crushed against his back as she reached her hands around to grasp his upper arms. She was shorter, of course, so she had to lift her arms in a fashion that only pushed her more closely against his back.

Alistair caught his breath and willed himself to breathe slowly and deeply.

Which only brought them more closely together.

He should have dropped the pizza box at the door, run upstairs, and barricaded the door.

"I really am fine," he said.

"If you're sure." She loosed her grip, but edged away only by an inch or so.

He nodded, although if she didn't let go, he wouldn't be fine.

Then she moved and sank gracefully to the floor, selecting another slice of pizza as if he hadn't been near death's door. Even more maddeningly, she displayed absolutely no reaction whatsoever to their physical contact.

"You should see an ENT about your choking proclivity," she said, a look of sweet concern in her eyes.

"It's not something that happens often," he said.

She nodded, but seemed unconvinced. "I've witnessed it at least three times," she said. "And I've only known you, what, a day and a half?"

Despite his best intentions, Alistair lowered his body to the floor and sat with his legs crossed yoga-style beside the coffee table. "Is that all it's been?" After draping a paper napkin across his lap, he took a slice of pizza.

Buster sidled over and hopped onto his knee, eyeing the food.

Lauren smiled, somewhat shyly. "Seems like longer, doesn't it?"

Alistair broke off a nub of crust and held it out to the bird, who accepted it with one claw and returned to the floor. "Much," he said, after finishing his first bite. He never should have sat down. It was too comfortable there, both of them on the thickly carpeted floor, her eyes all wide and trusting and more inviting than she could know.

Get up. Go. He applied his napkin to his hands, then said, "How's that calf muscle tonight?"

Her green eyes opened even wider. "I was hoping you would ask," she said. "Do you think you could do whatever that was you did to it last night?"

"Ask and you shall receive." He said the phrase lightly, but his body was already responding as she extended her right leg. Her feet were bare, and as she shifted, her dress fluttered and settled above her knees. Knowing full well she was almost naked beneath that fluffy bit of cotton she called a dress, Alistair forced himself to fix his attention on her foot, ankle, and calf.

He set down the rest of his pizza slice, wiped his fingers on a napkin, and lifted her leg gently, settling it across his legs as close to his knees as possible. He didn't want to scare her off by revealing the effect she had on him.

An effect he didn't completely understand. Yeah, sure, she was female and he was male and that alone was quite enough for, as Lauren would say, "most guys." But Alistair had never been indiscriminately sexual. As a general rule, he'd loved within relationships. And here he was, set on pursuing Barbara and all her competent perfection and his body was doing everything it could to derail him.

Go figure, he said to himself, stroking the muscles of Lauren's calves with a light touch.

"Ooh, that's nice," she said, dabbing her lips with a napkin.

"It's better with massage oil."

"This feels great. I don't know if it could get any better." She tucked the lid over the remaining pizza and leaned against the sofa. Her head tipped back and she lifted her arms and spread her long auburn hair over the cushions of the daybed.

At that moment, Alistair would have loved to perform a spell that transformed him into those cushions. Instead, he said, "Don't move. I'm going to get some oil."

"Whatever you think," she said, sighing contentedly.

The apartment consisted of the one room where he and Lauren were seated, which was the area he reserved for the magickal practices that he hadn't pursued much lately. There was also a bedroom and bath, and what passed for a utility kitchen. Sesame oil made a great massage medium, but he had no hopes of finding any there. The bathroom held none, but in the bedroom he hit pay dirt. He thought he'd left a bottle there last year, back when he'd been involved with a woman who'd been between jobs and husbands.

He stopped, one hand about to lift the bottle from the bedside table. Just like so many of his other lovers, she'd gotten her life back together, thanked him profusely, and sent him an invitation to her wedding.

"Haven't you learned anything, Alistair?" A large

mirror hung over the bed, but Alistair turned away before he could check his reflection. He knew, as he knew more things than one could usually be comfortable with, that there was a price to pay for hiding from truth. But this time he was safe; he had no intentions of letting Lauren get under his skin or into his heart. And even better, she was completely impervious to him. Unlike the other women, Lauren was straightforward in her needs. Job, shelter, food. She wasn't trading her body or trying to play with his mind.

These things he felt for sure. Lauren was an innocent.

Holding the massage oil, he turned from the bedroom, past the small bathroom and the one long counter with its tiny fridge that served as the kitchen, and stepped back into the front parlor.

Lauren was exactly where she'd been when he'd gotten up, but the lights had been dimmed. Only the flame of the cherry red candle he'd situated in the center of the love spell altar lit the room.

Gazing at Lauren's delicate skin in the glow of the candle, Alistair said a silent thank-you that he'd not burned that candle in the perfect match spell. His heart beat faster; Lauren lay on that sofa waiting for him of her own accord.

The next step for them—and Alistair knew what he wanted that to be—would happen only if Lauren trusted him enough to give herself to him.

Fourteen

Under normal circumstances, Oliver would have been more than happy to attend the Downtown Business Alliance Awards dinner with Daffy Landry. The two of them had had their diapers changed by the same nanny, played together as toddlers, and graduated from kindergarten together. Their paths had diverged with each attending same-sex schools for the next twelve years, but they'd been in the same freshman class at Tulane. Of course, Daffy had been a student at Newcomb, the women's college, while he'd enrolled under the auspices of the all-male college, a tradition of officially separating the sexes that simply ignored the social upheaval of the latter half of the twentieth century.

Daffy, or Daffodil as noted on her birth certificate, fit perfectly within the sedate traditions of her socially elite New Orleans upbringing, except that she'd never settled into marriage. Instead, she went into journalism, after a fashion, accepting the torch of society gossip columnist passed on to her by the venerable Betty Gillaud.

When she needed an escort, she often called Oliver. As she and Oliver had long ago agreed that any alliance between the two of them would smack of incest, theirs was a most platonic relationship. It had been Oliver who'd asked Daffy to accompany him to the Business Alliance dinner. He was receiving an award and expected to sit at the head table, where everyone else would be one half of a couple. There were plenty of eligible women he could have invited, but he hadn't had the heart to get any of their hopes up. With Daffy, there'd be no speculation that Oliver, one of the city's most eligible bachelors, was thinking of tying the knot.

It was in Oliver's nature to be prepared for any contingency and as a result, he kept evening attire at his office. He'd just made it back inside the bank from the Quarter when one of the guards called his name. Oliver turned. "Yes, Bill?"

"Miss Landry's here to see you. She's in your office, waiting with Ed. Seeing as it was her, we didn't think you'd mind."

Daffy here? It must be later than he realized. "That's fine," he said, then raced toward his office. Between the two of them, those two bank guards had taught both him and Daffy how to shoot. Of course they'd let Daffy into his office. But why she'd come to meet him he didn't understand.

Ed, the thin and lanky guard, was shaking his

head over Daffy when Oliver opened his office door.

"You've sure got a bad case of it," he said. "Best go home and take some Benadryl."

"Oh, Oliver!" Daffy leapt up from Mrs. Walling's desk chair. "Just look at me! I came to show you so you wouldn't think I was putting you off."

Oliver stared at his friend's face and arms, taking in the red welts almost obscuring her fine features. Daffy suffered from hives, but he'd never seen her this badly affected. "You sweet, silly thing," he said fondly, yet concerned, "you could have phoned. And you certainly didn't have to get all rigged up," he added as he noted the graceful lines of her knee-length cocktail dress. It showed enough cleavage to entice yet covered enough to whet one's imagination. "As usual, you are the picture of elegance, hives or not."

"Oliver, I'm a mess!" She sighed, and said, "I am sorry, but it's been getting worse over the last hour, and I simply won't make it through the dinner. I've been trying to think of someone else we can get to stand in for me."

"Did you give in and eat seafood?" Oliver stripped off his jacket as he asked the question, ignoring her suggestion of a substitute date. Too late for that; he'd simply go alone.

She nodded. "Soft-shell crab. And it was so-o-o good. It's just not fair to live in New Orleans and be allergic to shellfish."

Oliver's thus-far unsuccessful pursuit of the elusive Lauren filled his mind. What if she'd returned to Alistair's place by now? Would she go with him?

He reached for the phone, then caught himself. What a poor impression—asking a woman on a first date as a last-minute stand in. "No, Daffy," he said slowly, "some things just aren't fair."

The door to the conference room opened.

Oliver and Daffy jumped. Ed slapped his hand onto the gun at his waist.

Barbara stepped through the door, her purse over one shoulder and her laptop in her other hand. "Oh, excuse me," she said, glancing from Oliver to Daffy.

Ed lowered his gun hand.

"You're still working?" Oliver felt bad that he'd abandoned his consultant in his rush to go after Lauren.

"It's only seven," she said. "And I didn't have any other plans."

"Oliver!" Daffy jumped up and grabbed him by the shirtsleeve. "She's perfect!"

Barbara gripped the handle of her laptop case. She took in the coatless bank president and the incredibly beautiful woman in one of the loveliest cocktail dresses she'd ever seen. Beautiful, that was, aside from some horrible red blotches. She concluded she'd interrupted a moment of intimacy, but that didn't exactly equate with the presence of the guard.

Bemoaning her faded lipstick, Barbara straightened shoulders clad in the serviceable blue suit, and said, "Perfect for what?"

The other woman tugged again on Oliver's shirt. "What do you think?"

"It's a lot to ask."

"She said she didn't have plans."

"That's one thing; what you're suggesting is quite another."

"Yes, I know." She smiled brilliantly, and Barbara couldn't help but notice how close she stood to Oliver and how easily they understood one another. Thankful that she'd quelled the initial rush of interest she'd felt upon meeting and working with the bank's president, Barbara set down her computer and purse and leaned against the doorjamb. She'd let them finish their discussion, then take a polite leave. If she were interested in Oliver, it would be far too difficult for her to stand there watching him with this vision of perfection, communicating in what seemed their own private language.

"No time to change," Oliver was saying.

The woman turned to her and smiled in a friendly way. "Hi, forgive me. I'm Daffy Landry. Are you a six?"

"Barbara Warren," she replied. "Is my dress size relevant?" She hadn't intended to sound so brusque, but she felt awkward, a bit as if she were the tennis ball in a game of singles.

Oliver smiled and moved over beside the woman called Daffy. When he smiled like that, the effect produced a slow lighting of his features that reminded Barbara how comfortable and welcome he made her feel. She'd done consulting jobs all over the country and never responded to any of the scores of men she dealt with in quite the way she'd reacted to this man. "I'm in a bit of a bind," he said. "A social bind."

"And it's entirely my fault," Daffy—if indeed Barbara had heard her name correctly—said. "He needs a beautiful, intelligent woman to sit by his side at an incredibly boring but important awards dinner that begins in"—she checked a delicate watch ringed in diamonds—"fifteen minutes."

"Oh," Barbara said. Oliver was looking at her, his rueful expression indicating he would understand completely if she said no. Or better yet, Are you nuts? "Well, I'm more than happy to help you," she said, "but I'm not dressed for an evening social event."

"But I'm right that you're a size six?" Daffy turned around and patted the back of the neckline of her swirling cocktail dress. "Undo me, Oliver."

Barbara realized the two of them must be more intimate than she'd initially assumed. Wishing herself anywhere but still at the bank, she said, "You're correct that I usually wear a six, but I fail to see what that has to do with Oliver's dilemma." As a matter of fact, she'd swiftly seen where Daffy was going with her suggestion. An only child, Barbara had never swapped clothing. She hadn't even exchanged accessories with her high-school girlfriends.

"Hold on a sec, Daf," Oliver said. He moved closer to Barbara and spoke so that only she could hear. "Please don't feel you have to say yes, but now that the idea has come up, I find it rather appealing."

As close as he was, and as brilliantly blue as his eyes were gazing into hers, Barbara had trouble breathing in her normal steady fashion. Funny, but at lunch with Oliver's brother, she'd never once experienced that heady sort of sensation.

"It would mean a lot," he said.

She lowered her eyes, considering that she really had nothing to lose. An evening spent in Mrs. Merlin's company, as sweet and obliging as her godmother had been, couldn't compare to dinner with a man who'd gone out of his way to make her feel at home in his city and at his family's bank.

Raising her head, she drank in one more long look of those beguiling blue eyes. "I'll go with you," she said.

Oliver brushed the back of her hand, the barest skimming connection. "Thank you," he said.

"Great!" Daffy bounced over. "I sent Ed to get my gym bag out of my car. Let's pop into the conference room, and I'll slip out of this dress."

"I said I'd go, but I don't know that I should wear your dress." Barbara spoke hesitantly. Her blue suit was definitely not evening wear, but Daffy's dress seemed much too expensive to pass off to a total stranger.

"Don't be silly," the other woman said. "I've known Oliver all my life. That makes you practically my sister. Besides, don't worry about the dress. I have a cousin who runs them up for fun in her own design shop. If you spill coffee on it, it'll make her happy, give her something else to do making a new one." Daffy herded her into the conference room as she rattled on.

Acknowledging that she'd met an irresistible force, Barbara let her shut the door behind them.

A duffel bag was shoved through the door. In a flash, Daffy slipped the dress over her head and laid it over a chair. "Better hurry. Oliver's the guest of honor, and it will be awkward if you're late."

Barbara exchanged her suit for the dress, feeling very much like a postmodern Cinderella freed from a bank vault. Daffy insisted on touching up Barbara's makeup and slipping several of her bracelets onto her wrist. She whipped a butane-powered curling iron from her gym bag, all the while chatting about what a trouper Barbara was to help Oliver out of this bind.

Afraid of the answer but determined to have it, Barbara said casually enough, she hoped, "So you and Oliver, you're, um, friends?" Really, Barbara, she scolded silently, you have no business prying into Oliver Gotho's private life.

Busy turning under the ends of Barbara's hair, Daffy said, "From the cradle."

"I see."

Daffy tipped Barbara's chin upward and surveyed her handiwork. "Friends," she said, "not lovers. Never have been, never will be."

"Oh." Barbara colored slightly. Well, she'd gotten the information she wanted and pursuing the subject beyond that point would be unthinkably rude.

"Take a look," Daffy said, turning her gently toward a mirror hung over a walnut sideboard.

Barbara stared at the reflection of a stranger. She accepted she was attractive, even pretty, but never had she felt as magical as she did right at that moment.

Her lips gleamed, her eyes sparkled, and her hair swirled around her shoulders. The neckline dived prettily to reveal cleavage Barbara rarely showed, spending as much time as she did in business attire.

"You're a beautiful woman, and you look much better in that dress than I ever have," Daffy said. "I hope Oliver has the good sense to appreciate you."

Barbara laughed, slightly breathlessly. "He seems to value my computing advice."

Daffy widened her eyes, but whatever she was going to say was cut off by a knock at the door.

"Time to go," Oliver said.

Daffy opened the door, revealing Barbara. Oliver stepped forward, admiration in his gaze. "You look fabulous." Continuing to study her, he said, "Daffy, I have to hand it to you. Just like you said, she's perfect."

The candlelight showed Lauren to even better advantage. Alistair wondered whether she realized what a beautiful picture she created, curled on the floor, hair spilling every which way over her shoulders, a sweet smile on her face.

The flame from the candle leapt in a weaving spiral dancing motion. The candle casting that lovely play of light and shadow on Lauren's features was an extremely powerful magickal one, but as no spell had been rendered over it, the only magick in the room was the enchanting woman waiting for him by the sofa.

Advancing the rest of the way into the room, Alistair hid a rueful grin. The magickal balance of the universe might be undisturbed, but his very male body had certainly reacted to the effect of the scene. Pausing beside the far end of the daybed, he said, "Found it."

She stretched her arms over her head and yawned. "Oh, good. Massage does feel better with oil. And look how pretty this candle is."

He nodded, then realized something was definitely amiss. Matches were never used in candle magick. He kept special incense for lighting the wicks. Sitting down on the far end of the sofa, he said casually, "What did you find to light it with?"

She pointed to her bag. "I always have matches with me. You just never know when you might need one."

"Ah."

She must have picked up on something in his tone, because she twisted around, and said, "Were you saving it for a special occasion and now I've ruined that?" Her expression was so woeful, Alistair felt guilty. No harm had been done and, if anything, her burning the candle reinforced his own decision not to perform Mrs. Merlin's love spell.

Patting the cushion beside him, he said, "If it was meant for a special moment, I can't think of a better time than right now. Stretch out and I'll fix that calf before I get out of here and let you catch up on your sleep."

Lauren moved easily onto the daybed, lying on her side facing the candle, her bare legs offered to his touch. "This is even nicer than last night," she murmured, snuggling her cheek against one of the throw cushions.

"Being rescued from a mugger is pretty high up there on my list of favorite things," Alistair said, dribbling oil into his palms and rubbing them lightly together before smoothing his hands over her right leg.

"I was thinking of earlier. All I did was walk. And walk. And walk."

"Did you visit that address you asked me about?" He supposed it was unfair of him to ask when he already knew the answer, but he was curious as to Lauren's take on his brother, who would have been more than happy to keep her feet comfortably ensconced on Philip Street.

"Not so hard, please," Lauren said.

Alistair loosened the pressure of his hands. "Sorry." Thoughts of Lauren with Oliver had driven his massage technique straight to the dogs. Oliver had been captivated by Lauren—what man wouldn't be?—but she wasn't right for him. If Alistair had believed in his heart his brother was meant for this woman, he would have walked out the door after delivering the pizza.

"I had to return a man's wallet," she said. "A man I now know is your brother, which you might have told me when I asked for directions. Anyway, I was afraid he'd think I'd stolen it—which is ridiculous, because no matter how desperate I might be, I'd never steal. Not a dime. Not a penny." She'd lifted her head and shoulders. Her eyes flashed as she poked the daybed with an adamant forefinger. The determined effect was somewhat spoiled by the way her dress slipped off one shoulder.

"I believe you, and I apologize for withholding his identity. I was attempting to let matters take their own course," Alistair said, guiding her back down with a gentle hand, but leaving the dress askew. "Did he believe you?"

"Hmm," she said, seeming to accept his explanation. "He was quite charming and didn't even count the cash. He offered me lemonade and—"

"Oatmeal cookies?"

"How'd you know?"

"'Cause they were Columbina's famous?"

Lauren smiled. "Is having a housekeeper that mothering a Southern thing?"

"I wouldn't know about that. New Orleans isn't really Southern. It's a world unto itself."

"It sure is different from Illinois."

Alistair lifted her leg and eased it onto his lap, treating the bottom of her foot with alternating long strokes and caressing circles. "Did he offer you anything other than cookies and lemonade?"

"Dinner." She closed her eyes briefly, then opened them, a more closed-off expression in her eyes. "But I said no."

"Weren't you hungry?"

"Oh, I'm always hungry. But when a man offers you dinner, it always means he wants something else."

Alistair paused, his hands stilled on the back of her shapely ankle. He glanced toward the pizza box sitting in the shadows of the dancing candle flame. "Always?"

She followed his look. "Don't ask me why, but you're different. Not like—"

"—Most men." He finished the phrase for her. This point was pretty much as far as they'd gotten in the wee hours of the prior morning. He'd still yet to determine her reasoning for her conclusions about men. "What is it about all those other guys you so distrust?"

She wrinkled her nose. "Well . . ."

"Yes?" He moved to the other leg, pressing long strokes along her calf and stopping just above her knee. Any higher and he was asking himself to withstand a temptation he wasn't sure he could.

"There's an expression that sums it up but it's pretty crude."

"Try me."

"Most men are all 'wham bam, thank you, ma'am.'" She laughed in an embarrassed way. "See, it sounds awful just saying it."

Clearly she'd never known any but the lousiest and most selfish of lovers. "So most men use you and never think of giving you any pleasure?"

She'd turned her face into the pillows. Her shoulders had tensed. Alistair recognized he was treading on sensitive ground. "Hey," he said softly, placing one hand on her shoulder. "It's okay."

Lauren ground her face into the cushion and wished she'd never let Alistair lead her down the path of this topic. Embarrassed yet curious to see what he would say, she said in a voice that was pretty much muffled by the cushions, "I'm not sure there is any pleasure to be had."

"What do you mean?" His fingers were circling her upper back in a lazy, gentle motion.

She hated to turn over and lose that pleasurable sensation, but slowly she eased around. Pulling her hair up so she could twist it into a loose knot above her head, she said, "You always hear people talk about how great sex is, but I've yet to experience that. I've only had one serious boyfriend . . ." Lauren frowned as her words trailed off. She tried never to think of the way Brad had used her.

"And he was good-for-nothing?" Alistair's sympathetic tone comforted her.

"Rotten."

"Want to tell me about it?"

Strangely enough, she did want to. And she'd never told another guy about Brad. "It was a long time ago," she said.

"How old were you?"

She waved one hand, trying to dismiss the rush of feeling gathering within her. "Only twenty. A mere baby."

Alistair stroked her ankle. "Babies can be hurt."

"Yeah, that's for sure." She laughed shakily, wondering what it was about Alistair that made her feel so safe. "His name was Brad. He was doing his residency at the hospital. I was home from college for the summer. We met one night when I'd gone to the ER to take a snack to my father." Lauren smiled. "I used to do that, fuss over him."

"Sweet," Alistair said, continuing to soothe her ankle even as he drew her in, closer and closer.

"Anyway, Brad and I dated, and I fell in love with him and kept thinking how pleased my father would be with me for marrying a doctor." Lauren sighed. "Brad barely had time for me, and when he did it was sex for him, and then he'd fall asleep until he had to be back at the hospital. He made up to my father, got a great recommendation from him for a spot he wanted at another hospital, and packed his bags. When I said, 'What about me?' he actually laughed. I was such an idiot."

Alistair shook his head. "No, he was."

Thankful for being able to share that story with him, Lauren gave Alistair a heartfelt smile. It sure would be easy to spend more and more time with him. "You're so easy to talk to," she whispered, then a little bit frightened by how much she'd revealed, she wiggled around so that she lay on her tummy.

Alistair sensed her retreat. Rather than pushing her beyond her emotional comfort zone, he let his fingers convey his reassurance and understanding. Easing one hand onto her bare skin where the dress had slipped off her shoulder, he massaged her back with a rhythmic caress.

Her skin was warm and soft, and, with the sheen of oil, his hands moved almost as if by magick.

She sighed and said, "I know I'm a little bit nuts, but I don't know how to be any different than I am. I'm me." She half turned and stared up at him. "Do you understand that?"

Alistair nodded. "I've never admitted this to anyone else, but I've felt like that much of my life." He touched the tip of his index finger to her forehead.

Before he could move his hand, she grasped his finger and placed a feather-light kiss on it. Then, looking almost surprised, she gave him a crooked smile, and said softly, "I think I'm comfortable with you because sometimes you act like you don't like me, but you accept me anyway."

Alistair thought of her incredibly messy ways and

of her penchant for letting the bird share her table space. He smiled despite himself, and said, "Not everyone agrees on every point."

"No?" She wriggled against the daybed and shifted just enough to loosen the top of her dress completely off that enticing shoulder.

Without thinking what he was doing, Alistair bent over and kissed the hollow above her collarbone.

She held her breath.

Slowly he lifted his head, realizing what a mistake he'd made. In her eyes, he had probably become like all those other men, something he had intended to prevent.

"Forgive me," he said.

She blinked and took a tiny breath. "Is this over before it starts?"

"What do you mean?" He'd edged off and returned his hands where they belonged—or at least were safer—upon her lower legs.

"It's nice feeling safe with you," she said wistfully.

"Then safe you shall be." He said the words lightly, holding back what he'd rather tell her. *You're a beautiful, voluptuous woman and I'm a horny, appreciative male. Let me show you the pleasure you've been missing.*

"Thank you," she said, then added, in a shy voice that drove his resolve out the window, "I think."

Watching his hands on her legs, he imagined touching her in far-more-intimate places. As she sighed and relaxed even further, Alistair considered his dilemma. He could leave the room immediately and find whatever release he could on his own, locked safely upstairs in his own apartment. But he didn't want to leave, and Lauren didn't want him to leave. His body was calling out to him to stay by her side. He had to find a way to show her—without violating her trust—what she'd been missing.

"Have you ever let yourself be pleasured, just for you?" He asked the question pretty certain the answer was no, but not at all certain as to how she would react to it.

Her eyes widened. Then she shook her head.

"Sex can be a beautiful experience," Alistair said softly. "Let me show you how beautiful it can be for you."

Fifteen

Lauren gazed up at Alistair, unable to take her
eyes off his face, even though she was pretty certain
she was blushing. Had she understood him correctly? He wanted to pleasure her—and her alone—
to show her what she'd been missing out of this sex
mystery?

Was it possible?

Was what possible, she asked herself, the ecstasy
or that this man wanted to give her that experience?

As he talked, he kept up those circles on her leg,
circles that had started at her calf and now had
moved to the very sensitive skin of her inner thigh
just above her knees. "Think of it as a lesson that
there's more to life than all those other men ever
knew, and that you should never settle for less than
the best."

"That's pretty profound. Why would you do that? For me, I mean?"

"It's the least I can do to thank you for saving my life."

"All I did was interrupt the guy."

He shook his head, and some of his long silky hair slipped from the band. "At what I'd call a crucial moment," he said dryly. "Look, I'm not sure I understand this thing myself, but I know I'd like to."

"Buy low. Sell high." Buster squawked his favorite pronouncement, his first utterance in almost an hour, then tucked his head under one wing.

Alistair smiled and Lauren felt herself melt in a funny way she couldn't remember experiencing. "You won't hurt me?"

He shook his head. "Never."

"What do I have to do?"

Again, he touched her forehead with a fingertip that moved as lightly as a feather. "Nothing you don't want to."

Lauren wiggled her massaged toes and considered his offer. She was curious. She'd always felt there was enough wrong with her without being deficient in the matter of sex. And here was an opportunity to learn from someone who wasn't after her, didn't have designs on her body, and even more importantly, a man she sensed she could trust. Looking him in the eye, she said, "You'll stop if I say stop." It wasn't a question, and to his credit, he seemed to understand that.

"That goes without saying, but I'm glad you said it if it makes you more comfortable."

"If sex felt as good as massage," Lauren said, "I don't think I'd be celibate. My feet feel so good I've almost forgotten I tromped the streets for hours."

He grinned. His face lit up in a way that pleased her, but also made her slightly anxious. "You look a little bit like a satyr," she said.

He bent and lifted her bare foot to his lips, placing the gentlest of kisses atop the arch of her foot. "Satyr of pleasure, at your service."

Despite her nervousness, or perhaps because of it, Lauren giggled. Then she took a deep breath, lay back against the cushions, closed her eyes, and said, "Okay, I'm ready."

Her legs were still draped across his knees, and she felt him move closer. Breathing faster, she squished her eyes even more closely shut. She wasn't sure what she could learn to make all the groping and sweating of sex any more pleasant. To her surprise, rather than reaching for her breasts, she felt her right hand lifted and cradled in his. She eased her eyes open.

He had turned her hand palm up and was staring at it, studying her hand as if it were the most fascinating object in the world. She waited for him to squeeze it, or move it toward his own body in some suggestive manner, but he just kept on staring at her hand.

Finally, she said, "Why are you doing that?"

He didn't move the focus of his attention. "Getting to know you better."

"Ah," she said, not understanding at all.

"You have artist's hands."

"Of course I do. I'm an artist."

"And you have the hands of a gypsy."

Lauren started to sit up. Only then did he glance up.

"Please?"

Something in his gentle request eased her shoulders back down against the cushions. He smiled at her and went back to studying her palm.

If this was a lesson on how to enjoy sex, it sure wasn't what she'd expected. But he'd caught her attention with the gypsy comment. "Why a gypsy?"

"Your hands never stay still."

"That is true."

He nodded and lifted her left hand. He studied both together for a long moment, then placed them palms together touching and clasped within his hands. She wriggled, but he kept her hands quietly in place. Fixing his eyes on hers, he said, "Join me on the floor?"

Her hands still in his, Lauren rose and walked with him around the low table. He paused and stared into the flame of the cherry red candle. She did the same, noting that the candle seemed to burn even more brightly as they stood close by it. Then Alistair led them to the other side of the table and together they moved to their knees, still facing, still joined by their hands.

Lauren figured this was where things would turn sweaty. He was inches from her breasts, and she held her breath waiting for him to move his hands there. She didn't know why, but she hated for a man to touch her breasts. Guys were always into kneading or grabbing or sucking, none of which she'd ever found the least enjoyable. But at the same time, they'd be saying how great her boobs were.

"Lauren, you're okay," Alistair said. "Remember, this is a lesson."

"Did I say anything?"

He shook his head. "You didn't have to. Your body spoke to me."

She wrinkled her nose. "You're a funny man, but I like you."

"Thanks. Feel your shoulders, the way you're hunching forward. Listen to your breath. That's your mind talking to your body."

She had tensed up just thinking about him touching her breasts. Easing her shoulders back, she said, "Sex makes me nervous."

He moved one hand away and guided her right hand with his to her forehead. "Thoughts make us nervous," he said.

"Is this sex or psychotherapy?" She giggled, again, despising herself for doing so. Goodness knew she could probably benefit from both, but she hated even the suggestion.

"Sex is the best mood-altering drug I've ever known," Alistair said. "Now, sit down with your back to me and lean against my back."

"Are you sure you're giving me a lesson in sex? I mean, if we're back to back . . ." She trailed off, wondering why she was so impatient to get to the part she'd never liked.

Almost as if he could read her thoughts, he grinned, that devilishly knowing grin of his. "Your mind, Lauren," he said softly, "is just as essential as your body. But don't worry, we'll get to both. Unless, of course, you say stop."

She nodded and absorbed his image, the long hair slipping past his shoulders, the broad shoulders that rose above her own, the dark blue eyes that were almost the color of midnight in the shadows created by the light of the candle. Slowly, she turned and sat down.

He did the same, which she could tell when his back touched hers, solid, strong, and steady. He was taller, so of course their shoulders didn't match up. She held her body somewhat stiffly, until he said, "Lean into me, and I'll do the same."

"Won't we tip over then?"

He didn't answer. Lauren gingerly leaned back and realized he must be doing the same. They settled against each other, fitting perfectly. Oddly content, she sighed, and said, "Now what?"

She could feel him smiling by the way his shoulders moved slightly. That in itself was remarkable, almost as if her body was now reading his mind. "Hey, this is pretty amazing," she said.

"Good."

She sat for a moment or so, then started to turn her head around.

"Close your eyes," Alistair said.

"I just had a question."

"You can ask it without turning around."

That was true, but Lauren liked to move. He'd been right when he'd called her a gypsy. Trying to go with the flow, she closed her eyes, leaned into his back, and said, "If this is sex, aren't we supposed to be naked?"

His shoulders jerked. "Not necessarily, but would you like to be?"

She nodded.

He must have been reading her body gestures, too, because he said, "Lean forward and slip out of your dress."

Suddenly nervous again, Lauren inched her dress up over her hips, then pulled it over her head. Alistair remained sitting upright, facing away from her. She wasn't shy about nudity, which he knew from the night before, but somehow taking her clothes off with them sitting back to back seemed much more intimate than simply dropping her dress for a body massage. Puzzling over that one, she leaned back, anticipating flesh upon flesh.

Instead, her skin met cotton. The softly worn cotton of his T-shirt, but it certainly wasn't the warm body she'd expected.

"Um, aren't you going to get naked, too?"

No response.

Lauren crossed her legs in front of her and leaned forward, hands resting on her knees. "I think sex calls for an even playing field."

"But I'm not the one getting the lesson."

"There's no better way to teach than by example."

He chuckled. "I guess you got me there."

She heard the soft rustling of fabric. When the sound stopped, she leaned backward slowly. He was there, meeting her, his skin warm and smooth against hers. She realized he'd left his shorts on, and hesitated. Why hadn't he taken them off? Should she ask him to? She'd sketched more live nude males than she could count. Bodies meant nothing to her.

But this wasn't art; this was sex.

"I thought," Alistair said, interrupting her tumble of thoughts, "that I'd leave my shorts on. It helps to remind me I'm only giving a lesson."

"How did you know that's what I was thinking about?"

He shrugged. Lauren liked the movement of his muscles against her own. "Okay, I know," she said. "Just a lucky guess."

He nodded, which she experienced as a lengthening of his neck. "Now, let's feel the moment," he said in a low, slow voice. "Let your eyelids drift shut and sense the beating of your heart. And as you do, open your heart to the beating of mine."

Lauren took a deep breath and closed her eyes. Sitting still was hard enough for her under normal conditions, so she had no idea how she'd manage to be quiet long enough to do what he'd just described. But so far everything Alistair had suggested had been perfectly harmless, and, if anything, she was more content and relaxed than she could recall ever feeling.

She knew there was nothing logical about trusting a stranger the way she did Alistair, but logic didn't stand a chance of overruling her feelings on this question.

At first, as she tried to relax, all Lauren heard were her own restless movements. As she shifted this way and that, trying to ease into the spirit of the experience, even the sliding motions of her feet on the carpet sounded loudly in her ears.

Unlike Lauren, Alistair sat unmoving, and slowly the warm, solid stretch of his back formed a wall of peace between them.

"Listen to your heart," Alistair said softly.

His words stilled her mind and she quit fretting. To her surprise, she began to sense the blood coursing through her heart. Eyes gently closed, she pictured the steady rhythm, the blood collecting oxygen in the lungs, filling the chambers of her heart, then returning through her arteries to nourish her body.

She began to hear the swishing thump of her heart. Her head drooped back slightly and as she settled more deeply against Alistair's back, she sighed.

And that's when she felt his heartbeat.

"Alistair!"

"I know," he said. "Just let your body listen to mine."

As suddenly as she'd felt it, she lost it. Then she realized that her own excitement at sensing the tempo of his heart had disrupted the connection.

Alistair sensed when Lauren once more relaxed enough to let her senses take charge of her mind. He felt her lean more closely into him. Her shoulders eased, teasing him as they brushed his skin to settle slightly lower against his back. Her hair cushioned them and tickled him in a most pleasurable way. He'd pulled his own hair forward over his shoulder and reveled in the silky texture of her thick hair on the back of his neck.

Earlier, when they'd still been on the couch, as he watched her throw her head against the cushions, clench her teeth, and say, "Okay, I'm ready," he'd known it would take every slow and gentle technique he could devise to lead her to the blissful state of sexual release.

Orgasm, contrary to what many men and women assumed, was centered in the brain, not in the genitals. And unless he could capture her mind, Alistair knew he had no hope of releasing her sensuality.

"Mmm." She uttered the breathy sound, and Alistair smiled. Lauren was proving to be a pretty fair pupil in the art of Tantric sex. For someone who rarely kept still, she was doing a good job of listening to their bodies.

A better job than he was, actually. But then, he had to stay in control. The last thing Lauren needed was Alistair ripping off his shorts and jumping her bones.

So it was a good thing he'd kept his ancient purple-and-gold LSU shorts firmly in place. The warmth of her skin on his, the rhythmic tempo of their breath, which was starting to move in unison, plus the vision of her gleaming skin, with her rose-tipped nipples and thatch of dark hair competing for his attention—

Alistair stirred as his arousal pressed against the restraint of his running shorts.

"Listen to your heart," Lauren said softly.

At that he grinned. The apprentice was overtaking the master.

But her reminder helped him to release his mind. He stilled the jumble of thoughts and opened his senses to their bodies.

Sweetness flowed from her into him. He breathed deeply, even as she did the same, then they continued in harmony. Alistair let the feelings of union and peace fill his heart and mind.

Slowly, ever so slowly, he released the moment. Achieving the unity of Tantric togetherness even for a small amount of time was a pleasure to be savored. But he didn't want to press Lauren's ability to be still, and he wanted her to be thoroughly relaxed when he shifted his focus to directly pleasuring her body.

"Slide down on the floor and lie on your back," he said, careful to speak slowly and softly. As he said the words, he followed his own instructions until they touched only head to head.

The intimacy of quiet contact was having its effect on Alistair. Having been so near and so nearly naked and so in tune with the flow of her energy made him want her beyond all reason.

What he needed to know was whether the prolonged relaxation and withholding of direct sexual stimulation was whetting Lauren's appetite in the same way.

For better or for worse, it was time to find out.

Alistair was only human. He might not be like all those other guys Lauren referenced, but he was a hundred percent hot-blooded male.

He eased upward.

"Do I sit up now?"

"No." Alistair shifted so all of Lauren's body stretched out in front of him. He absorbed the image slowly, feasting on the sight of her. Her arms rested at her sides, her eyes were closed, and a bare hint of a smile lit her face.

With every slow and easy breath, her lush breasts

rose, seemed to pause, then lowered as if beckoning his touch.

Alistair stifled a groan of desire. He had to be out of his mind. Giving a lesson, my foot! He was playing with fire and should have been out the door an hour ago. Drop the pizza and run. But he hadn't, and now look where he was.

What man would blame him? Alistair moved so that he lay on one side, close by Lauren. Her eyelids began to flutter, and he reached and brushed the fringe of her thick lashes with the tip of one finger. "Just feel the moment," he said.

She seemed to accept that suggestion, as she left her eyes closed. Her lips parted slightly and Alistair wanted to lean over and fill his senses with the taste of her mouth.

Instead, he circled her belly button with the side of his thumb. She quivered and sighed.

Alistair smiled. Judging by that tremulous reaction, she'd been as affected by the breathing postures as he had been. He puffed a tiny breath of air onto her belly button and circled it again.

"Mmm," she murmured.

"Oh, yes, good enough to eat," Alistair said, lowering his thumb to the inside of her thighs. Would she tense or would she continue to let him skim his hand, teasing her until she had no idea what had led her to the brink of passion?

When she continued to lie with her eyes closed, Alistair realized he could proceed.

His only problem was, the longer he protracted the explosion of her desire, the greater chance he stood of violating his own self-imposed control.

A control he had to maintain. He had no right to take this woman; no right to violate the trust she'd placed in him. Even more than that, he had no intention of pursuing a relationship with her. He might best plead temporary insanity for offering this "lesson" to her; but he wouldn't be able to pardon himself if he took his own pleasure with her. And added to all of those good reasons, tomorrow he was spending the day with Barbara. Sweet-natured, competent, intelligent Barbara, who he hoped to get to know much, much better, in what he intended to be the most mature relationship of his life.

That thought steadied him, but his body was buying none of the rationalization. He had to shift slightly away from Lauren, lest his desire show itself far too physically. Wondering how in the universe he'd gotten himself into this pickle, he continued his lighter-than-feather touching of her lush body, a body that was responding visibly now to his touch.

Her legs had relaxed, opening outward at the knee with an inviting curve that caused him to catch his breath. Skimming his thumb up her inner thigh, he paused just at the curve where her leg met the trunk of her body. Moving ever so softly, he traced a circular path toward the dark thatch of hair. Rather than dipping his fingers into her inner lips that he knew would be damp, quivering, and yearning for more stimulation, he kept his attentions on her pubic mound, touching lightly, then exerting the gentlest of pressure.

He knew, whether she did or not, that with the

prolonged intimacy and the subtle stimulation he'd been giving her, she could reach the peak of passion without him touching her beyond that.

But he wasn't sure he wanted to stop there.

Lauren wanted to open her eyes, yet she wanted to keep them closed forever and ever, or at least as long as she could continue feeling as marvelous as she was at that moment. She had no idea how Alistair had conjured such sensations within her, but she was very thankful he'd volunteered to teach her all about pleasure.

The smile that had been hovering on her lips blossomed. Never had she felt this comfortable with a man. Why, she and Alistair had been together for what had to be at least an hour, and he hadn't even tried to make a move on her. She sighed and stirred against the pressure of his palm, aching to rise into the warmth and strength of his hand.

And more than that, she wanted him to keep touching her. Wriggling her hips, she lifted them. As she did, she eased her eyes open. He was half lying, half sitting beside her, a dreamy-eyed expression on his face. His hair had fallen across the front of his shoulders, and, as she watched, he shifted lower and his hair skimmed her breasts, setting off a most delightful sensation.

The sensation joined with the heat his touch was building within her and she lifted her hips even higher. As she did, his hand slipped between her legs and she registered, in some blissfully removed way, that one of his fingers had eased inside her.

As smoothly as he'd entered her, he was out again. Bereft, she cried out, "Don't leave!"

She wasn't sure, because what with her overload of sensation and with the veil of his long hair, she couldn't see too clearly, but she thought he smiled.

And as he did, not one but two fingers eased back inside. And with a waltzing motion, they began to dance.

Drugged by the sweet rhythm of his fingers and the silky torment of his hair whispering over her breasts, Lauren gave herself up to a torrent of sensation she would never, in her wildest of fantasies, ever have imagined.

She rose with the tempo of her own ecstasy, paused on the brink of what she couldn't quite name, then cried out as her body convulsed around Alistair's fingers. Reaching up blindly, she drew him to her and held on, crying, laughing, and saying over and over again, "Oh my."

Sixteen

*H*e hated to do it, but he had to.

Or so Alistair told himself later, once again sitting on his balcony in the middle of the night, attempting to find solace in his cigar.

Rather than hold Lauren close and slip into the inviting heat created by her explosion of passion, he'd rolled away at once, stood up, and said, "Not bad for one lesson."

She'd blinked her eyes, hazily, awash in the afterglow of her sensual release. "You're going? Now? I mean, isn't there more . . ." She'd trailed off, looking slightly embarrassed.

He'd nodded, halfway to the door, backing away as quickly as he could. There was no way she could miss his erection. He'd intended not to frighten her; the joke was on him. She had frightened him.

Her passionate response had unsettled him.

More was exactly what he wanted and what he wasn't going to get.

So he'd said something curt, his exact words he couldn't recall, and then slammed the door behind him.

Alistair realized he hadn't yet lit his cigar. Just as well. He rationed his smokes and less than twenty-four hours had passed since he'd been sitting on his balcony with a lighted cigar and looked down and spotted Lauren.

Playing with fire. That's what he'd been doing down there in the lower apartment. He shook his head, wondering at his own blindness. He'd told her he offered the love lesson to thank her for saving his life, yet he admitted that wasn't the reason. Worse, he hadn't done it simply out of desire for her.

He'd done it to rescue her.

That a woman as luscious as Lauren had never once enjoyed sex struck him as such a shame that he'd been determined to help her understand what she was missing.

Rescuing others was definitely his fatal flaw. The only time in his life he had held out against the urge was the case of his father and following his footsteps into banking. He'd known his father wanted the succession, so to speak, ensured. It had cost Alistair agony upon agony to resist the ingrained reaction to do what someone else needed for him to do.

He and his father had quarreled badly, and things between them had never been quite the same after it had been Oliver who'd stepped into their father's wake. And Alistair had spent more months and years—more than he cared to admit—delving into people's lives and leading them out of their difficulties.

Rescuing women, mainly.

It was time to put an end to this pattern of behavior.

He'd made that promise to himself, and he wasn't going to fall back into it now, no matter how appealing, vulnerable, and needy someone might be. Particularly that unbelievably beautiful redhead he'd left lying naked on the floor only two stories below him.

Still in a sweet hazy fog, Lauren moved only as much as it took to blow out the candle, tug a chenille throw off the daybed, wrap it around her, and curl up on her side, cradled by the floor where she'd experienced the most amazing sensation she'd ever known.

Alistair had given her that.

He'd also hurt her feelings before he'd dashed out the door.

"Men," she said aloud.

Buster stirred but didn't lift his head from under his wing.

"Not you," she said, more softly. But honestly, here she was thinking he was different from other men, and he was, but why couldn't he have stayed beside her and savored the moment? She'd been hovering on a cloud of sweet passion, and he'd leapt up, charged to the door, and made that crack about one lesson.

It certainly wasn't the harshest thing anyone had ever said to her, but it had taken away the bliss of the togetherness she'd felt with him, a unity she'd never, ever experienced with a man.

Well, she might enjoy another lesson with Alistair, but she certainly didn't need one. Why, now that she knew everyone else had been going about the whole business in such a topsy-turvy fashion, she'd be able to take care of matters herself.

She settled her cheek against one hand, and slipped the other between her legs. Smiling at the memory of how wonderful he'd made her feel, Lauren drifted to sleep.

"Is that you, dear?"

Barbara could have sworn she hadn't made a sound. Oliver's BMW purred so quietly she didn't think her arrival in his car could have tipped off her godmother to her presence. She'd slipped off her shoes before edging open the front door of Mrs. Merlin's house.

She didn't want her to think a burglar was gaining entrance, so Barbara called softly, "Yes, it is." The last thing she wanted to face was a postmortem of her evening courtesy of her godmother.

A light flickered on in the kitchen, and Barbara knew she'd been trapped.

"I'll just brew us a cup of kava kava tea," Mrs. Merlin called. "It's just the thing to put one to sleep after a lively night out on the town."

"It was a banker's dinner," Barbara answered, walking down the hall toward the kitchen, deciding she might as well face the conversation. Then she could curl up in the quaint four-poster bed in the guest room and drift off to sleep on a cloud of what-if's.

Tomorrow was her date with Alistair and if she enjoyed that half as much as she had her evening with Oliver, she would have two tempting reasons to extend her stay in New Orleans. Though after the fabulous time she'd spent with Oliver, she'd almost forgotten why it was she thought it was the other brother who was the one destined to liven up her life.

Mrs. Merlin wore a cherry red caftan and a silver nightcap over her orange hair. Barbara blinked, thankful the overhead kitchen light was on the dim setting. Her godmother puttered by the stove, then turned around. When she saw Barbara's dress, her mouth formed an "O."

"Now that's the sort of dress you should wear more often. Did you go shopping instead of going back to that stuffy old bank this afternoon?"

"Actually, it belongs to the woman who was supposed to be Oliver's date, but she insisted I wear it." Barbara had telephoned Mrs. Merlin to let her know she'd be back late, but hadn't had time then to explain the circumstances.

"A generous woman." Mrs. Merlin's eyes twinkled. "And not a woman in love with your Mr. Oliver, I'd say."

"What do you mean by that?" Barbara tried not to sound too curious.

"Take a look at yourself in a mirror, dear. You're quite a feast in that dress, and no woman would offer it to you to spend an evening with a man she wanted for herself."

Barbara colored both from embarrassment and pleasure. "It is a nice dress, isn't it?"

The teakettle chirped, and Mrs. Merlin turned to the stove.

Barbara smoothed the silky fabric of the dress. She'd felt a little bit like Cinderella. Everyone at the dinner had been so nice to her. Oliver had accepted his award and given a brilliant speech about the importance of small businesses holding their own against corporate takeovers. Afterward, they'd gone dancing with two other couples in a club done in the style of a 1940s cabaret.

"There's no need to tell me you had a good time," Mrs. Merlin said as she sat down two cups of steaming bran-colored tea. "I can read it in your aura."

"Really?"

She nodded. "Almost purplish tonight. That's lovely."

Barbara wasn't sure she believed in auras, but Mrs. Merlin said it so matter-of-factly it made her think such things might be real. "What color is my aura at other times?"

Mrs. Merlin played with the handle of her teacup. "Well, dear, that's a hard question. It doesn't come through too clearly. You're not brown or muddy, which is good, but you're usually not vivid one way or the other."

"And that's bad?" She heard the wistful tone in her voice.

"Not necessarily, but this change in you tonight, now that's a very good thing!" Mrs. Merlin rubbed her hands together, and said, "I knew I could count on Alistair."

"I spent the evening with Oliver," Barbara said, wondering if her godmother had been paying attention.

"Oh, yes, I know that," she answered, a twinkle in her eye.

"But I do have a date with Alistair. He's taking me to the French Quarter Fest. And Oliver's going, too, with the woman who was at Alistair's place at lunchtime."

"What a perfectly interesting foursome." Mrs. Merlin lifted her cup. "Now sip your tea. You'll want to be on your best form tomorrow."

Maybe it was seeing her in Daffy's dress, but Oliver felt as if he'd known Barbara for years. He wouldn't have believed he could have gotten through the evening as calmly as he had, what with his mind all in a whirl over locating Lauren, but with Barbara by his side, all had gone as smoothly as a nectar snowball.

He tucked himself under the covers in his four-poster bed, one that had been in his family for five generations, more contented than he'd been in ages. For years he'd been the slow and steady Gotho. Here he was living in his great-grandparents' house, being waited on by his grandmother's housekeeper, going to work at his family's bank, sitting in his father's old office.

Tonight he'd felt like a new man. Barbara had been excellent company and had fit in perfectly with the bankers' group. But tomorrow was the day he was waiting for.

Tomorrow would bring him face-to-face again with the woman who had captured his imagination, the woman he just knew would set him free from his lamentably stuffy self.

Slivers of pink slipped into the sky over the city as the long night came to an end.

Lauren had slept like a baby, Alistair almost not at all. Barbara had been lulled into a dreamless night, and Oliver had tossed and turned worse than a sailor on a rough sea.

Mrs. Merlin was up with the sun. She wanted to finish planting the new herbs in her circle bed. She'd never attempted any magick other than the candle spells that always went just a bit askew. But the gardener and the mystic aspects of Mrs. Merlin appreciated the white witch or wiccan tradition of an herb bed shaped in a circle and planted with the herbs most necessary for wiccan spells. Not that she planned to pursue those arts. No, indeed. Matchmaking by earthly means was proving to be far too fulfilling.

She did suspect, though, that Alistair had given in and performed the perfect match spell she'd requested for her goddaughter.

Why, the difference in her aura was remarkable, not to mention the sparkle in her pretty green eyes.

It would be just like Alistair to reconsider and do

the spell. He was always so helpful and so good at looking after others. And he'd never once yelled at her, not even the time she mistakenly changed that nice lady lawyer into her precious tomcat.

Today she was going to help out Alistair by driving Barbara to the Quarter so he didn't have to get his car out of the garage where he stored it (parking in the Quarter was so hard to come by and so shockingly expensive!).

Grubbing in the dewy soil, Mrs. Merlin admitted she might not be quite so helpful if she didn't think it best for her to keep a motherly eye on the progress of the matchmaking.

Lauren awoke feeling like a new woman. She yawned and rolled onto her back. For a moment, she had no idea where she was, then as she noted the red candle, the pizza box, and the fact that she'd slept on the floor all the details of the night before flooded back.

"Oh, my," she murmured. Had Alistair really roused that reaction in her? And could he, or anyone else, do so again?

Hoping the answer was "yes" Lauren jumped up. Buster eyed her somewhat critically.

"It's not as if you haven't seen me naked before," she said. She opened the lid of the pizza box and poured a ration of the seed Alistair had kindly provided on one side of the inside cover. Eyeing the two leftover slices, she realized she wasn't her usual starving self.

Oddly satisfied, she set out to explore the bucket-sized apartment. Not much space was wasted on the kitchen, she noted with approval. She turned on the water to fill the claw-footed tub, then opened an armoire in the bedroom.

Two dresses and a rose red sweater hung there. Reflecting on the crumpled state of her dress, she fingered the fabric of a purple print linen sheath and wondered if its owner would mind very much if she borrowed it. Just for the day, of course.

Lauren knew Alistair had had his own eccentric reasons for giving her such pleasure last night. He hadn't been interested in her as a woman, or he wouldn't have raced out the door. She might be sexually unresponsive, but she wasn't ignorant of male sexuality.

Not Lauren the doctor's daughter.

He'd only offered her a job because the shop girl had pinned him to the wall. And Lauren knew the job wouldn't last long. She'd give someone change for a hundred rather than a twenty, or misring or mischarge purchases, or tell a customer what she thought of him. Then Lauren would be history.

When it came to jobs, Lauren was always history.

So she was back to the realization she'd had after her father's harsh news.

She had to marry and marry well.

And Oliver Gotho fit the ticket.

Lauren turned the taps off in the tub. Facing herself in the mirror, she admitted she couldn't marry just anyone. She'd have to at least like the man, and, of course he'd have to be nuts over her, but then, men always were.

Except for Alistair.

Frowning at that thought, she climbed into the tub and eased into the lovely warm water. She almost hated to bathe, as it seemed as if she were washing away some of the magic of the evening before. But this was no time for fancifulness; she had to be sensible.

Time to get ready for the day ahead—she thought with both a hint of anxiety and the thrill of anticipation—a day that could change her life.

Barbara bumped into Oliver within a block of the Bayou Magick Shop. Surprised to see him again so early in the morning, she halted on the sidewalk and wished Mrs. Merlin had consented to let her wait at her house until Alistair arrived to pick her up. It was awkward, going out with one brother one night and the other the next day. And Barbara did not know how to handle such situations.

Oliver, or so it seemed, did not have any such difficulties.

"Oh, it's you," he said. "Good morning. Are you on your way to meet my brother?"

She nodded. She couldn't help but notice he looked just as dashing in khaki slacks and a polo shirt as he had in his evening attire.

"Why didn't he pick you up?" Oliver had stopped, and was frowning at her in a way she found vaguely disconcerting.

"Well, he was going to, only my godmother offered to drop me off."

"I'm sure that was thoughtful of her, but it doesn't excuse my brother's behavior."

"No, really, it's okay," Barbara said, feeling as if she needed to apologize, as much for her god-mother as for Alistair. Truthfully, she felt rather awkward, approaching a man she scarcely knew along a street that looked as if it hadn't been swept in at least a generation. Not quite certain where the idea came from, she said to him, "Would you like to start the morning with a cup of tea?"

His face brightened. "An excellent idea." He came even with her on the sidewalk, and said, "I know the perfect place."

She fell into step beside him, feeling more at home than she had since she'd left him to tiptoe into Mrs. Merlin's house the night before. "Thank you for a lovely evening," she said. "If you'll give me your friend's address, I'll arrange to have her dress cleaned and sent back to her."

"That you will not." Oliver looked down at her, indignation in his blue gaze. "Pop it in a bag and bring it back to the bank. I'll take care of anything that needs to be done. You did me a great favor, attending that boring business banquet with me. You know, I've never had such a good time at one of those things."

Barbara knew she colored up in a way that prob-ably set her pale complexion off to poor advantage, but she couldn't restrain her reaction. "I'm glad," she said, simply enough.

"Do you really like tea, rather than coffee?"

She nodded. "I expect it's my British upbringing."

"Well, that makes sense. Much more than my own reasons, I suppose." He pointed toward the corner, and they turned their footsteps, walking comfortably in step with one another. "This place doesn't have the best selections of tea, but it's comfortable and convenient." He grinned, and Barbara's heart leapt in some inexplicable way. "It's not Twinings' Tea Room, so don't get your hopes up."

"You've been to Twinings'?" She asked more eagerly than she'd intended, but she loved the centuries-old tea shop tucked into a corner of Fleet Street in the City of London.

Oliver nodded, and launched into a tale of the last time he'd been in London. Before she knew it, she was telling him the story of her life, her anticipation of spending the day with Alistair completely forgotten.

Alistair was steamed.

He'd gotten up early, after a night of almost zero sleep, and taken himself off for a frenetic run along the riverfront. Then he'd slipped back into his building, showered, and left again to find breakfast out somewhere.

He hated to admit it to himself, but he was determined to avoid Lauren. When it was late enough to collect Barbara for the promised day of activities, he'd called for his car at the Monteleone Hotel parking garage. He'd waited impatiently while the valet had gone in search of it, then driven away from the Quarter, anticipation rising in his spirits the farther away he got from his own neighborhood.

Perhaps he'd walked the wild side for too long. Perhaps he'd lived in the French Quarter longer than a native New Orleanian should. The party lifestyle of the constant playground worked well at first, but the congestion, the continual noise and attitude of drink, eat, and fall down on the sidewalk because tomorrow never comes had worn on him. Today he found himself grateful to drive out toward the more sedate neighborhood of Mid-city, sedate, of course, unless it was the last week in April and the first week in May, when Jazz Fest at the Fairgrounds overtook the entire neighborhood.

But it was mid-April, and the only festival taking place that weekend was in his own backyard. Alistair pulled his Mercedes convertible to a halt in front of Mrs. Merlin's house and blinked twice, quite rapidly, as he studied the bright purple color she'd painted it since he'd last visited.

No one, he considered, was quite like Mrs. Merlin.

For some odd reason, that thought led him to Lauren. He pictured her beside him on the floor, abandoned to the sensual pleasure he'd introduced her to, and the remaining crumbs of calm he'd felt that morning fled like dew before a July sunrise.

Suddenly cranky, he got out of his car, let himself in through the front gate, and made his way through the forest of foliage to the front door. He rang the bell, waited, then lifted the knocker.

When no response was forthcoming, he followed the stepping-stones around the side of the house.

All was silent.

The garage, he realized, sat empty.

Alistair rolled his eyes and shook his head.

No one, he repeated, was quite like Mrs. Merlin. It would have been just like her to drive Barbara to the Quarter, determined, in her own peculiar fashion, to have interfered with any plans he might have. He wasn't psychic, but he was pretty certain Mrs. Merlin didn't think he was the right man for her goddaughter.

For once, Alistair told himself, climbing back into his car, Mrs. Merlin had another think coming.

Seventeen

The only thing right so far that morning was that Kara stood behind the register, looking as detached as always as she rang up a counterful of purchases. Alistair said good morning, smiled at the middle-aged woman handing over her platinum American Express, and glanced around the shop, counting heads.

Busier than usual for a Saturday morning, but that was to be expected during the French Quarter Festival. The event, featuring local musicians and restaurateurs and craftspeople, had been started for locals but the word had spread and now thousands of out-of-town visitors flooded into the city for the long weekend of food, music, and, of course, drinking.

No tourist's pilgrimage to the Quarter would be complete without a stop for a beignet at Café du

Monde, a pause for a hurricane at Pat O'Brien's, and a visit to the Bayou Magick Shop to purchase a souvenir voodoo doll. Consequently, Alistair found himself counting twelve customers in the cramped quarters of his shop at this early-morning hour.

He frowned. Kara couldn't handle this volume by herself. What had he been thinking when he'd asked Barbara to spend the day with him?

"Vah-voom!"

Alistair swung around at the appreciative sound uttered by the male customer standing in front of the display touting the legend of Marie Laveau, voodoo priestess. The man had his gaze fastened not on Marie's image, but on the redhead who had just emerged from the back of the shop.

Alistair couldn't blame the man for his vocal admiration, even though it elicited in him a jealous irritation he had no cause and certainly no claim to feel.

Lauren stood just inside the back of the shop, wearing one of the dresses Erica had left behind. Or maybe it had been Sharon's? Alistair's memory of those other women was fuzzy, but the picture Lauren made in the flowing lightweight dress came sharply into focus. He remembered the dress as shapeless, but on Lauren, it had acquired curves and a shape that gave it—

Alistair paused, searching his mind even as the jerk next to him continued to ogle Lauren.

Personality.

On Lauren, the dress took on personality.

Attitude.

Flair.

No matter her quirks, Lauren brought a dress to life.

"Good morning," Alistair said, moving forward just as the man next to him started to do the same. Blocking out the stranger with his back, he smiled down at Lauren, forgetting all about being irritated with Mrs. Merlin.

No man could be irritated when Lauren was looking up at him, lips parted, creamy skin fresh from the bath, and a glow in her eyes he knew he had kindled the night before.

"Hi," she said, slightly breathlessly.

He wondered how she managed to sound as if she'd just been kissed so thoroughly she couldn't catch her breath. Staring at the way the dress clung to the curves of her body, the body he had teased and prompted to last night's sweet release, Alistair found that he'd lost the power of speech.

Finally, realizing she was staring at him the way one would a street-corner mime, he said, "Where's Buster?" *Witty, Alistair, witty.* One would think she's making you nervous, which is ridiculous. Why should she make you act like a twelve-year-old with a crush on the baby-sitter?

"In the apartment," she answered, peering around his shoulders. Looking nervous all of a sudden, she said, "Are you usually this busy?"

"On a good day." At least he sounded more normal. What was wrong with him? His mission was to find Barbara and head over to Woldenberg Park for the world's largest jazz brunch.

"Oh." Her voice had gotten very small. Too quiet.

"Are you nervous about the job?"

She nodded.

"Don't worry," he said. "There's nothing to handling the customers. People in a magick shop tend to be on their best behavior."

"Afraid you'll cast a spell on them if they don't behave?" She grinned up at him.

He grinned back. She was ditzy, but fun. "Have you eaten?"

She shook her head.

"Barbara's not here yet. Want to get some café au lait with whipped cream on top?"

Her eyes widened. Then to his surprise, she said, "I'm not sure."

Ignoring the customers beginning to fill the shop, Alistair studied Lauren. Last night had changed her. And him, too. "Can I persuade you?" He wanted her company before his date began with Barbara.

In a low voice, she said, "Tell me why you ran out last night."

Of course, Alistair chided himself. He'd hurt her feelings. "I'm sorry I spoke so harshly. But if I'd stayed one minute more, I might not have left."

"Oh!" She moistened her lips, and it was all he could do to keep from kissing her.

Instead, he said, "Now how about that coffee?"

She nodded.

He led the way out of the shop, pausing at the door to tell Kara to call over to CC's Coffeehouse if she needed him for anything.

To Lauren's annoyance, she actually felt shy around Alistair this morning. The comfortable-pal status had evaporated sometime between the start of last night's massage and the culmination in that mystifying crescendo of passion.

Shyness wasn't a state she knew much about. And this in-between sort of place in which they'd been intimate but not technically had sex put her out of sorts, also. She was used to guys using her, then losing interest immediately. But Alistair wasn't like that. Here he was taking her out for coffee when he should be getting ready for his date with Barbara.

They had descended the steps and turned down Bourbon Street, and still Lauren kept her eyes fastened on the passersby and her lips sealed shut.

She longed to ask Alistair what was going through his mind, but she didn't know how. Before she'd entered the shop and seen him standing there in all his glory, she'd actually been thinking any man could do what he'd done last night.

One look at his deep, all-knowing eyes, his broad shoulders that radiated strength, the flowing hair that reminded her of Sunday school stories of Samson—and Lauren had known she'd been fooling herself.

No one else could do for her what this man had done.

Still, she had to try to learn from the experience and move on with her life. Like he'd said, it was only a lesson, just a bone thrown to a charity patient.

For some reason that thought infuriated her. She stumbled on a pitted crack in the sidewalk, which irked her even more.

But as she started to tumble gracelessly forward,

a rock-steady hand shot out and caught her by the shoulder. "Easy," Alistair said. "The streets are dangerous."

Not just the streets. Lauren smiled her thanks and picked up her pace. His hand dropped to his side. "So, how'd you sleep last night?"

"Beautifully!" She answered the question impulsively, immediately embarrassing herself with the honesty of the response. But she had slept the sleep of the charmed, enjoying a rest like she couldn't remember. Of course, he would think it was because of the way he'd brought her to sexual release, which prompted her to add, "For a strange room and all."

"Oh, yes, a strange room." He smiled, but it was more of a grin, a wicked grin.

Lauren's heart skipped a little faster. Could one devilish smile have that effect on her? Still, her body was warming, reminding her of the sensations touching him back-to-back had fired off in her.

Alistair easily matched her pace. Even closer to her, he said, "I'm glad everything was to your satisfaction."

She stopped smack in her tracks. A gray-haired woman bumped into Lauren, muttered an irritated, "Well, excuse you!" and hurried around them.

Lauren squared off and looked Alistair straight in those beautiful dark eyes. "Are you trying to humiliate me?"

"No!" He looked genuinely surprised. "Why do you ask that?"

"Your choice of words," she answered stiffly, already feeling foolish and wishing she'd kept her reactions to herself, "seems selected to remind me of certain intimate, physical details—"

"Details? That's how you think of last night?" He loomed over her, and the kind and gentle Alistair whose heart had fused with her own had disappeared.

"Yes. Details. Just like the elements of a lesson plan. A lesson you deliver and then disappear." Lauren's temper flashed. She'd known he hadn't cared about her when he'd offered to teach her how to enjoy sex. She knew it was illogical for her to be angry when he'd done nothing but show her that she could indeed experience the pleasure she'd assumed was beyond her. So it was wrong of her to expect him to show some tenderness or at least respect toward what they had shared.

He was staring at her, but he didn't seem angry. His eyes were roving her face and body the way Lauren had gazed at that pizza last night.

"I regret the abrupt way I ended last night's session." His voice had lowered and he just kept on staring at her as if he were absorbing her through his eyes. He leaned even closer. "There are a few more pages in the lesson plan."

"What do you mean?" Her anger had spent itself, too, or perhaps she just couldn't maintain it when his mood had shifted so dramatically. Especially since she didn't want to be angry with him. She just wanted him to . . . to what, Lauren? To pay attention to her, she answered her own mocking inquiry.

"I left a few *elements*," he stressed the word with another flare-up of that wicked grin, "out of last night's lesson. What do you say we cover those to-night?"

"A-another lesson?" There went her heart again, skipping way too fast. She'd have to have that checked.

"Think you can handle a few more details?"

Lauren flipped her hair back over her shoulder, met his gaze, and said cheekily, "If you can handle the pupil, I can handle the homework." Then she started walking, her feet moving almost as quickly as her racing pulse.

She was pretty sure that Alistair kept his true feelings bricked up behind a padded wall. He was kind, he had friends, even among the cops, and he was talented and clever. But despite all those qual-ities, he maintained an emotional distance from oth-ers that both concerned and frightened Lauren.

Why had he challenged her to another lesson? And why had she said yes? She'd learned all she could learn from a man who was only going to share his body and not his heart.

Alistair let Lauren get a few feet ahead of him, so he could stand on the sidewalk and ask himself at what point that morning he had lost his mind. It was Barbara he should be planning to spend the evening with, not this sprite who had blown into his life like a storm out of the Gulf.

Take it back, he told himself. Catch up to her and tell her you were only kidding. Better yet, tell her she had to find another place to stay. The apartment two floors beneath his own home was too close for comfort, not to mention sanity.

"Lauren." He called her name as he caught up to her beside the open door of CC's.

Framed in the doorway, she paused, then a smile brighter than any he'd yet to see on her face lit her features. She waved to someone inside the door, then said, "Alistair, look who's here!"

And without giving him a chance to say another word, she skipped inside the coffeehouse.

Given no choice, Alistair followed.

There sat his date for the day and his brother, as cozy as two kittens, both with hands cupped around mugs of tea. At that moment, all Alistair could remember was just how much he hated tea.

But as the scene before him played out, he watched it as if he were the projectionist in a theater. When Oliver saw Lauren, he broke off his conversation with Barbara in mid-sentence. That wild and crazy expression he'd worn that day at the bank sprang full-blown onto his face.

Scraping back his chair, Oliver knocked it over. It fell onto the seat behind him and sent it skidding across the stone floor. Rather than setting the chair to rights, Oliver leapt forward, took Lauren's hand in both of his and kissed it with greater reverence than any bishop had ever shown to any pope.

"What an honor," he said.

Barbara said a brief hello to Lauren. Alistair wondered whether she was wishing Lauren to the devil or whether the engrossed way she'd been listening to Oliver only a few moments earlier merely reflected a savvy consultant wooing a client.

Lauren's reaction to Oliver surprised the heck out of Alistair.

Rather than tugging her hand free as he'd expected, she clung to Oliver, fluttered her lashes, and said, "At last we meet again."

On that line, Alistair barged in. He nodded to his brother, then landed a kiss somewhere to the back of Barbara's left ear. When she didn't slap him for his bold greeting, he flashed her one of his best smiles and pulled out the chair closest to her.

Before he could sit down, Lauren plopped into it. "Great to see you again, Brenda," she said, talking way too fast. "Wherever did you get that hat?"

"Barbara," Barbara said. "And I borrowed it from my godmother. I don't do well in the sun."

"No?" Lauren repeated that act with the fluttery lashes, and Alistair wondered just what had gotten into her.

"I'd think with your complexion, you'd have a similar problem," Barbara said.

Lauren shrugged. "In some things I'm just plain lucky."

Oliver smiled in a beatific way that made Alistair want to kick him.

Turning her head, almost completely hidden under the floppy straw hat, toward Alistair, Barbara said, "Mrs. Merlin did tell you she was giving me a ride this morning?"

Alistair hesitated, and Barbara, no dummy, picked up on it. "Oh, no, did you drive all the way out to her house?"

"It's not far." Alistair righted Oliver's toppled chair and guided his brother into it. Someone had to play the role of the responsible sibling here.

"It's a very long way." She motioned toward Oliver. "We bumped into each other looking for you. And Lauren, of course." She flashed a smile Alistair knew was as false as his own cheerful attitude toward a scene that held all the elements of disaster.

"All I've been doing is looking for you," Oliver said, gazing across the small table and into Lauren's eyes.

"Get a grip," Alistair said. "Better yet, get her some coffee."

"Oh, of course." Oliver blinked and had the grace to blush. "We already have our tea, but what would you like?"

Lauren clapped her hands together. "Café au lait. And Alistair knows just how I like it."

Alistair shrugged. He knew exactly how Lauren liked it. Nice and slow and building to a heat that overtook itself and ignited into a flaming passion, almost catching both of them unawares. Then he shook his head. He had to stop thinking about sex with Lauren. Barbara was his date, and not only that, she was the woman who was going to break his past pattern of mistakes.

"I'll get it," Alistair said. "Would you care for a fresh cup of tea, Barbara?"

She said no, thanks, quite prettily, and Alistair let his hand brush against the back of her shoulder as lightly as a mosquito dancing over an azalea bush. He wanted to demonstrate possession, and he wanted both Barbara, and Lauren, to see it.

Not to mention Oliver.

Alistair ordered two café au laits, one topped with whipped cream, and an assortment of pastries.

When he returned to the table, Lauren said, "Wow, talk about déjà vu."

"You've been here before?" Oliver asked the question of Lauren as Alistair observed that his brother had edged his chair so that he sat almost in Lauren's lap.

Lauren nodded. "Yesterday. No, wait, the day before. Gosh, I'm getting all confused in my head over what day it is. Does that ever happen to you?"

Oliver gave the question his usual quiet consideration. Alistair could tell this because he'd known his brother all his life. He also knew the answer. Until the day before yesterday, Oliver had never suffered confusion of any sort. At last, he said, "No." Then he turned to Alistair. "Were you two here the day before yesterday?"

"It's possible." He backed away, returning to the counter for the plate of pastries.

He set it down, amused by Lauren's appreciative look but contrite when he saw the obvious dismay on Barbara's face. "Don't worry," he said, "we're still going to brunch. Lauren just needs refueling."

"Oh. Of course. But this is fine for breakfast. You don't have to take me anyplace special."

"Special?" Lauren pointed to a cherry cheese croissant on the plate of pastries. "This place *is* special." She tore off a piece and offered it to Barbara. "Here, try this."

"No, thanks," Barbara said, in a polite but firm tone.

"Oliver?" Lauren handed the bite toward him.

Alistair had to smother a smile. His brother was tempted, in order to please his goddess, but he never touched croissants. He expounded on the layers of butter baked into the pastries. Ever since their father's heart attack, Oliver had become a cholesterol hawk.

"Thanks, but I'll wait for the brunch, also," he said.

When she turned to him, Alistair dipped his head, careful to hold his hair back with one hand, and took the bite from her with his teeth.

She grinned.

He winked at her, enjoying the intimacy, feeling strongly connected despite the presence of both their "dates."

His sense of well-being lasted only a moment, as Oliver said, "Alistair, am I correct in figuring that you and Lauren were here at CC's the very same time I was looking everywhere for her?"

Barbara's eyes widened, as did Lauren's, but Alistair couldn't tell whether Lauren was surprised at the question or ecstatic over the chocolate éclair she'd just tasted.

"That is technically correct," Alistair said. "However, I did not definitely know that Lauren and the goddess you were raving over were one and the same."

Oliver set down his cup of tea. "As if there could be two women like Lauren! I think you owe me an explanation, Alistair."

Alistair nodded. "I'll concede that, but perhaps another place and time—"

"No. Now." His usually placid brother had squared his shoulders and lowered his brows.

Barbara fiddled with her mug of tea, and Lauren

switched her gaze from brother to brother. Alistair sighed. "You can be a stubborn son of a gun."

"As if you can't?"

"Again, I concede. I didn't tell you because I didn't think it was the right thing to do."

"Right for you or right for me?"

Alistair hesitated. "For both of us."

Oliver slammed his fist against the opposite palm. "Let me make my own decisions for myself, okay, big brother?"

"I'm an only child," Lauren said, "but is this what you call sibling rivalry?"

Her question seemed to break Oliver's fit of temper. He smiled at Lauren, and said, "Yes, I guess you could call it that. Big brother likes to boss and protect, but kid brother has to find his own path, in his own way."

"Well stated," Alistair said.

Oliver punched him lightly on the shoulder, and said, "No hard feelings?"

Knowing he'd been wrong to shield Lauren from his brother, Alistair shook his head. "I apologize for hiding your goddess from you."

"Hey, I'm not a goddess," Lauren said, talking around an éclair. "I am a mess, though." She licked chocolate off one finger and Alistair had to suppress a very strong urge to offer to help.

He had to get control over himself. Turning to Barbara, he said, "Are you ready for the world's largest jazz brunch?"

"That would be lovely."

He slid one arm over the back of her chair. She leaned against him, her pretty hair brushing his arm in a way that helped him not mind so much that Lauren had turned to Oliver and was doing that lash-fluttering routine again.

Not only was she pulling that, she was actually getting him to take a bite of éclair. That change of behavior boded ill, for whom, Alistair didn't want to analyze too closely. Instead, he smiled at Barbara. "Ready?"

She nodded, almost with relief, he thought, which made sense after the tension of the scene she'd witnessed.

"But I haven't finished my coffee," Lauren said.

Eighteen

*N*ot a foursome.

Barbara couldn't clear that thought from her mind as she looked from Alistair to Oliver. Surely one of them would set Lauren straight.

Time hung suspended. Barbara listened to the rustle of newspaper as the couple at the table next to theirs turned the pages of the *Times-Picayune*.

Alistair and Oliver exchanged glances, but Barbara couldn't begin to interpret the mysterious nonverbal language of the two brothers. The morning had started out nicely. When it had been just her and Oliver, Oliver had been attentive, witty, and entertaining. Now he was acting like someone had cast a spell over him.

Not someone, Barbara amended. Lauren.

"I'm done," Lauren said, setting down her coffee cup and casting the crumbs off her skirt.

At least then Alistair reached for her hand. Barbara normally would have found a graceful way to avoid the contact; she was in New Orleans on business and never had she crossed the professional line with a client. Of course, Oliver was technically the client. And some feminine control mechanism in her brain wanted to show Oliver that someone else could be, if not gaga, at least interested in her as a woman and not only as a computer whiz.

So perhaps the foursome wasn't such a bad idea after all. Managing a weak imitation of the redhead's eyelash swooping, Barbara snuggled her hand into Alistair's and walked with him out of the restaurant.

At last Oliver found himself face-to-face and alone with Lauren, the woman who'd captivated him from the first moment he'd set eyes on her in the Square what seemed a lifetime ago.

"Lauren." He said the name aloud, testing the sound of it, a rather silly thing he'd never felt the need to do with any other woman's name.

"Yes?" She dabbed at a few crumbs on the plate with one forefinger.

"What's your middle name?"

"Grace."

"Grace." He tested that name, too, but found it didn't fit her as well. "And your last name?"

She wrinkled her nose in her best imitation of Samantha from *Bewitched* and said, "Stevens."

"Are you from the Midwest?"

"You didn't get it." She sounded disappointed.

"Get what?"

She wrinkled her nose once more, twisting it

right to left. "Don't you ever watch Nick at Night? Those *Bewitched* reruns are so droll."

He honestly didn't catch the connection. And Oliver was not used to feeling dim-witted. "I'm afraid I don't understand your reference point."

"Darren and Samantha *Stevens*."

"Right." He laughed along with her, rising from his chair at the same time.

She stood, too, and they headed for the door. "I think it makes my name less boring and middle-of-the-road to associate it with the *Bewitched* characters."

"There's nothing middle-of-the-road about you," Oliver said, longing to take her hand the way his brother had captured Barbara's. But he sensed he had to move slowly with this woman. When he'd invited her to dinner the other day, she'd bolted like a duck after a shotgun blast in a blind.

She had encouraged him more today, even to the point of flirting with him when she'd first entered CC's. Emboldened by that thought, he said, "That's a very pretty dress you're wearing today."

She shifted her carpetbag of a purse to her opposite shoulder, which allowed Oliver to walk more closely beside her. "Thanks. I borrowed it from Alistair's closet."

"From my brother!"

"Well, from one of his female friends, obviously. At least, I don't think he's into cross-dressing."

"My brother?" Oliver was amused at the thought. "He has a thing about not cutting his hair, and he dabbles in magick, but he walks the straight and narrow heterosexually speaking."

"Oh, yes." Her lips curved up in a reminiscent smile that set Oliver's back up.

"So you're staying with Alistair?"

"He's letting me camp out in an empty apartment, but I don't think he means for me to stay for long."

"Then you'll need a place?"

"Yes." Her shoulders drooped. "And I'll need another job as soon as your brother sees how I always mess things up."

"You're working for him, too?"

"Well, in the magick shop. I gather he manages it?"

Oliver could have set her straight on that point, but he couldn't quite grasp that his own brother had not only let the woman of Oliver's dreams stay at his apartment, but he'd given her a job. Those actions were Oliver's responsibility, not Alistair's. He should have spoken even more strongly to his meddling, interloping brother. They'd never come to blows before, not even when Alistair had upset their father by refusing to have anything to do with the bank, but Oliver would be damned if he'd let his brother waltz in and steal Lauren. Why, Alistair didn't even care about her. There he was, only a block ahead of them, trying to make time with Barbara. And Barbara wasn't the type of woman to be trifled with. She was one of the nicest, most intelligent, and caring women he'd ever met. And Oliver would be willing to bet his brother was only aiming for another notch in his belt of conquests. No way Alistair could truly be interested in Barbara; she was the complete opposite of any female he'd ever been involved with.

"Your mind sure has gone away someplace," Lauren said.

Slowly, Oliver unclenched his fists and his jaw. "Excuse me," he said. "I was just surprised that Alistair had taken you under his wing."

"It's just because I saved his life," she said, pausing to glance into a shop window.

From another block, sounds of jazz battled with zydeco. The streets were growing more crowded with others who'd come out to enjoy the French Quarter Fest. But Oliver wasn't in a very festive mood. "You saved my brother's life?"

She nodded. "He says so, but all I did was interrupt him when he was being mugged."

"Alistair neglects to share the oddest details."

"Oh, he didn't make much of it. I think he thought it wasn't his time to leave the planet, or something like that." Lauren started walking again.

"More likely," Oliver said, "he was embarrassed to tell me that a woman saved him from a street criminal."

"Oh, most men would be," Lauren said. "But Alistair isn't like most men."

Oliver refused to ask her for more details. Quite frankly, he didn't want to know. He admired his brother, looked up to him, but never once in their lives had they been interested in the same woman. This competition—and Oliver knew in his gut that Alistair preferred Lauren no matter how proprietary his behavior toward Barbara might be—cast things in a whole new light.

Instead, he changed the subject. "Why do you think you can't work for Alistair?"

She sighed and shook her head as if the weight of the world were on her shoulders. "There's a cash register involved."

"And you don't know how to work it?"

"Oh, I know how." She wrinkled her brow. "But have you ever known something but even though your brain processed all the dots and dashes, when you did it, it came out in circles and loops?"

Oliver considered her questions, but had to shake his head. "I can't say that's ever happened to me."

She sighed again. "It's the way my brain works." She kicked at a stray oyster shell. "I can't handle cash or numbers. That's why I have to finish my dissertation, so I can get a job as an art professor. Or at least that's the plan my father has for me."

Without his realizing it, he and Lauren had caught up to Alistair and Barbara. Standing on the corner, waiting together to cross, Oliver wondered whether his brother had heard Lauren's statement about mishandling cash. He had to be nuts to let her work in his shop.

Of course, he wasn't the only one who was nuts. Leaning over, he whispered to Lauren, "Don't worry about anything. You can always come to work for me."

"In a bank!" Lauren went off in a peal of laughter, and both Alistair's and Barbara's expressions demanded some explanation of her mirth.

Not wanting to share her at all, Oliver tried to ignore them.

Lauren, however, had no such scruples. "Can you

believe it?" She was laughing so hard she slapped her thighs and whooped. "Oliver said I could work in his bank. I'm sorry, Oliver, it's so sweet of you, but I would probably get you closed down in about two minutes."

"And why is that?" It was Alistair, rather than Oliver, who asked the question.

The WALK sign went unheeded as Lauren calmed her outburst. Suddenly much quieter, she studied her feet. Oliver waited to see how she'd work her way out of this situation. Really, he'd only meant to be helpful and generous. And, too, he admitted, to keep her close by him.

"Uh, I'm not very good with numbers," she said.

"Remind me about that tomorrow," Alistair said. "I'll run the register and you can work the floor."

She smiled at him with such a brilliant sense of relief that Oliver wanted to remind her that he'd just offered her a haven at the bank. But pride kept him quiet.

Instead, he moved beside Barbara. "Is this your first visit to the Quarter?"

"Second," she said, "but I really didn't get to see anything yesterday. Though so much of it seems familiar from my mother's descriptions."

"Your mother grew up here but never returned with you to visit?" Alistair asked the question before Oliver could.

Barbara shook her head. "There was no family left here, and my mother had made her life in England with Tops."

"Tops?" This time Oliver got the question in ahead of Alistair.

"My dad," Barbara said, her expression softening even more sweetly. "I called him that because he was such a number-one dad."

Oliver moved closer to Barbara's side, his sense of protectiveness stirred by the wistful note in her voice and the shadow of sorrow that had passed over her face. He knew from a comment she'd made last night that both her parents were dead.

"It's hard enough to lose one parent without losing both of them," he said softly.

She smiled up at him and at that moment, Oliver knew there was no other woman in the world as perfect as Barbara Warren.

Feeling almost dizzy by the realization, Oliver said, "Let me walk you to Woldenberg Park. I'd love to hear more about your mother and father, and if you'd like, I can tell you some of the city's history."

Again, she smiled at him and nodded, and Oliver led her across the street, ignoring the flashing DON'T WALK sign.

"Well, that's a first," Alistair said, staring after his brother and his date.

"You can still go after her," Lauren said, feeling generous and trying to keep a wistful edge out of her voice.

"I'll let Oliver give his history lesson."

They stood there for a moment, jostled by the passersby trying to catch the light. A calliope sounded nearby and Lauren smiled. The sound always delighted her.

Alistair seemed to come out of his reverie. "Well, what would you like to do now?"

"Are we still going to brunch?"

"Oh, yes. Shall we head straight there?"

She hesitated. She'd left Buster behind out of deference to Oliver's rather starched countenance. "Would you mind terribly if we went back for Buster? He hates being left alone."

"You're a funny creature," Alistair said, but his voice was kind and not at all critical.

"I've been trying to tell you that," she said, turning and leading the way back toward the Bayou Magick Shop.

The streets were filling up, and she and Alistair couldn't walk side by side. Music drifted from every block as street performers joined the ranks of the special events scheduled for the festival. Lauren was eager to collect Buster and get back outside to enjoy the day, and the much-anticipated brunch.

They could barely squeeze into the shop.

"Am I glad to see you," Kara exclaimed.

"A busload at once," Lauren murmured, then as Alistair moved quickly toward the counter, she made her way through the group of mostly middle-aged women wearing name badges.

Buster glared at her with a baleful expression when she slipped into the lower apartment. "I'm sorry," she said, "but at least I've come back to get you."

The parrot squawked once or twice.

"Forgive me?" Lauren extended her hand.

Buster examined it. "Buy low. Sell high," he pronounced, and walked his way up her arm.

"Let's get some fresh air," she said, and left the building by the walkway that ran from the interior courtyard alongside the shop. As crowded with customers as the shop had been, Alistair would be in there for a while.

Once on the sidewalk, she paused. This section of Bourbon Street was so much nicer than the sleazier blocks full of topless, bottomless, and charmless offerings. The April sun warmed her head and shoulders, and she smiled from the pure pleasure of a pretty day.

"Mom, look at the bird! Can we take a picture?"

Images of her scrape with the police filled her mind. On the other hand, as she looked at the eager face of the girl standing in front of her, all thoughts of law and order fled.

She saw, too, that the girl's mother carried a vivid purple bag with the distinctive Bayou Magick Shop lettering on it.

"Everything has a price," the mother was saying to the daughter.

"For a picture?"

The mother nodded. "Ask the lady and then you can decide if you want to spend your money for a picture of a bird."

Clearly the mother didn't think it worth one dime. Lauren tried not to take offense; she'd never handed over cash for such a thing, either.

Then an idea came to her in a flash. What a great way to pay Alistair back for helping her!

"Your bird is beautiful. How much does a picture cost?"

"Normally it's five dollars," Lauren said.

"Five dollars!"

"Buster is a very rare bird," Lauren said. "But I

see you've been shopping at Bayou Magick. For customers who purchased at least twenty dollars' worth of merchandise, the photo is free."

"Mom, it's free!" The girl skipped over to her mother and tugged at her hand. "Come take our picture."

The woman moved closer, looking at Lauren somewhat askance. Lauren smiled at her, and said, "For customers of Bayou Magick, the photo is what we call lagniappe, or a little something extra."

"Thank you," the woman said, and focused her camera.

Mother and child went away, the child, at least, happy.

And Lauren set about advertising that morning's lagniappe to every passerby, succeeding in sending a steady stream of customers, especially those with children in tow, into the shop.

She'd gathered quite a crowd and collected receipts for fifteen purchases from letting Buster pose on fifteen different children's shoulders before an angry-looking man burst out of the store next door and barged into the Bayou Magick Shop.

From behind the register, Alistair glanced up as the bells on the door clanged violently. Mrs. Merlin made almost that much noise whenever she swept in, but the man advancing on the counter had nothing in common with that genial woman.

"I demand to see your manager!" The burly man glared at him and pushed up the sleeves of his pullover shirt.

Alistair considered the man, assessing his level of temper. On a busy day like today the last thing he needed was a scene. Even for a day with a special event going on in the Quarter, they'd been busier than Alistair could have dreamed. He'd sent Kara to the back for a brief break, and as soon as she returned, he planned to go in search of Lauren and apologize for abandoning her.

But now he had this irate man to handle.

"How may I help you?"

"You can go get your manager for me."

Alistair smiled pleasantly. Honey always caught more flies than vinegar. "I am the manager, sir."

"Impossible. You are too young. I demand the owner."

Alistair suppressed a sigh. This man could use some powerful aromatherapy to clear his aura. "I am both. Alistair Gotho, at your service. And you are?"

"I am the man who runs the poor shop next door, just trying to earn a living." The man took in a gulp of air, and Alistair knew he was building up steam for another outburst.

The bells clanged musically as a group of four women strolled in laughing and chatting. Alistair could have sworn he heard one say something suspiciously similar to "Buy low. Sell high."

His senses went on alert. There were no coincidences. He added up the angry man and the overheard reference to Buster and called Kara to come up front.

Then he led the irate man toward the door.

"Your shill is blocking my store to the benefit of your business and the detriment of mine." A vein on his nose glowed.

Alistair opened the door. "Please, let's discuss this outside. So, you've just taken over the jewelry shop and you're my new neighbor?"

"Yes. And I do not need these troublemakers—" He gestured to a group of four children dancing around Lauren and Buster. Just as the man had claimed, they were blocking the narrow front of the next-door business.

Lauren spotted him and waved, but her smile foundered as she saw the man beside him. Alistair couldn't help but enjoy the image of her with the kids, while two sets of indulgent—or perhaps relieved for the respite—parents sat on the stoop of the angry man's store.

"Can I talk to you a minute, Lauren?"

"Sure." She said good-bye to the children, collected Buster from the smallest one's shoulder, and walked over to his side.

"Lauren," he said, hoping all was as innocent as it looked, "our neighbor is bothered by all the commotion. It would be better if you played with the children directly in front of the Magick Shop."

"Play with them?" The man spit out the words. "She is not playing. She is stealing business from me."

"No I'm not." Lauren glared at him. "These children don't want any jewelry."

"But maybe their parents do. Only by the time you get through with them, they don't have money for my store!" He jabbed a thick finger toward Lauren's face. "You should go away. Where did you come from, anyway? You weren't here when I came to run this store."

"Hey, that's not very nice," Lauren said.

Buster gave one of his haughtiest looks to the man.

"Is it nice that you are making money off this circus, and I am not?"

"What do you mean?" Alistair was puzzled by the man's behavior. Then a thought hit him. "Lauren, you're not charging money for photos, are you?"

"Honestly, Alistair, I may get things confused but I'm not stupid. Of course I'm not doing that after the police . . ."

"Ha, the police. I knew you were trouble."

"Everyone knows that," Lauren said. Looking pretty pleased with herself, she said, "I'm more clever than to get in trouble for the same thing twice."

"Ha, I told you she's making money."

Alistair wondered why he was standing here mediating this circus rather than strolling along Woldenberg Park, sampling brunch offerings and chatting with Barbara. He looked from Lauren to the man, wondering how to settle the guy down. Just then the group of four women exited the shop. He moved out of their way, but to his surprise the white-haired matriarch of the group marched straight up to Lauren.

Flashing a Bayou Magick receipt, the woman said, "My turn, dear. I bought twenty dollars' worth of those funny-looking dolls."

Nineteen

*B*efore Barbara had finished her first bite of the small sampler dish of Eggs Bienville at the Taste of New Orleans booth the riverfront in Woldenberg Park, she knew three things. She liked jazz a whole lot more than she'd ever thought possible; remaining in New Orleans longer than two weeks would find her gaining at least ten pounds; and last but certainly not the least significant, she was the most fickle woman on earth.

She licked the plastic fork coated with a delicious sauce she couldn't identify and reflected that only yesterday morning she'd been fantasizing about the mysterious, unorthodox, silver-haired social pirate Alistair Gotho.

Right now, she couldn't remember why she'd felt that way. She'd been hanging on Oliver's every word all morning, not to mention during the awards dinner the night before.

She'd told herself she needed to step outside the comfortable, albeit rigid boundaries of her personal preferences and seek out a man who could stir up a wildness in her she longed to experience but never had. And she'd thought Alistair might be that man.

But seated in the shade of a canopy that Oliver had found for her, waiting for him to return with refreshing bottled water, Barbara had to admit Oliver stoked fires within her she hadn't known she'd banked, let alone ever laid.

Oliver had noticed, in his thoughtful way, that she'd begun to perspire and her skin to blotch even with the protection of Mrs. Merlin's hat. He'd suggested, right after their stop at the Taste of New Orleans booth, that rather than strolling through the collection of outdoor tents featuring offerings of local restaurants they escape the sun for Brennan's, a restaurant famous for its food and service and particularly renowned for its breakfasts.

The restaurant would be booked, but he knew the family and was confident he could get them in.

Barbara had settled gratefully in the shade, conscious of a degree of attention she'd never experienced in her life. Oliver knew how to spoil a woman. And to top that off, her tour book had featured Brennan's prominently, and Barbara had noted it as one of the places she wanted to visit.

Oliver reappeared just as Barbara's conscience reared its head. She accepted the cool bottle of water, appreciating the droplets of condensation that dampened her hand.

Oliver twisted open a matching bottle, drank deeply, and then said, "I called Brennan's, and they'll take us in thirty minutes."

"That's lovely," she said, hesitating. She had to admit she preferred having Oliver to herself, and in a civilized air-conditioned environment. Sharing him with the redhead, no matter how nice and friendly she appeared, certainly didn't whet her appetite one bit. Still, she had agreed to spend the day with Alistair, and she wasn't quite sure how the switch-around of escorts had occurred.

Slowly, she asked, "Is it wrong to run off when Alistair and Lauren may be looking for us?"

The array of expressions that crossed Oliver's face enlightened, confused, elated, and depressed Barbara, pretty much in that order.

"I'll call the shop and leave a message. If he's there"—he paused—"I'll ask them to join us. If not, I'll suggest we meet up later today. Say, before dinner?"

Barbara nodded, interpreting his decision. Before dinner implied he assumed the two of them were spending the rest of the day together. That thought pleased her. Joining up for dinner was an unknown, but as it seemed far too many hours ahead into an unpredictable future to worry about, she let it go.

She rose and fell into step beside Oliver. They headed away from the bustle and activity of the riverfront, back into the equally noisy streets of the Quarter.

Across the street from where they threaded their way through the hordes out to enjoy the food and music festival, on a second-floor balcony covered with plants sat a man and a woman. Seated beneath an umbrella atop a table, they were calmly reading a newspaper.

"They don't even seem to notice the crowds," Barbara said.

"I think the residents grow immune to the commotion," Oliver said. "Take my brother, for instance. He's lived on Bourbon Street for almost ten years and claims to like it there."

"Claims?"

"Sometimes," Oliver said, a pensive expression on his face, "it's hard to tell just what Alistair is thinking."

Barbara could believe that. Had Alistair wanted to spend the day with her? Was he even mildly attracted to or interested in her? Or, had he thought to entertain the banking consultant as part of his entry into the family business?

Funny, but even as she asked herself those questions, she realized the answers didn't matter much to her. She did, however, want to learn more about the man who'd just paused to admire the window display of a store featuring nineteenth-century European oil paintings.

"Have you ever lived in the Quarter?"

He shook his head and made a slight face. "Too noisy for my taste. We get enough tourists wandering through the Lower Garden District, which is what my neighborhood is known as, but they generally come around in daylight. And," he added dryly, "they're usually sober. That's a nice painting," he commented, as they began walking again. "I don't know the artist, but I like it."

"It's reminiscent of Renoir. Quite lovely."

He smiled at her, appreciation in his expression. "What about you? What's it like where you call home?"

She thought of her expensively decorated but rather bland condominium where she spent her time between consulting trips. Funny, but after a few days in Mrs. Merlin's purple house, she could see that her own home lacked zest. "Home is a high-rise condominium. I do have a penthouse view, and it doesn't lend itself to porch-sitting, but it is quiet."

"Maybe too quiet?" He spoke softly.

Over the cry of a buggy driver passing by, she wasn't sure she'd heard him correctly. She hesitated.

"Maybe that was too personal of an observation on my part, but I was wondering if—" He looked down at her left hand bare of any ring and with a rush of warmth Barbara understood what he was trying to ask.

"I live alone," she said.

"No Mr. Warren?"

She shook her head, a fuzzy rush of heat creating flip-flops between her eyes and the back of her head.

"Has there ever been?"

"No," she said, wondering if he'd answer the same question as to his own status. If not, she knew she wouldn't have the nerve to ask.

At that moment, he paused and pointed to a building across the street. They stepped from the sidewalk onto the pavement. The street had been blocked to automobile traffic, and they moved with the flow of the other pedestrians to a pair of double doors painted a deep pink.

Itching to ask the question and not knowing how, Barbara wondered where her appetite had gone. Then, smiling, he put one hand on the door pull and, looking into her eyes, said, "Me either."

Three hours after he and Lauren had returned to the shop to collect Buster, Alistair opened the front door of the jewelry shop next door and stuck his head in. Lauren had agreed to help out the guy to calm him down, but as Kara had yelled for him to come back and figure out what was wrong with their charge card system, Alistair had no idea how the two of them had worked things out.

What he saw inside the tiny shop made him smile. There sat Lauren, her face puckered in concentration as she wielded a thin paintbrush across the cheek of a young girl. Another child and an adult, sporting works of art on their faces, were handing the beaming proprietor cash for a tidy mound of purchases.

He waited until Lauren put the last flourish on the purple-and-green butterfly and handed a mirror to the girl, then slipped inside the store.

"Cool!" The girl dug a crumpled bill from her shorts' pocket and gave it to Lauren before dancing out of the shop with the other girl and the adult, both kids debating who had the coolest butterfly.

Alistair found himself gripped in the embrace of the man who only a short time ago had been as cross as a leopard that'd lost its spots. "Your friend is so talented," he said, finally letting go. "She saw the paints I had traded for a bracelet, and look what art she has been making."

Not only art. Money. Lauren handed the five-dollar bill over to the shop owner. "Alistair, Jo-Jo had face paints!" She jumped up, almost oversetting the tray table holding a few pots of paint and a jar of water. "Oops."

If he'd known paint would make her that happy, he would have bought out the entire stock of Dixie Art and Supply. He smiled at her and his arm slipped naturally around her shoulders.

"So everyone is happy?" Alistair glanced at his neighbor and then down at Lauren.

"Peace is made," the man said. "And please, call me Jo-Jo." He beamed again. "That is what my friends call me."

Alistair tucked Lauren just the tiniest bit closer to his side, savoring the feel of her soft body molding to his. "Wonderful," he said, adding, "Jo-Jo."

That seemed to seal the deal because the shop-keeper smiled and with a flourish returned the much-folded five-dollar bill to Lauren. "And this is for you."

"Thanks!" She stared at the bill as happily as if Jo-Jo had given her a hundred, and then slipped from Alistair's embrace and bent to clean the brushes in the jar of water.

Lauren, Alistair realized, was terribly naive and possibly too willing to help others at the expense of her own good. Jo-Jo had clearly rung up a good deal of business from the face painting and the other purchases. She'd been doing the same thing to help him in front of the magick shop. And she'd even rescued a parrot and sacrificed her possessions and the roof over her head in the process!

She needed someone to look after her.

Oh, no.

Without being aware of it, he backed toward the door.

"Are you going back to work?" Lauren was drying the brushes on a rag and looking slightly anxious.

Say yes. Tell her Oliver called and escort her over to Brennan's, not that his brother would still be there. Alistair had gotten his message some time ago and purposefully not told Lauren, telling himself it was for his brother's own good to keep Lauren away from him. The two of them weren't suited for each other, and the sooner Oliver got over his infatuation, the better off he'd be.

"Alistair, are you okay?"

One hand on the doorknob, Alistair looked at Lauren's perfect face and body that hid a five-foot-five bundle of confabulations and tribulations and tried to remind his brain that he was out of the caretaking business.

Slowly, he shook his head, smiling even as he did so. "No," he said, "I don't think I am okay, but I also don't think I've ever felt better."

"Great! Then let's go eat." She shook Jo-Jo's hand. "If Alistair will give me time off tomorrow, I'll come back as we discussed."

"And Mr. Alistair says?" Jo-Jo looked at him the way a dog eyed a bone with a lot of meat still hanging on it.

"Whatever the lady wants." Boy, did he have it bad.

Lauren collected her carpetbag, stepped toward him, then stopped. "I can't believe it. I almost forgot about Buster!"

"Where is he?" Alistair glanced around. He, too, hadn't even thought about the bird, but as occupied as he was with trying to figure out how he was losing his battle to stay detached from Lauren, that wasn't surprising.

"He's visiting with Jo-Jo's cockatiel."

"Visiting?" Only Lauren would think in those terms.

"Come, see," Jo-Jo said, pointing to a door at the back of the shop. Just then, two women walked in and he greeted them, waving Alistair and Lauren to the back as he did so.

They skirted around the display cases and into the back office. Sure enough, inside a fairly large cage sat a white bird, smaller than Buster, but with that same sharp-eyed stare, a stare that was fixed solidly on Buster.

The parrot had fastened his claws around the metal lines of the cage and was engaged in trying to reach in and peck at the smaller bird's food. He must have recognized Lauren, because when she entered the room, Buster quit trying to squeeze his beak through the bars and called, "Buy low. Sell high."

The white bird preened its feathers and sidled closer to Buster.

"Look, they've made friends." Lauren was smiling, and that made Alistair smile, too. Only two days ago he'd crossed the threshold of the responsible world of banking and now here he stood matchmaking for birds in the back of a French Quarter shop.

Only two days ago he'd been on the road to normalcy.

Only two days ago he could have sworn he wouldn't be standing three inches away from a redhead who needed food, clothing, and shelter, not to mention kissing.

She was in front of him in the cramped quarters of the office. Alistair lifted a strand of her long thick hair from her neck and with the tip of one thick strand, gently teased her bare shoulder. As she turned slightly, her face moved upward toward his. Bending forward, he feathered his lips over hers.

When she didn't stiffen or draw away, he pulled her around to face him and before he could think better of his actions, captured her lips in a kiss whose hunger shook him.

She moaned softly and wriggled against him, her lips parting as she mirrored his own urgent passion.

He forgot all about treading carefully and not scaring her away like all her other men. No other men had ever existed. She was his and his alone as he claimed her mouth with his tongue, branding her, drawing her essence into his through the intimate dance of their mouths.

She kept on moaning and snuggling closer to him until he was wild enough to back her onto Jo-Jo's desk and take her there and then. He caught her derriere in his hands and ground her to him, beginning to moan himself.

He was as hard as the drilling shaft of an oil rig and he knew he had to have her. But some semblance of sanity returned; at least enough to make him let go of her bottom before he lifted her dress. Knowing she wore no underwear and feeling her skin through the thin fabric of her linen dress had set off a fire he knew only one way to quench.

"So, what do you think?"

Alistair froze at the sound of Jo-Jo's cheerful voice, thankful Lauren hid his aroused body.

Lauren had slipped her arms around Alistair's neck and despite the interruption, she kept on sucking on his lips. Gently, he pulled away. "Lauren, sweetie," he whispered to her, "we have company."

"Oh." She fluttered her lashes and slowly her eyes came back into focus. Then as she looked down where their hips locked in a greedy embrace, she raised one hand to her lips. "Oh!"

Alistair edged back, and said, "Sorry, Jo-Jo. Got a little carried away."

The shopkeeper rubbed his hands together. "What a couple of lovebirds. Run along and leave Buster with me. He and my little Priscilla will be quite happy together."

Lauren looked a little anxious.

"Do you want to do that?" Alistair could still feel the heat generated by their bodies even though they were no longer touching. All he wanted to do was sweep Lauren out of the shop and into his apartment before she had time to think too much about how passionately she had reacted to his kiss. If she stopped to analyze it, her feelings might not come as naturally and her old fears would probably resurface. And, too, he admitted ruefully, he needed her to keep on feeling the same way. Either that or he was going to be taking one long cold shower the rest of the day.

Buster had gone back to pecking at the edge of the food container. The other bird sat there grooming one claw while keeping an eye on the parrot.

"Okay," Lauren said. "Buster seems happy, and it's very good of you to bird-sit."

"No problem." He held open the door, and Alistair let Lauren walk in front of him. As he passed by Jo-Jo, the man said to him with a wink, "Today I bird-sit for you, maybe tomorrow I baby-sit."

Alistair let it go, but as the man's words sank in, he remembered thinking only last week he ought to restock the condom supply that he had let run dry. And now here he had Lauren melting in his arms.

He groaned, and Lauren glanced back, smiled shyly, and tucked one hand into his. "Time for that second lesson?"

Determined to think of some solution, he nodded and guided her out of the jewelry shop. As he had often told Mrs. Merlin and other students of magick, "Trust in the universe and it will provide."

"Yoo-hoo, Alistair!"

Alistair swiveled his head sharply in the direction of that piercing and all-too-familiar voice. Mistake. Too late he realized ducking back into Jo-Jo's shop would have been the wiser course of action.

Mrs. Merlin bore down on them across the street crowded with merrymakers.

Lauren sighed. Alistair almost joined her in the gesture of exasperation. He started to reassure her they'd find a way to slip off, but at that moment a mule drawing a buggy bolted and charged straight toward Mrs. Merlin.

Heedless of the effect her swirling caftan and bouncing parasol might have on the animal, Mrs. Merlin had dashed across the street in the path of the mule. Whether the mule frightened her or she tripped on something, she landed with a splat face-down on the asphalt.

The buggy driver yanked on the reins but that only aggravated the situation as the animal reared backward, tipping the carriage and its shrieking occupants at a precarious angle. The man and the woman in the passenger seat clung to each other as Alistair rushed for the mule's bridle and Lauren raced to Mrs. Merlin's side.

With a lunge of its head, the mule evaded Alistair's grasp. He tensed to grab for the bridle again, when a deep and commanding voice said, "Allow me."

A sprite of a man with a fringe of silvery hair had appeared beside Alistair during the commotion. In one smooth motion, the man tossed his jacket over the mule's head. As quickly as it had bolted, the animal stopped, all four hooves planted on the street, inches from Mrs. Merlin's prostrate body.

Mrs. Merlin blinked and clasped her hands over her breasts. "My hero," she cried. "You saved my life! How ever can I thank you?"

Alistair exchanged a glance of relief and appreciation with Lauren, who was gathering items scattered from Mrs. Merlin's handbag.

The stranger bowed over Mrs. Merlin and offered

his hand. Again, he said, "Allow me," but this time it was more of a request than a command as he gazed at the openly admiring expression beneath Mrs. Merlin's wild orange-and-silver hair.

"My honor," Mrs. Merlin said, accepting his hand.

For such a small man, he lifted her effortlessly to her feet, then turned and flicked his coat from the mule's head. "You may move on," he said to the openmouthed driver. He ushered the foursome to the side of the street. Looking straight at Mrs. Merlin, he said, "General Wisdom, at your service."

Mrs. Merlin fluttered her lashes, and again Lauren's glance shot swiftly toward him. He grinned, enjoying that Lauren had caught Mrs. Merlin's girlish reaction also.

"Maebelle Merlin," she said. "And these are my friends Alistair Gotho and Lauren—dear, I don't believe I know your last name."

"Stevens," Lauren said, shaking hands with the general. "How did you know how to stop that mule?"

"Cavalry training."

"They still have that?" Lauren looked surprised.

"In my youth," the man said, smiling gently. "And that's quite some time ago."

"But you look so young." Of course Mrs. Merlin couldn't help herself from commenting. Alistair waited for the man's reaction. Were he and Lauren witnessing a budding romance at first sight?

"Vitamins and herbal remedies," he said.

"Ooh," Mrs. Merlin said, "that's right up my alley."

The general smiled. "We must exchange fountain-of-youth secrets. But I mustn't keep you from your friends. Perhaps I can call you later?"

Alistair wasn't sure who spoke first.

"Oh, we're through visiting," Mrs. Merlin said.

"I was just leaving to collect Buster," Lauren said.

"I was on my way to the shop," Alistair said, pointing to the Bayou Magick Shop sign as he uttered the first excuse that popped into his mind. He wanted to be with Lauren—alone—and Mrs. Merlin was more than capable of taking care of herself. If he had any reason to distrust the older gentleman, he would have stuck by Mrs. Merlin's side like a cocklebur. But the man's air of command and erect posture gave credence to his military title. His clear eyes and even clearer thinking as he'd stopped the mule spoke well of him. Alistair noted the expensive cut of his suit and the Presidential Rolex on his left wrist. Mrs. Merlin could do a lot worse.

"Then perhaps you'll have tea with me at the Windsor Court before I escort you home?" The general looked as if Mrs. Merlin's answer would make or break his day.

"Are you staying there?" Lauren asked, eyes wide.

The general nodded.

"That's an incredibly fancy hotel. You must be very . . ."

Lauren caught herself before she completed her observations of his financial well-being. Alistair smiled at her, encouraging her as she attempted to smooth some of her rough edges.

". . . comfortable there," she finished.

"Very," the general said with a smile. Then he said good-bye to them and offered his arm to Mrs. Merlin.

They strolled off, heads bent toward one another. Alistair wasn't sure, but he thought he heard Mrs. Merlin describing the benefits of kava kava.

Lauren clasped his arm. "Oh, Alistair, that was amazing. Love at first sight!"

He brushed a lock of her hair from her cheek. "Mrs. Merlin would be the first person to assure you that some things are meant to be."

Lauren blushed slightly, bringing a delightful rosy tint to her cheeks.

Alistair fished the key to the side gate out of his pocket. He didn't want to risk entering through the shop and getting sidetracked. "Ready?"

She nodded, but he sensed her hesitation. She glanced back toward Jo-Jo's shop. "Would you mind if I pick up Buster now instead of leaving him next door?"

He realized their rush to share their passionate reaction to one another had gotten trampled in the drama of the moment. He gazed into her eyes, trying to read her feelings. Reluctant to let her out of his sight, he brushed his thumb over her lips, an unspoken promise that they would take up again later where they'd left off. "Go ahead. I'll wait right here."

She touched her lips with the tips of her fingers, looking confused, and dashed toward Jo-Jo's.

Wishing Mrs. Merlin had found any other time to materialize, Alistair watched as Lauren hurried into the jewelry shop. She was racing after Buster as if her life depended on it, but Alistair understood, or thought he did, her dilemma.

She'd enjoyed their intimacy, found great pleasure in their kisses. Yet she couldn't reconcile those feelings with her prior experiences. Alistair wasn't sure he could either, but he knew two things.

First, he relished those kisses with Lauren as much as she did.

And second, before they got too far into their interrupted lesson, he'd make sure he paid a visit to the Royal Street pharmacy. He might miss a perfect opportunity once, but only a fool got caught short a second time.

Twenty

$\mathcal{D}$r. Lawrence Stevens had never felt so desperate in his life. Not even the time he'd faced five surgeries of five children under age ten in the space of one evening in the ER had he felt so helpless.

He'd only been trying to do what he thought was best for his daughter when he'd told her she'd have to stand on her own two feet and not come running to him for rescue once again.

But as soon as he'd put down the phone and seen his fiancée's expression, he realized he'd muffed the most important crisis of his parenting years. Even the first weeks and months after his wife died hadn't been as difficult as the past thirty-six hours as he'd wrestled with his decision to let Lauren land on her feet without his aid.

At last, walking off the plane in New Orleans, Bonita Bristol at his side, Dr. Stevens felt as if he could begin to try to correct the mistake he'd made, a mistake wrought only out of a wish to make up for his past overindulgent behavior.

Bonita had concurred with his decision to go to New Orleans, which at first confused him, as it had been Bonita who'd pointed out, in her gentle fashion, that he encouraged Lauren's dependence and it would be healthier if he let her find her wings in her own way.

It wasn't as if Lauren weren't capable of taking care of herself, but she'd been a child with special needs. Schoolwork had never come easily to her. He and her mother had spent countless evenings with young Lauren helping her master her numbers and letters, precious hours together as a family, during which time Lauren never gave up. After her mother's death, she'd been even needier.

Or maybe, Bonita had also suggested, he had been the needy one.

Whatever the case, he'd overreacted when he'd left her hanging on the other end of the phone in a strange city with no funds and no way of contacting her.

The only address he had was that of her last employer, Mrs. Plaisance, the woman she'd been sobbing about and saying she'd died when he'd tried, in his misbegotten way, to practice a dose of tough love.

Being a father, Lawrence reflected, grabbing one of their two suitcases off the carousel, was far harder than being a surgeon.

Two hours later, having reached a dead end with the unconcerned and downright unhelpful Plaisance family, he climbed back in their rental car and gripped the wheel.

Bonita soothed his arm with gentle strokes.

"They were more concerned over that damn bird they said she stole than they were over what might have happened to Lauren!"

"Evidently the relatives only showed up when Mrs. Plaisance died," Bonita said.

"To pick her bones and collect the cash." Lawrence shook his head. "No wonder Lauren bolted. And, of course, she took the parrot with her. As a child she rescued everything from kittens to lizards, even snakes." His eyes clouded slightly, and he blinked to clear his vision.

Bonita took one of his hands from the wheel and clasped it in hers. "You're going to find her."

"You know I believe that. What confuses me is I ask myself whether I should be searching for her, then the next second I think of course I should be and curse myself for my harshness on the phone."

"Changing behavior isn't easy."

"Tell me about it." He gently freed his hand and started the car.

"Where to?"

"Where everyone goes in New Orleans. The Quarter." He'd been to the city many times over the years, always for some medical convention or another. Two years earlier, he'd noticed that the area known as the French Quarter seemed even more populated by lost souls, primarily youngsters living on the streets and moving about in groups that formed substitute families. Some had dogs with them, for whom they panhandled to feed.

He'd thought at the time how fortunate he was that Lauren continued to stick to the mainstream of life, despite her penchant for problems.

The irony wasn't lost on him now.

Dogs.

Parrot.

"Bonita, she's got the bird with her!"

"Yes?"

"A redhead with a bird—and knowing Lauren, the thing's riding on her shoulder—won't be hard to find." For the first time, he felt optimistic.

Bonita only nodded, and he knew she wasn't as convinced. But he knew he could find his daughter. It would take only a short time to post some flyers. He had his laptop with a recent photo scanned in. He'd sketch in a parrot, print off some copies, and start working the area around Jackson Square.

Of course, finding her might be the easy part. Winning her forgiveness for the way he'd abandoned her could be much more difficult.

Buster on her shoulder, Lauren followed Alistair into his apartment. She'd opted to collect Buster to give her a few minutes alone to examine her feelings. Over the last few hours her emotions had swooped and dipped and peaked and plummeted, reminding her of the sole time in her life she'd been talked into riding a roller coaster.

But unlike the roller coaster, she wanted to take another chance with Alistair.

Alistair's cat greeted them at the door, meowing. "Sorry, old fellow," Alistair said, picking him up, "but it's into the bedroom with you. Make yourself at home, Lauren. Be right back."

Pleased at the familiar air of his invitation, Lauren settled on the sofa. Buster perched on the arm. She could still hear the howling protests of the cat when Alistair reentered the room. He stopped at the refrigerator and approached with a glass of lemonade, managing to touch her hand as he gave it to her.

To her surprise, he claimed one of the facing chairs rather than the space beside her, but the reassuring—and undeniably sexy—smile he gave her warmed her heart. She smiled back and sipped her lemonade. Today was turning out to be one of the best days of her life, though in a topsy-turvy sort of way, to be sure.

"I heard from Oliver. He and Barbara ended up at Brennan's for breakfast. They invited us to join them, but I declined. I hope that's okay."

Lauren nodded, pleased, though she supposed she should be disappointed. If he and Barbara really had hit it off, there went her plan to pursue the eminently marriageable Oliver Gotho as her port in the storm. But she was happy to think Barbara, who seemed nice as well as intelligent, successful, and pretty, would be otherwise occupied if Alistair ended up spending time at the bank with her.

Anyway, she'd decided she couldn't marry Oliver no matter how desperate for protection she was. She couldn't marry anyone who didn't make her feel the way Alistair made her feel.

Lauren sighed and stirred on the sofa.

Her mind danced from Barbara and Oliver to the wild yet sweet feelings Alistair had awakened in her in Jo-Jo's shop. Her lips curved in a smile as she tasted his kisses in her mind. Again, she shifted on the sofa, wondering why Alistair hadn't joined her.

Even as she voiced the question in her mind, Alistair rose, took her empty glass from her, placed it on a side table, and sat down beside her.

Lauren's heart up-tempoed.

"There are a few things I'd like to share with you," he said.

"Things?" Her imagination raced until she realized he meant he wanted to tell her something.

He took her hand. Gazing into her eyes, he said, "I'm very attracted to you. I know you've heard that before. But I'd like you to know a little bit more about me, just in case . . ."

He was circling her palm in a sensuous motion.

Lauren said, "In case I keep on thinking you're not like other guys?"

He smiled and nodded. "I'm at a crossroads in my life. I'm thinking of selling the magick shop and going to work for the family bank."

She puckered her brow in thought. "Wait a minute. I thought you said you were the caretaker here."

He looked slightly embarrassed. "Technically correct, but I do own this building and the business."

Funny, but it hadn't even entered her mind to marry Alistair for protection from the realities of the world. Gazing into his deep blue eyes, she knew no woman would ever get away with such a thing. Alistair could read her mind, she was sure of that.

Besides, it wasn't for riches that she liked Alistair Gotho.

"Would doing that make you happy? Will it give you satisfaction?"

Alistair rose and walked to the windows of the parlor that opened onto the balcony. He stood with his back to her for several minutes. She waited in silence, thrilled to be with him, honored to be sharing his decision-making process. Why, it was possible that she might actually be helping him by listening.

She hesitated, then decided to ask the question that had popped into her mind. "Did you reject banking not because you disliked it but because you were supposed to do it? I mean, because your father just assumed you would choose his path without exploring any of your own?"

Slowly, Alistair turned around from the window. He smiled ruefully. "Well, I think you've pegged me right there."

"So you might actually enjoy the business?"

"I might. And I also want to help Oliver. It's not fair to leave the burden on his shoulders. He may actually discover one day he acted to please our father, not himself."

"What did you just say?"

He was walking back toward the couch, and Lauren stared at him as she digested his last sentence. He'd spoken of Oliver, but he might as well have been describing her.

"His need to please our father was greater than his—"

"Yes." Lauren shook her head. "That's exactly what I've been doing with my life. I've been trying to earn my Ph.D. to please my father. I mean, I always sort of knew that, but just hearing you say that about Oliver really put it into perspective."

He joined her on the sofa and sat sideways facing her, watching her face as she spoke.

"I keep trying, even though I keep failing, because deep down I'm afraid he won't accept me for who I really am, an artist, not an academic."

"My father didn't reject me when I said no," Alistair said softly. "He yelled and screamed and raised the roof, but he came around."

"But you had a brother who stepped in."

"Yes, and that's one of the big reasons I'm willing to help him now."

"Wow," Lauren said, drawing out the word. "I feel so much lighter." She tapped her chest. "But we're discussing your choices, not mine. What is it you like about running the shop?"

"Ah, I think it's about both of us, as any good exploration should be," he said, running a hand lightly over her hair. "The shop, Lauren," he said slowly, "isn't just a store. I don't just sell souvenirs of voodoo dolls to tourists. I practice magick, specifically candle magick. It's not something I sought out, but it's a gift, or sometimes not such a gift, that I happen to have been given. What Olin Desque taught me was how best to use those gifts."

Lauren wasn't sure she understood what he meant by candle magick. Her life was centered squarely in the earthly. Science, medicine, and even her art—all those influences in her life were reality-based. "Magick?"

He nodded.

"Do you mean you could cast a spell over someone, and they would have to do whatever the spell made them do?"

"I could do that, but I don't."

She wrinkled her brow. "Could you make someone fall in love with you?"

"By performing a candle spell?" He had taken her hand and was stroking the top of it in gentle circles.

She nodded.

"I could, but—I haven't."

"I see." But of course she didn't.

"There are better ways to fall in love," he said softly, tipping her chin up so that their eyes met.

"Natural ones?"

He nodded. "When each person chooses the other of his own free will."

"Hmm." Lauren wondered whether she had chosen to respond to Alistair's kisses when he'd held her close and plundered her mouth, or whether she'd reacted instinctively. She'd almost felt as if some other creature had taken possession of her mind and her body when he'd drawn her to him. And not once had she sensed a sneeze coming on.

"Choice." She repeated the word, and wondered whether Alistair would choose to keep holding her hand.

"Did you ever consider performing a perfect match spell?"

Alistair let go of her hand, rose, and regained his seat in the chair opposite the sofa. When he left her side, Lauren felt as if the world had tipped sideways.

"I went so far as to set up the altar," Alistair said. "Just the other day."

"Yet you decided not to do it?"

"At the time I wasn't sure why not," Alistair said. "I tried to tell myself it was all right to do it to help Mrs. Merlin's goddaughter or Oliver, yet I knew if I went through with it, it would have truly been for my own benefit."

"And that's a bad thing?" She heard the wistful note in her voice.

Lauren wasn't sure that she believed in spells one bit, but she was curious about the possibility. If he really could conjure his perfect woman, what would she be like? Would she have anything at all in common with Lauren Grace Stevens?

Almost apologetically, Alistair said, "Well, as most of us do, I have been seeking my own perfect match." His eyes lit on her face, but Lauren couldn't decipher the look. Was he sending her a message? She wanted to believe that he was actually interested in her, but her sense of insecurity when it came to men held her back. He sure had seemed keen on getting to know the proper Miss Barbara. She sighed and decided she lacked data to draw a conclusion.

He leaned forward, hands on his knees. His hair fell around his face, and he raised one hand and dashed it back over his shoulder. "If I had performed the spell, I wouldn't have known whether the woman I conjured truly wanted me."

"And vice versa," Lauren added softly, understanding him perfectly. "One wants to be wanted for one's good, one's bad, and yes, even one's ugly."

"Yes," Alistair said, "and it was better for the spell to be left undone and for Barbara or Oliver or anyone on this planet to remain alone than always to have that question in the back of their mind."

"It would be beautiful to be wanted, flaws and all."

"Hey," he said, moving back to the sofa and reaching for her hand, "it *is* wonderful."

Lauren nodded. Of course he would know that. Alistair Gotho could crook a finger and have any woman he wanted. She'd seen the evidence of his former lovers—why, she was wearing a dress she'd found in one of his closets!

But who wanted her—a dyslexic, hyperactive, unemployed doctoral student? Wistfully, almost afraid to ask the question, but dying to know the answer, she said, "If you were going to conjure your perfect match, what would she be like?"

Alistair shifted closer. Waiting for his response, her feelings of vulnerability mounted. She grabbed the hem of her dress and started rolling the fabric between her fingers.

Alistair paused. His silent scrutiny only fed her nervousness. Earlier, when he'd been kissing her, she hadn't been at all anxious, but holding her breath for his answer, plus remembering what he'd said about taking up where they'd left off once they were alone, she was paralyzed. What if she disappointed him? What if the feelings he'd roused in her last night and again in the shop had been a fluke? What if she was a failure at being with a man?

Yet, oddly enough, coupled with all her fears came the crazed wish that he would describe her to a "T" and then sweep her into his arms and kiss her senseless.

"My perfect match?" The words rolled slowly off his tongue even as he lifted one strand of her hair. "Definitely a redhead," he said.

"Really?"

"Oh, yes." He glanced away, then shifted his gaze back. "Funny, but I've never dated a redhead before."

Tracing his finger lightly over her forehead, he said, "My perfect match is wise and witty." His hand moved lower, hovering above her breast. "And warm and loving."

"And kissable," he added, lowering his lips to hers.

Her lips parted magickally and she trembled as he drew her close. He hadn't exactly described her to a "T," but if she worked on the wise and witty part, she might match up.

Slowly he lifted his lips from hers, only to waltz kisses along her throat. She sighed blissfully, and said, "Does this mean it's lesson time?"

"Yes." He kissed the hollow of her throat, then slowly lifted his head. "Unless you'd rather have lunch first."

And for the first time in her life, Lauren said, meaning every word, "I couldn't swallow a bite."

He reacted to her statement with a grin that lit his face charmingly. "I think," he whispered before he captured her lips again, "that means it really is lesson time."

Twenty-one

*A*listair started with the kiss, tasting the sweetness of her lips, drinking her in like the starving man he was. Starving for connection. Starving for the tenderness and protectiveness Lauren aroused in him.

He inhaled the scent of her hair, smiling as he detected the faint aroma of the herbal-blend shampoo he stocked in his own shower.

She sighed and shifted so that her body draped across one of his legs. The kisses alone had him aroused, but as her dress slipped above her knees and her bare leg caressed his thigh, Alistair made a sound somewhere between a growl and a groan and pulled her fully onto his lap.

Their mouths still locked in their hungry dance, Alistair loosed the top two buttons of her dress. He could picture her creamy breasts and pinkish nipples, the duskier rose of the flesh circling the nipples pebbling from her own arousal. But picturing wasn't enough.

He opened the next two buttons, praising Lauren silently for her decision not to bother with underwear. Slowly, he lifted his mouth from hers.

Her eyes were shiny, and she had her arms wrapped around his neck. Snuggling against him, she said, "Why does everything you do feel so good?"

He regarded her rosy lips, kiss-swollen, and the blush on her cheeks, the sparkle in her eyes. She was holding nothing back, and he knew as surely as he knew his own name that she would give herself completely to him, free of any of her lack of desire or fear of performance. There was a reason. Or perhaps there was no reason, and it was complete coincidence that their sexual chemistry was perfectly matched.

"Just a minute and I'll tell you," he said, kissing her lips lightly once, then easing her breasts free and into his hands. "But I think I'd rather show you first."

She leaned back slightly, offering her body to his caress. Touched by her trust, he vowed never to betray it in any way. Then desire swept away thoughts of reason and logic and chemistry as he lowered his lips. With a feather-light touch, he lapped one nipple.

She clutched the back of his head. "Oh, that feels so good," she said in a voice full of marvel.

Before he could explore either her breast or why she sounded surprised that having her nipple kissed felt so good, a sharp rap at the door broke through the quiet room in which the only sounds were his and Lauren's own heavy breathing.

Willing whoever was there to go away, Alistair circled one nipple gently with his tongue as he moved one hand to stroke Lauren's hair. His own hair fell over his shoulder and onto her naked breasts. He teased her flesh with his hair as he shifted to kiss her other breast.

Knock. Knock. Knock.

Alistair lifted his head. "Go away."

"It's Oliver."

Alistair rolled his eyes and muttered, "An even better reason to go away." Then he glanced at Lauren. Her eyes were half closed, and he wasn't sure she was paying attention to anything other than the progress of his mouth and the reactions of her body.

But to his surprise and disappointment, she sat up and said, "Shouldn't you see what he wants?"

Slowing his breathing, he considered the question. Maybe she wanted the interruption. Or worse, maybe she wanted to see Oliver. He'd been about to explain in specific detail how perfect they were for one another and that being the case, why let Oliver into the picture?

"Kara sent me up here," Oliver called through the door.

Groaning, Alistair pulled away. He leaned down and fastened the buttons of her dress. "I promise you we'll take up where we left off."

She nodded, eyes shining in a way that gave him hope she really had no desire to see his brother.

"But if Kara needs help in the shop, I'll have to go downstairs."

"I understand. Do you want me to help?" She was pulling down her skirt and smoothing her hair.

"Just wait here." He didn't want her escaping. This interruption was good for one reason and one alone. He'd dash to the pharmacy as soon as he checked on Kara.

Alistair crossed the room and opened the door. Oliver and Barbara stood there, standing close together, looking every bit as comfortable with one another as an old married couple.

Relieved to see that, and realizing he shouldn't abandon them on the stair landing, Alistair invited them in, then raced down to the shop.

The moment Alistair stepped out the door, Lauren bolted from the sofa. In her dash not to be discovered, she made for the first shelter she saw—the island counter separating the living room from the small kitchen.

She felt as guilty as a shoplifter caught with a purse full of compact discs. She wasn't behaving rationally, and she knew it. Even as she crouched down behind the counter rather than come face-to-face with Alistair's brother, she knew she was being silly.

But she couldn't help it. The sensations Alistair had unleashed in her had to show on her face. Why, her lips were all puffy, and she couldn't stop smiling, not even as she hid between the sink and the barstool. It was just too embarrassingly personal to face anyone—especially the brother of the man who'd produced those effects!

Lauren caught the sound of a second voice, lower-pitched and female. She cringed. Of course Barbara was with him. Get up now, she commanded her body. Pretend you dropped something and stand up, and say, "Why, hello, I didn't hear you come in."

Her knees remained firmly tucked over her ankles despite the signals of her brain. The longer she hid, the more foolish she would look.

Only if they find me.

That thought was her undoing.

Staring at her toes and counting the dismaying number of chips in her Ripened Raspberry polish, she prayed for them to sit down or better yet, pen Alistair a note and go away.

She heard a rustling and a slight creak of springs and let out the breath she'd been holding. They'd sat on the sofa; she knew because she'd heard the same faint metallic groaning before Alistair had started kissing her and she'd lost all track of earthly reality.

"That's odd," Oliver said.

"What's that?" Barbara murmured.

"Lauren's parrot is here, but Lauren isn't."

In her hiding spot, she stiffened. They were bound to start looking around for her. How, how, did she get herself into these fixes?

"Are you sure that's the same parrot?"

"Of course it is. Why else would Alistair have a bird in his living room when he has a cat that's a hundred percent predator?"

Barbara laughed, but it was strained. Lauren wondered what Oliver had said to put her off. She certainly was no cat lover; Lauren had observed her drawing away from Midnight the other day, so it couldn't be the predator comment.

"You do pay a lot of attention to her, so I guess you'd recognize her sidekick."

Meow, Lauren thought, intrigued by the exchange as she eavesdropped shamelessly. Why, Barbara is jealous of me! If only she knew what a pain it was to have men go gaga over one without the slightest provocation. Surely she had some inkling; she was quite pretty. Lauren would like to ask her, and if she weren't pretending not to be there, she might have spoken out right then and there.

Silence followed Barbara's snippy comment, and Lauren bet she was wishing she'd kept her last observation to herself. Jealousy turned guys off, and fast. Lauren knew 'cause she'd used it to get rid of guys who didn't know how to take no for an answer.

"Come here," Oliver said in hushed tones. The words sounded a lot more like an invitation than a command, and Lauren knew she was about to overhear more than she should.

The sofa creaked, more loudly this time.

"I only have eyes for you," Oliver said.

Lauren gasped. Why, he'd been fawning over her only that morning! What kind of switcheroo was he pulling?

Immediately, she realized she had no call to stand in judgment. She'd been on the verge of using Oliver's infatuation with her to grab herself a husband to pull her out of her personal tailspin, and only minutes earlier, she'd been half-naked in Alistair's arms.

"Did you hear something?" Barbara asked the question, but in a dreamy way as if she didn't really want an answer. Oliver must have answered her with a kiss as the sofa creaked even more and no more words were exchanged.

Darn. Now what? She didn't want to sit and listen to the two of them doing what she and Alistair had just been doing on that very same couch! But surely they wouldn't do more than kiss. It wasn't as if they were in their own living room.

But as long as they were in a clinch, maybe she could make it around the corner and down the hall to the bedroom. She rose slightly, afraid to breathe for fear of being detected.

The door to the apartment opened.

Lauren froze. Oh, no! Just when he'd started to like her, Alistair would think she was a complete idiot. Should she crouch down or bluff her way through it?

Fear of looking a fool ruled, and she dropped to her knees, determined to postpone the inevitable for as long as possible. Maybe Barbara and Oliver would leave, and she wouldn't get caught in front of all three of them. Ever the optimist, Lauren thought, her father's words echoing in her head. She clenched her eyes shut, wishing she hadn't remembered that expression. Every time she'd landed in trouble, she'd always found some happier interpretation to cast on the situation. Even the time she'd been expelled her freshman year in high school, the year after her mother died, she'd explained to her father that it was good to get in trouble a little 'cause it was like a vaccination. Besides, it hadn't been her fault that the gunpowder she'd made in the lab exploded and smoked the school out for half a day.

"I'm back," Alistair said, fairly unnecessarily. Lauren thought he sounded very out of breath, as if he'd run up the stairs. But he was in too good shape for that to put him out of sorts.

"So," Oliver said, "business must be booming. Everything okay down there?"

"Sure. She just needed some change and more charge slips. Where's Lauren?"

"Lauren?" That was Oliver, naturally.

"You know, long red hair, legs to die for. I left her sitting right there where you two are."

"Are you sure you're feeling all right?" Oliver sounded concerned. No wonder, Lauren thought. He had every reason to think Alistair had gone nuts.

"I've rarely felt better." Alistair sure sounded happy, despite being puzzled. "But if you can tell me where Lauren went, I'll be even better."

Legs to die for. Lauren mulled over Alistair's description. She'd always thought of her legs as one of her least attractive features. Most men raved over her face, her hair, and her breasts. She stifled a sigh that did battle with a smile as she concluded it was just like Alistair not to describe her the way all those other guys did.

"If you're sure she was here when you left, then maybe she's in the bathroom." That was Barbara. Sensible, logical Barbara.

"Of course."

As silly as the gesture was, Lauren squeezed her eyes shut tight as footsteps crossed the living room, veered beside the kitchen area, and headed down the hall.

She still had her eyes closed as the feet retraced their path and came to a halt in front of her.

Slowly, slowly, she opened her eyes and let her gaze travel from Alistair's sandals up his khaki pants to his belt buckle. Staring at the intricately entwined silver prongs of what looked like a hand-made silver buckle, she said, "Were you looking for me?" Odd she hadn't noticed the unique design of the buckle before, but then she'd been concentrating on his lips and the way he made her want to dance her tongue in a pas de deux with his.

"Uh-huh."

"Oh." She sat back on her heels, letting her hands fall to the tops of her thighs. She was at a disadvantage here. He was staring down at her, a puzzled expression on his face, but she could tell he was distracted by the way her dress had slipped lower in the front, revealing the tops of her breasts.

But would her body be enough to distract him from how odd a duckling she truly was?

Lauren sighed. She wanted him to like her, want her, and not mind that she was a mess. If he only wanted her body, he really was no different from all the other men in the universe.

She waited for him to ask her what in the world she was doing crouched on the floor of his kitchen. She waited for him to fix her with the look of disbelief she'd seen so many times before, the look that told her she was too different from everyone else to fit in.

Instead, he said in a gentle voice, "Were you meditating, Lauren?"

Amazed and grateful, she lifted her eyes to meet his gaze. He did look concerned, but not disturbed with her. Taking the excuse offered her, she rose, accepting a hand from him to help her up. "I must have lost track of time," she said.

He put an arm around her. "Barbara and Oliver are here." He guided her to the living room, and she'd never been so grateful in her life.

"Hello," Oliver said. "I hope we didn't disturb you."

She shook her head. "Oh, no, I assure you I didn't hear a word you two said." And then of course she blushed, because her statement as much proclaimed that she had overheard their entire conversation.

"Well," Barbara said, shifting slightly away from Oliver and folding her hands in her lap.

Lauren noticed that Barbara's lips had that same puffy, rosy look to them her own had after Alistair kissed her. But if that was the case, why pull away from him?

Duh. Lauren wished she weren't so dumb. Barbara was probably just as embarrassed at being caught in such a private situation as Lauren had been. And Barbara had at least held her ground and not dived under the couch.

Lauren smiled sweetly at the other woman, trying to signal her solidarity with her sisterhood, but Oliver intercepted the look.

Alistair must have seen it, too, and misinterpreted

its intended recipient, because he let go of Lauren and sat down in one of the two chairs opposite the couch. Feeling stranded, Lauren took the other one. Surely Alistair hadn't thought she was flirting with his brother?

Why would she do such a thing when he'd been so open and intimate with her? But as she pondered the question, her temper flared. Did he think he owned her? Possessed her every thought and feeling? Why, because he'd rescued her from a displaced and loveless life? Chafed by the questions, she squirmed in her chair.

"Kara confirmed that you really are going to work for Alistair," Oliver said.

Lauren nodded. Right now she wished she could quit and run out the door. She wanted Alistair to desire her purely for the person she was, not as a charity case who owed him gratitude.

"My brother does it again," Oliver said, with a grin.

"What do you mean by that?" Alistair's voice chimed in with Lauren's as they both asked the same question.

Oliver looked slightly uncomfortable. "Well, you know how you always rescue lost souls. And now you're rescuing . . ." He trailed off as Alistair shot him a look darker than any Lauren had ever seen him give.

So was that it? He had a track record of picking people up and dusting them off? Lauren bristled, but only because she fit the pattern so perfectly. Why, oh, why, did life have to be so complicated? She shifted in her chair and fixed Oliver with a smile more brilliant than she'd delivered that entire day. "So, Oliver, are you good at rescuing helpless females, too?"

"I've never gone into that line." He glanced sideways at Barbara, who'd folded her arms over her chest.

Lauren fluttered her lashes. She'd be darned if she'd be another charity case for Alistair Gotho. He'd made her feel things she'd never experienced in her life, and he'd made her want more of those soaring heights of pleasure, made her believe he was the only man who could give that gift to her.

She thought of the dresses in the closet, the massage oil he'd found in the bedroom. Glancing down at the dress she wore, she wondered what other woman or women had worn it before her. No, she didn't want to be just another helpless cause in Alistair's dance card of aid to the troubled.

She wanted to be his only one, or she wanted nothing from him, nothing at all.

It was a bad idea, but all that occurred to her was flirting with his brother. That would show him that she didn't need him to set her life to rights. She didn't need him to rescue her. She didn't need her father or any other man. Her life would work only when she learned to set it right on her own. But in the meantime, she wasn't beyond using Oliver to help her prove her point. Lauren had never known the luxury of being the perfect angel.

"But you would show a person around the French Quarter Festival, wouldn't you?" She kept her eyelashes moving and crossed one leg over the other, leaning forward enough so that her dress dipped just a touch more in the front. She wasn't sure, but she thought she heard Alistair catch his breath.

"Well, that was the plan for the day."

Poor Oliver. Lauren was insightful enough to realize he couldn't disregard logic. He wasn't a banker for nothing. "That's right," she said with a pout she'd almost forgot she knew how to produce. "And you did ask to escort me today."

He nodded and pleated the fabric of his neat khaki slacks, pants that were almost a double of the ones Alistair wore. Trying not to think of that, Lauren kept her gaze fixed on Oliver. "I'm ready when you are," she said.

Twenty-two

Of all the pissy things to do. Alistair fixed his brother with a steady glare that would have sizzled a more perceptive man. But as logical and orderly and intelligent as his brother was, he was not the intuitive sort.

Nevertheless, Alistair kept pinning him with his gaze, thinking Oliver just might notice he'd done the wrong thing by offering to show Lauren around.

Showing Lauren around was Alistair's job.

Just when that had happened he couldn't say for sure, but it wasn't the same as the rescuing he'd done in his past. He wanted to walk side by side with Lauren, watch her reactions, marvel at her open-armed approach to life. And he most definitely did not want Oliver snatching her out from under his nose.

But what did Lauren want?

Alistair relaxed the grim stare that wasn't producing any results and rubbed the side of his cheek, wishing he had the luxury of time to consider the possible answers to that question.

His brother, though, was making his excuses to Barbara and rising from the sofa. He moved with a fair degree of reluctance, and he was probably reacting as any properly bred Southern gentleman would in agreeing to the escort she'd claimed, rather than out of a preference of Lauren over Barbara.

But Alistair didn't trust him not to succumb to Lauren's charms once he was out of range of the banking consultant's less vivid flame.

The image of the altar he'd erected for the perfect match spell flashed in his mind, and Alistair pondered the message. He'd acknowledged the strong urge to work the spell for his own benefit; he'd overcome that. But had he as successfully learned from his own past mistakes?

Each time one of his former girlfriends had begun to move away from him, he'd clung to the known, the comfortable, and tried to hold her to him. He hadn't wanted to go through the process all over again, the hunt, the search, the meet, and the plunge into passion only to discover he'd fallen yet again for the wrong woman.

He'd walked away from the spell.

That choice had been the easy one.

The difficult one was letting go of his own past behaviors. If Lauren was meant for him, she would come of her own accord. Alistair took a long, deep breath and smiled at his brother and at Lauren.

"You two have fun," he said, managing a fairly nonchalant tone. "Barbara, I was thinking of taking in the impressionist exhibit at NOMA. Would you like to join me?"

Her face lit up. "Oh, yes. That and breakfast at Brennan's were the two things on my to-do list." Then, for whatever reason, she blushed and glanced over at Oliver.

But Oliver had his head tipped, listening to something Lauren was saying to him, and he missed the look.

Barbara's face fell.

Alistair had always considered that expression a cliché, but as he watched Barbara's aura shift and her body language close off protectively, he knew he'd never seen it more clearly demonstrated.

"I'd love to go with you to the museum," she said. "If you'll excuse me for a minute to powder my nose, I'll be ready."

Marveling that anyone still used that expression, he nodded. Pointing to the hallway, he said, "First door on the left."

If Barbara's face had fallen, Lauren was launching daggers at him from her beautiful green eyes. Alistair suppressed a grin at the crazy tack his thoughts had taken, and said, "Don't forget to take the key to the gate. I may be out late."

That statement cost him a lot of effort, but he'd be darned if he'd sit back like an overturned turtle and grasp at hope.

* * *

Watching Lauren eat actually made Oliver queasy. He'd never spent time with a woman who could stand in the sun and devour a dish of spicy crawfish tails and pasta followed by a plate of shrimp étoufée. True, both those foods were New Orleans' specialties, but the ladies he was accustomed to ate them in minute portions in air-conditioned environs.

It hadn't taken Barbara more than a taste of the hot food earlier in the day and she had sought the shade and the cool water he'd retrieved for her. Then the two of them had enjoyed a delightful, if indulgent meal at Brennan's. The food had tasted especially good, but Oliver had long since concluded that the magic ingredient had been the woman by his side.

Barbara.

"So," Lauren said over the blare of a very loud and none-too-musical band, as she tossed a small Styrofoam bowl and a plastic fork into a trash barrel, "what's next?"

"You're not still hungry, are you?" Oliver realized as he said the words just how impolite they sounded, and tried to amend them with, "I mean, would you like dessert? I saw a booth with strawberry shortcake."

She seemed to consider the question, then shook her head. "No, thanks. What I need is a nap."

"Do you want me to walk you back to Alistair's place?" He tried not to sound too eager.

"That's the last place I want to go." She set her jaw mulishly, and Oliver wondered just how many hours his fit of gallantry would take out of his day. Or more specifically, away from Barbara.

Funny, but only yesterday—no, only this morning—he would have given an arm and a leg to have the honor of spending the afternoon with the beautiful redhead at his side. Even now that he'd realized he must have been suffering from heat stroke or a curious case of early mid-life crisis that had resolved itself before he'd created any harm, he still admired the beautiful woman strolling by his side.

If her half-hopping along, half-walking steps could be called strolling.

But no matter how overactive her movements, or partially perhaps because of them, she attracted attention.

He spotted the sidelong glances, and the bolder men ogled her openly.

And it was no wonder.

Lauren was a sight to feast one's eyes on.

Even though the sheath-style dress she wore flowed around her body, it was very much defined by the luscious curves that mounded her breasts and rounded her hips. And Oliver was quite certain that beneath the soft floral fabric, she wore not a stitch of clothing. Whenever she bent forward, his eyes met cleavage that made him catch his breath. Even though he'd recovered from his fit of infatuation, he could still appreciate the female form, and appreciate Lauren's he did.

And he'd be willing to bet his brother did, too.

So why had he stolen Barbara from under Oliver's nose?

"Why does he do it?"

"Excuse me?" Oliver, addressing only his own thoughts, hadn't been paying a jot of attention to his surroundings as he and Lauren had walked along the riverfront.

She halted in front of the Moonwalk, a boardwalk along the river that had been fenced off for renovations. Oliver frowned at the sign pronouncing the mayor's plans to improve the walk. He'd never felt the simple walkway needed any changes.

Some things didn't need improving.

His love life, though, could sure use some. Here he was with a woman he'd fallen for at first sight, yet he was spending every moment wishing he were back with someone who was not only a consultant for his bank, but a woman who'd told him that morning that she always fell for the nice, dependable, intelligent guy. Something about coming to New Orleans, she'd said, had shown her she needed to add some spice to her life.

She'd smiled when she'd said that, the bowl of her brandy milk punch glass cradled in her hands, and he'd set out to prove to her just how full of spice and zest he could be.

But obviously it hadn't been enough. What had she said to Alistair? There were two things she wanted to do in New Orleans—have breakfast at Brennan's and visit the impressionist exhibit at the art museum.

Why, if Oliver remembered correctly, Alistair didn't even like the impressionists!

"I said," Lauren said, speaking as if she were addressing a nearly deaf person, "why does Alistair rescue people? More specifically, women?"

"Does he?"

Lauren caught Oliver by the front of his starched short-sleeved shirt, so different from the much-washed blue denim one Alistair had worn. "Don't try to put me off. You're the one who said he did that. You're the one who implied that's exactly what his interest in me is." She bit her lip and slackened her grip on his shirt. "Or maybe I should say was," she added.

Oliver was staring at her. She couldn't read his expression, but after having only enough appetite to sample two of the myriad of food choices available, she knew something was different with her. The image of Oliver's face, only a few inches from hers, wavered and she blinked. She wasn't herself. Perhaps she should get out of the sun.

"Do you care about my brother?"

He kept on bobbing around in her vision, and Lauren dashed away a drop or two of perspiration. It must have been that last dish, with that spicy sauce, that had done her in. "I think I need to sit down," she said.

Rather than making light of her situation, Oliver was solicitude itself. "That's more like it," he said, leading her to a shady spot beneath a tree. "Let me get some water."

She grasped his sleeve. "No."

He looked surprised and she couldn't blame him.

"I'd rather you not leave me. Sit!" She patted the ground directly in front of her. "This spot is just perfect."

Oliver reluctantly folded his legs and settled on the grass, wondering as he did what was going on in her mind under that beautiful surface.

He had no way of knowing she'd just spotted two ghosts.

"Do you want to cover the Square again?"

Lawrence Stevens patted Bonita's hand, grateful for her unceasing support. They were standing on the grassy fringe of park that ran along the Mississippi River where it bordered the French Quarter. That day was another cause for local celebration, judging by the food booths and stages for bands that were lined along the way. The whole area was mobbed, and Lawrence's neck ached from searching every which way for a sight of telltale bright auburn hair.

He nodded.

"You sense she's somewhere around here, don't you?"

"Thank you for understanding that," he said, as they began walking again, this time away from the river. "I'm a man of science and medicine, but I can't shake the intuition that I'm almost close enough to reach out and touch her." He laughed without mirth. "And I don't mean over the telephone."

She said nothing. The two of them had been over and over that last call from Lauren. Stevens regretted with every ounce of his being that he'd cut her off over the phone, yet in some way, he still felt he'd done the right thing.

It was very confusing.

They covered the several blocks back to Jackson Square in silence. The noise of the streets, with cars cruising slowly, mules clopping along in front of buggies, and music dancing from shop fronts, pretty much made talking a luxury anyway.

At the edge of the Square, he said, "Let's make our way around the artists and fortune-tellers one more time, then how about I take you back to the hotel? I don't want to wear you out."

Bonita squeezed his hand. "I'm not tired, and I'm staying with you."

"Always were stubborn, weren't you?" But he smiled gratefully. How he wished his daughter could know Bonita the way he did. Maybe once they found her she'd agree to come home for a visit and spend some time with them. He'd loved Lauren's mother, but he'd been so young then and spent so much time away, first in medical school then the long hours at work, that they'd never developed the closeness he had with Bonita just over the past two years. He knew some of his friends would say that closeness came from Bonita having been his therapist, but he'd discontinued treatment with her more than a year ago. Once their feelings had blossomed, they'd decided it was wise for him to switch to another counselor.

"There are a lot more people out now," Bonita said, gesturing toward the row where artists had set up to paint and peddle their works to the tourists.

They walked past the first several outdoor work areas, recognizing the artists from their earlier surveillance.

Lawrence stopped at the next spot. A rickety card table covered by an orange cloth held two flickering candles. An older woman draped in shawls despite the warmth of the sun sat behind the table idly flipping through a deck of cards. Her sign read SISTER GRISWOLD KNOWS ALL.

"We didn't talk to her before," he said, and pulled one of the flyers with Lauren's picture from the folder he had tucked under his arm.

The old woman's eyes lit up as Lawrence approached her, the flyer face out.

"You seek the sight of Sister Griswold." It wasn't a question, but a statement.

He paused. "Yes. I'm looking for—"

"Shh. Don't tell me."

"If I don't describe who I'm looking for, how are you supposed to tell me whether or not you have seen my daughter?" Stevens put stock in his own sense of intuition but the efficacy of fortune-telling was pretty much beyond the pale of believability to him.

Bonita laid a gentle hand on his arm, and he realized his frustration at not yet finding his daughter was stripping away his usual good manners.

The card reader had closed her eyes and had begun humming a low, not very melodic tune. She spread the cards she was holding facedown on the table but did not turn any of them over.

Just as Lawrence was thinking about trying the grizzle-haired cartoonist to the right of them, she began to speak.

"You and your daughter have suffered pain. She has run away from you, but not because she does not love you or the other woman in your life. She is afraid of what she will make of her own span of years on this earth, afraid that she will never know the bonds of love that you have woven not once but twice."

"How do you know all this?" He was truly amazed. He checked Bonita's reaction and saw that she looked pretty fascinated, too.

The old woman shrugged her shoulders and waved a hand over the cards. "I report what I see."

"But you haven't turned any of the cards over," Bonita said, not in an argumentative way, but as if she was trying to understand Sister Griswold's technique.

At first the woman's only answer was another elaborate shrug. Then she sniffed, and said, "One can see without seeing if one knows how." Indicating the two chairs in front of her table, equally as rickety-looking, she said, "Come. Sit and let me read the cards for you."

Stevens glanced at Bonita, and silently they pulled out the two webbed lawn chairs and seated themselves.

"What's this cost?" Stevens liked to get to the point when it came to money, rather than be surprised after all was said and done.

She glanced at him in a sly, sideways fashion. "What is the value of the information you seek?"

His jaw tightened and his stomach clenched simultaneously. He'd let his desperation to find Lauren and set things right with her lead him straight into a swindler's trap. This woman was a fake.

Everything she'd said so far, he realized with a sick thudding of his heart, she could have guessed from observing them.

Stevens scraped the chair back. The sound of the metal frame scratching against the flagstones ricocheted around the Square. The artists on either side of Sister Griswold kept on painting. No doubt they'd grown accustomed to the shyster's irate customers. "Come on, Bonita, she's just trying to take us for whatever she can."

Bonita hesitated.

Sister Griswold, looking quite unconcerned with his reaction, turned over one card. "Your daughter's name is Lauren, and she was last employed by a Mrs. Plaisance."

He sank back into his chair. It rocked sideways on the uneven pavement then settled. Stevens knew his face was as white as the hospital coats he wore back home.

Back home where life flowed at a gentle, steady pace, his earlier workaholic tendencies having been tempered by Bonita's influence.

"How much?"

"One hundred dollars."

Without further hesitation he yanked two fifties from his wallet and tossed them onto the card table. From the chagrined look on the fortune-teller's face, he concluded she was wishing she'd set her price higher.

"So where can I find her?"

Sister Griswold placed a finger to her lips and bent over the cards, her face so low he couldn't read her expression. A hundred dollars obviously paid for the full show.

She turned over four cards and paused, steepling her fingers and muttering something he couldn't hear. Then she swayed side to side in her chair and began to speak.

"Love is in the cards for your only child, but she is in danger of choosing unwisely."

She stopped rocking and tapped one finger on one of the cards. The tapping seemed quite ominous. Stevens leaned forward, but he knew nothing of whatever art she was plying and could make neither heads nor tails of the convoluted images on the card.

"Not only is she in danger of choosing the wrong lover, but she has pursued a calling in life that is not true to her spirit. If she does not change this course, she will come . . . to grief." The fortune-teller spit out the last two words, then fell backward in her chair, hands flopping about her chest.

"What's wrong?" It was Bonita who asked the question. All Stevens could see was a huge ball of guilt about to roll and crush him. Lauren had never wanted the things he'd wanted for her. He'd pushed her into graduate studies; he'd wanted his only child to have those sacred letters behind her name. But what good was a Ph.D. if the pursuit of it made her miserable?

Bonita had risen and was leaning over the old woman, who was gasping for air. "Seeing the cards costs me my energy and my heart is weak. So weak." She moaned and clutched her chest with her hands. "I may need a doctor, and they are so expensive."

Stevens jerked out of his reverie. "I'm a doctor. ER physician." He reached for her wrist to check her pulse.

The old woman made a remarkable recovery. She straightened and pulled her wrist from his grasp. "Just your touch has healed me."

"Good," Stevens said, quite unfeelingly. He was getting pretty impatient with her trickery. "You still haven't told us where Lauren is." He pulled a twenty-dollar bill and a business card from his wallet. The bill he held between his fingers; the card he tossed on the table, along with an ink pen. "Write down where she is. Now."

She muttered something about interrupting the flow of a vision from the cards, but took the pen and slowly printed on it, every so often nibbling on the tip of his Mont Blanc.

When she'd finished, he snatched up the card and read aloud: "Oliver Gotho—1212 Philip Street." Glaring at her, realizing she'd also cost him one of his favorite pens because he certainly didn't want it back after she'd chewed on it, he said, "She's staying with this Oliver person?"

The sister arranged her shawls and said haughtily, "It is the name and address the cards have revealed to me."

He dropped the twenty-dollar bill and stood up, ready to track down the lead despite his skepticism. "Keep the pen."

She smiled, gracious in her triumph.

Bonita said, "This Oliver. He's the wrong choice, isn't he?"

Sister Griswold swept the four cards back into the deck, twirled the Mont Blanc, and smiled a most enigmatic smile.

Twenty-three

*B*arbara hadn't known it was possible to feel so dismal in a museum. She was no art expert, as Lauren had pointed out at lunch the day before, but throughout her life she had found museums a haven. The New Orleans Museum of Art was on a smaller scale than her favorite National Gallery, but the special exhibit should have provided her with pleasure.

Instead, she felt only a restless urge to have the visit over and done with. Funny, but during breakfast at Brennan's, the other experience she'd been so looking forward to, she'd wanted the day to go on and on and on.

The meal had been sublime, but that feeling had nothing to do with the food and everything to do with Oliver. Instead of expressing her appreciation of the seascape she'd been staring at for five minutes, she sighed. She might as well have been staring at a blank wall. All she could see was the imagined handwriting that proclaimed she was making a prime muddle of her life.

Alistair had gone to make a phone call to check on his assistant at the shop. When she caught sight of him crossing the gallery she straightened her posture and tried to look as if she were happy to see him. Not that she didn't like him; it wasn't his fault he wasn't Oliver.

From his glum expression it seemed something might be wrong. She brightened. Maybe they could cut the visit short and she could find an excuse to derail Oliver before he could spend any more time with the far-too-engaging redhead.

"Things bad at the shop?"

"Oh, no, everything's under control. There," he added, in a tone that matched Barbara's bleak mood.

"Is anything else wrong?"

Alistair indicated a bench in the center of the deserted room. "Rest a minute?"

She joined him.

"I thought Oliver might have returned by now." He scowled and twisted his long hair into a rope that he then yanked behind one shoulder.

"They haven't?"

"No." Another scowl.

An idea came to her. "Is that the real reason why you made that call?"

He glanced away, then made eye contact. "Well, I cannot tell a lie."

Barbara smiled and without knowing she was go-

ing to, reached over and patted his hand in a sis-
terly fashion.

They sat in silence for a few minutes. Gathering
her courage, Barbara said, "Your brother is very
nice. Is that why you encouraged Lauren to go off
with him?"

"Me? I didn't encourage any such thing."

"Well, there were four of us in your living room,
and I was with the man I wanted and you were
with the woman I'm pretty sure you want, but then
the next thing I knew, Lauren was making off with
Oliver and instead of stopping her, you were asking
me to go to the museum." She was gathering steam
and feeling much more comfortable speaking her
mind. "And the way I see it, your invitation pretty
much encouraged them to spend the rest of the day
together." There, she'd said her piece. She took a
deep breath and stared into Alistair's really marvelous eyes, wondering why they didn't affect her
the way Oliver's did.

Alistair was smiling, quite broadly. "I detest
logic," he said, "especially when it's so on point."

"Oh, yes, I agree."

"I've acted like a fool," he said.

"Oh, yes," she repeated, but then added, "me,
too. But it's not as if I don't enjoy your company."

Alistair sat back against the bench, bemused by
Barbara's insight and by the way she once again
patted his hand. Oliver would be well taken care of
by this sweet and sensitive woman. His life would
be orderly, yet passion would rule in private. He
smiled. Lauren would never know the meaning of
order, but she was well on her way to embracing

her passionate self. And in the process, she was helping him welcome new ways of experiencing life. He might not be able to invite Buster to eat on the table, but a little bit of clutter didn't seem like such a big deal anymore.

"I do have a confession to make," Barbara said.

"You do?"

She nodded. "It was most unprofessional of me, but I was hoping you'd notice me—as a woman—not as a consultant." Her cheeks warmed to a becoming pink and she said quickly, "And it wasn't because you were the type of man I usually fell for. In fact, it was because—"

"—Because I was the opposite of any man you'd ever been involved with." He couldn't help himself. He finished the sentence for her.

"You do understand!"

He grinned. "I guess we can call this a dual confession. I've been doing the same thing. You'd think just once in my life I could attract a woman who is not only beautiful, but competent, successful, and totally together."

"I'm not beautiful."

He tipped her chin up and studied her. "Oh, yes you are." He smiled, and added, "Oliver has a few things to teach you."

She smiled at that, as if picturing many things she'd like to explore with his brother. "Lauren's very bright," she said slowly. "And far more beautiful than I am."

Alistair sighed. "And troubled. And unemployed. And fighting off a horde of personal demons. But you know what? I'm beginning to learn that it's not up to me to fight those battles for her. But I want to stand by her, every day of the rest of our lives." He jumped up and offered Barbara a hand. "Opposites aren't necessarily the answer."

She rose, and said, "So what are we doing standing here? We've got our work cut out for us, winning them back!"

Columbina Jefferson had known Oliver Gotho all his life. She'd also known his brother and his father since the cradle.

Standing now in the broad doorway of Oliver's house, she watched impassively as the nicely dressed but rather anxious couple let themselves out the front gate.

She'd called the cab that stood ready to collect them.

She'd sympathized with their plight without telling them anything. Given the description, Columbina had no doubt that the woman who had sat on the front porch yesterday with Oliver and exclaimed over Columbina's oatmeal cookies was the man's daughter.

But it was up to Oliver to deliver that message.

Columbina managed the house and the business of running the house. His personal life she left strictly to Oliver. Or so she told herself, in between peeking through the curtains to see what woman he'd brought home and materializing at advantageous moments when he'd obviously chosen poorly.

She'd served lemonade and cookies and much

more sophisticated selections to a train of women. Instinctively, she'd known the redhead had been yet another detour on Oliver's path to happiness. What she wouldn't give for her Oliver to find the right woman.

The cab drove away and had just cleared the corner when another vehicle appeared. Recognizing Alistair's convertible, Columbina smiled. Oliver was her favorite but Alistair ran a very close second.

The passenger door opened and a petite blonde dressed in soft pink and carrying a straw hat stepped out. Columbina narrowed her eyes. Alistair emerged from the car, spotted her on the porch, and waved as he moved around the car to the woman.

He said something Columbina, despite her very sharp ears, couldn't hear, and the woman smiled up at him as if he were the cleverest man in the world.

Hmmph. Columbina folded her arms across her chest. She knew the way she knew whether a cantaloupe was ripe without even touching it that this woman wasn't Alistair's type.

Watching her dainty steps as she moved up the sidewalk and the way she smiled shyly as she approached the porch, Columbina knew her prayers had been answered.

Now if only Oliver had the sense to get himself home.

Temporary insanity.

Walking back to the Bayou Magick Shop next to Oliver, Lauren could think of no other excuse for her harebrained notion of pursuing Oliver to the altar.

They were as bad for one another as an unprimed canvas was for a beautiful fresh tube of paint.

"Here we are." Oliver spoke for the first time in blocks. Rather unnecessarily, he pointed to the door of Alistair's business.

"I hope you don't mind if I don't go in," Lauren said, shifting from foot to foot. Her poor toes and legs were killing her, but she needed to keep on walking. She thought so much more clearly when she kept moving, and did she have some thinking to do! Her mind was playing tricks on her. Back at the riverfront, she'd caught a glimpse of a man who reminded her so strongly of her father that she'd started to go after him. And the really odd thing was he was with a woman who looked like a twin of Lauren's mother.

Oliver didn't seem to mind one bit. He edged toward the door.

Lauren was sure he was embarrassed over the way he'd gone nuts over her. Impulsively, she reached out and laid her hand on his arm.

His eyes widened slightly. For just a moment, Lauren considered that it would serve him good and proper if she did come on to him. But truly she did wish him well. She gave his arm a light pat and said, "You and Barbara will be very happy together."

A grin split his face. "You really think so?"

She nodded.

"You must think I'm a fickle sort of fellow."

Lauren squeezed his arm, then dropped her

hand. "Oh, I like you so much better for having gotten over me so fast."

He looked a little puzzled at her comment. "I don't think my brother's over you."

"And that's why he's at the museum with Barbara?" Lauren couldn't keep the edge out of her voice. "Never mind. I've got to go."

She backed away, waiting until he disappeared inside the shop before she bolted into Jo-Jo's jewelry store. If Alistair was back, which she thought unlikely, she didn't want Oliver to tell him where she'd gone.

Quickly, she collected the face paints and brushes and borrowed two lightweight campstools Jo-Jo had traded for a man's ID bracelet. When he asked, she reassured him that she'd be back the next day—without knowing whether she would or not—and headed back toward the river side of the Quarter.

She longed to collect Buster, but the need to avoid Alistair until she sorted out her feelings was too strong. It was a shame, because the parrot was such a good draw. But without Buster, she'd be less visible to the police and as she didn't know whether face paint artists were required to have a license, she figured she ought to play it safe.

Safe?

Ha!

Lauren kicked at a pebble, tripped over the sidewalk, and barely saved herself from a nasty fall by using the campstools as a brace. Oh, brother.

Brother—specifically Oliver's brother—summed up her major problem. Forget that she was out of work and cut off from her family. Forget that she was on her way to setting a record for the most-delayed dissertation at Primalia College.

Her major problem was her heart.

Alistair had said she was safe with him, yet she felt at her most vulnerable with him. When he kissed her and held her close, she did feel physically safe. And he was kind and understanding. He'd even provided her with an alibi when he caught her hiding from Barbara and Oliver in his kitchen.

But safety was an illusion.

The more she allowed herself to care, the greater the pain would be when she lost him.

And lose Alistair she would, if she hadn't already.

Even her own father had given up on her.

Lauren started to stumble again, then righted herself quickly. Enough of her self-pity! She looked around at the throngs of people. She'd been so engrossed in her thoughts she hadn't even experienced the sights and sounds of the blocks she'd covered.

She crossed the street and followed the wave of people into the alley behind Café du Monde. The area was full of craftspeople showing their wares. Wedging into a spot between a woman selling hand-painted bandannas and a mime selling silence, Lauren set up her campstools and opened her paints. She dug in her carryall bag and fished out the cardboard backing of a sketchpad. Setting up shop, the first thing she lettered was her sign:

ANGEL FACES—$5.00

She wasn't sure what an angel face was but she thought the title looked pretty catchy on the sign.

And sure enough, a man and woman strolling arm in arm must have thought so because they stopped immediately. Lauren pocketed their money and began to paint her way to freedom.

Alistair offered Buster another seed. The parrot sidled closer, studying its benefactor. Alistair stretched his legs out where he sat on the carpet in the ground-floor apartment. "Yeah, Buster, I'd look at me funny, too. I'm a piece of work. I had Lauren in my hands, and I didn't just lose her. I pushed her away."

"Buy high. Sell low."

For a moment, Alistair thought his ears had deceived him. Then he laughed as he realized the parrot really had reversed its favorite phrase.

"Yes, I'm a genius when it comes to women." Buster accepted the seed from him. "I did have to let her go, you know," Alistair said. He picked up the silver pin he'd used to represent mind on the altar he'd never used. "If she doesn't come to me of her own choice, it's better that we're not together."

Buster crunched the seed. Alistair did believe what he'd just said aloud. 'Course that hadn't stopped him from searching the Quarter for Lauren since he'd left Barbara at Oliver's house. He'd returned to his place only a short time ago and it was now getting pretty close to midnight.

Someone else was searching for Lauren, too. He gazed at the flyer lying on the coffee table and then folded it and put it in his shirt pocket. He'd spotted the flyer taped to a light pole along Decatur Street.

Her father.

Alistair had called the number given and left a message for Dr. Stevens, but no one had returned the call. No doubt he was still out looking. Alistair ought to be sensible and go upstairs to his own apartment and wait for a call there.

Instead, he toyed with the pin and offered another seed to Buster. What he wanted was for Lauren to come back to him, and waiting in this room where they had been so intimate made him feel her return was not only possible, but also imminent.

The doorknob turned.

Alistair sat rock still. He knew he hadn't caused her to materialize but the timing amazed him. And gave him hope. He sat still, unsure whether or not to call out to warn her of his presence. She had no reason to think she'd find him sitting there waiting for her. Buster, though, didn't wait. He hopped down from the coffee table and headed across the room.

The door opened more slowly than he'd ever seen a door move.

Finally, Lauren stepped into the apartment.

She'd never looked more adorable. Purple and green paint smudges decorated her forehead and one cheek. She was lugging two aluminum stools and her carryall. Despite the late hour, she didn't look at all tired.

"Alistair?"

He nodded, watching her expression and her body language for clues to her mind-set. He needed to apologize for spiriting Barbara off to the museum, but he wanted to see if she was open to an apology. Had the evening with Oliver changed her feelings toward him?

"What are you doing here?" She sounded curious, not upset.

"Waiting for you."

"Oh." She looked uncertain and stood where she was, way too far away.

"To apologize," he added.

"Oh," she said again.

He rose and crossed to her. He reached for her bag and the stools and lifted those burdens from her, the way he longed to ease the other problems that weighed her down.

He'd always been inclined to help others, but his task was to learn when it was appropriate to help and when it was more appropriate to step back and let others help themselves.

She let him set her things down for her, but then she said, "I didn't expect to find you here. I only came to collect Buster."

"You're leaving now? It's almost midnight."

"I don't think it's right to impose on you," she said, her chin set at a stubborn angle.

Alistair ached to kiss away her objections but he respected her determination to take care of herself. "Well, you're not imposing on me. Besides, you're working in the shop tomorrow—"

"I have to resign." She said that really fast, almost all in one breath, but she faced him eye to eye.

"Why?"

"I have a new job. One I know I'll be good at! I've been painting faces and I met a woman who runs this children's program at the zoo and she asked me if I'd come to work there teaching art." At that, Lauren moved into the room and danced in a circle, her stiff formality evaporating. Then she caught herself and slowed to a stop, and said, "I am sorry to let you down, because I know Kara left on vacation."

"That's okay. I can handle it myself. The job sounds perfect." He was truly happy for her. "You can still stay here." Right, Alistair, why not come right out and beg? Tell her you'll never forgive yourself if you let her walk away?

"Thank you, but I also met a woman who is going to let me be her roommate. And I don't have to pay rent until the beginning of the month."

"You did all this tonight?" Alistair stepped back toward the couch. "What about Oliver?"

"Oh, I left him hours and hours ago. If he has any sense, he's with Barbara right now."

"Say that again?"

Suddenly, Lauren clapped her hand to her mouth. Eyes widening, she said, "I hope that doesn't upset you about Barbara."

He grinned and shook his head. "Oh, no, all's well that ends well, don't you think?"

She nodded, looking wistful and much more tired than when she first walked through the door. Stooping down, she scratched Buster on the head, then placed him on her shoulder and rose.

"I have to get my dress and other things from the bathroom," she said.

"Sure." Alistair let her walk by, thinking that all his gifts and supposed wisdom were worthless if he couldn't figure out a way to rekindle the magic that existed between the two of them. He'd tell her about her father's flyer before she left. But before he did, he needed to hold her close and show her how he felt about her. Maybe it was selfish to put that first, but for once in his life, Alistair was going to rescue himself.

Because he knew if he let her go, he'd be making the worst mistake of his life.

Twenty-four

*L*auren knew she should be happy. She'd found a job and a place to live. So why did she feel like sitting down on the side of the claw-footed tub and bawling?

She lifted her own dress from where she'd hung it to dry after rinsing it out only that morning. Holding it to her chest, she pictured Alistair in the other room.

So near and yet so far.

She wished she could go to him. Just that moment when she'd danced about and shared the news of her job with him had reminded her how quickly she'd come to enjoy sharing every moment with him.

Silly, you barely know him.

Maybe, but she knew enough to know he was perfect for her.

But could she trust her feelings? Would he cast her aside the way Brad had done, or grow impatient with her as her father had?

It was for the best he'd gone off with Barbara to the museum. That had been a lesson learned for her. Yet she still stood there in the bathroom wishing she could walk into the other room and throw her arms around him and give herself completely to him.

Something she'd never been able to do with any other man.

She sighed, and said aloud, "Don't be silly. You'll get over him."

When she spoke, Buster hopped from her shoulder to the edge of the sink, staring at her with that quizzical look of his.

"Well, I will," she said, and changed dresses.

In the midst of pulling her own dress over her head, she heard a clank. Free of the fabric, she looked down. Evidently Buster had knocked the soap off the counter.

Even the parrot knew she was fooling herself.

"So I fell for him," she said. "What am I supposed to do about that?"

"Love me?"

Lauren whirled around, just missing the edge of the tub and upsetting a faux crystal tumbler from the edge of the sink. She caught it in midair and saved it from the fate of the soap.

"Hey," she said in surprise, concentrating on the near miss because she had no idea what to make of what he'd just said. "I'm getting less clumsy. A day ago I wouldn't have saved it."

From where he stood just outside the bathroom door, Alistair smiled at her, admiration and respect in his eyes. "The new Lauren," he said softly. "You're coming into your own."

She loved hearing those words from him. Smiling shyly, she said, "I think maybe I am."

And then she fell silent. Even without actually standing within the doorframe, he filled it. The intensity of his dark violet-blue eyes deepened as he watched her. His shoulders had never looked broader or stronger than they did beneath the plain navy T-shirt. He had on the same purple shorts and Birkenstock sandals he'd worn the night she'd saved him from the mugger. He'd pulled his hair back with an elastic band.

She had the wildest inclination to reach up and slip the band off.

Running her tongue over her upper lip, she considered her options.

And Alistair, being the patient and wise man he was, seemed prepared to wait all night long for her next move.

"Buy high. Sell low." Buster flapped his wings and jumped up and down on the edge of the sink.

"What did he say?" Lauren looked from Alistair to the parrot and back.

Alistair was grinning. "He said it before you came in, too. I think he's trying to tell us something. You know, like we've gotten things mixed up and backward but it's not too late to straighten them out."

Lauren smiled. She still thought she should walk away now before her heart was even more lost to him. But she wanted this night with him. Whatever the consequences, she would deal with those emotions later.

She dropped the dress on the side of the tub and opened her arms. "Love me, Alistair," she whispered.

It might be the craziest thing she'd ever done, but as she watched him close the small distance between them and saw the desire and tenderness in his expression, she knew it might also be the happiest.

"Lauren, Lauren," he said, clasping her gently as she slipped her arms around his waist. "Thank you for coming back to me." He tipped her chin up and feathered a kiss over her lips.

He was being, she realized, extremely cautious with her. And the funny thing was, she didn't feel at all shy. Smiling into his kiss, she traced the tip of her tongue over the line between his lips and found her way deep inside his mouth.

He groaned and pulled her tighter to him.

Encouraged by his reaction, she tasted his mouth again and again, and his tongue began to move in a dance with hers.

His hands cupped her bottom and she pressed against his very aroused body, one corner of her mind registering that she'd never felt so sexually adventurous.

Emboldened by the very idea that she could gift Alistair with a similarly generous pleasure as he had given her the other night, she reached for the waistband of his shorts and began tugging them downward.

She inched first one side of his shorts then the other down his legs while she continued the wild kissing that was turning her completely liquid inside.

She cupped one hand around his arousal, enjoying a sweet rush of pleasure as he gasped and drove his tongue deeper into her mouth. His shaft was strangely silky to her touch, and yet at the same time huge and heavy with the urgency of his need for her. The heat and sensation of touching him so intimately drove her absolutely wild, and she wondered what it would feel like to place her mouth where her hand was.

Slowly she withdrew her tongue from his and slipped down beside him.

"Lauren."

She kissed the heavy warmth just next to where she cradled him with her hand.

He moaned. "Lauren."

She answered him by opening her mouth wide and taking him in. Amazed at the sweet, heated sensation, she enveloped him more deeply.

He was tapping her on the shoulder. Slowly she worked her mouth up the length of him, then lifted her face. "Yes?"

Eyes heavy with passion, he said, "Before we go any further, maybe we should go into the bedroom."

Lauren smiled. She'd completely forgotten they were still standing in the small bathroom.

He pulled her up to him, kicked his shorts off the rest of the way, and lifted her. "And I thought I was the one giving the lesson," he said, kissing her ear-lobe.

"Oh, Alistair, I feel so good with you, it's as if a part of me that never existed has come to life, and it's so wonderful."

"You are so wonderful," he said, and then sat her down beside the bed and reached for her dress. In one swift movement, he had it over her head. It disappeared somewhere on the far side of the bed along with his T-shirt.

When she reached out to cup him again, he said, "And a very quick learner, but let's not be too quick."

"What do you mean?"

He grinned and Lauren's pulse raced even faster. He pulled back the bedcovers and, lifting her, laid her on the cool sheets. He joined her, his body above hers. She reached up and pulled the elastic from his hair. It fell over her naked skin like a satin waterfall.

This was the part where she usually got really nervous and started wondering why she'd agreed to get in bed. But right then all she could do was feel—sweet, sensuous feelings that rolled through her body in waves that were building a craving for more sensation.

"Remember what we did last night?" Alistair had shifted so that he lay beside her. With one hand he was stroking the inside of her thigh in feather-light circles that were making her skin tingle.

She nodded. How could she forget?

"Are you ready to feel that good again?"

She smiled, but said, "I want to make you feel good this time."

He grinned. "I think we can work this out so we both feel great."

"You haven't been wrong yet," she murmured. "But are you sure you want to do this?"

"Oh, yes. There's no question in my mind. Why do you ask?"

"You did say you'd given up women." She hated to remind him of his statement at that moment, but she felt it was the honest thing to do.

He ran one hand from the tips of her toes, along her legs, grazing her inner thighs, and looping a heart around her belly button. "Only until I found the right woman, the perfect woman," he whispered, and then he retraced the path, this time with his lips.

Lauren sighed and stretched her hands over her head. "The right person does make all the difference in the world. I'm still amazed at how good you make me feel."

"And it gets better," Alistair said, teasing her inner thighs with his tongue.

"Better?"

"As we grow together," he said, "I promise you things will be even better."

Lauren closed her eyes briefly. She couldn't bear to think of walking away from this wonderful man, though that's what she'd made up her mind to do.

Tomorrow.

Tonight belonged to them.

Lifting her arms, she pulled him down for a long, slow kiss. At the same time, she fondled his arousal.

After a very long moment, Alistair said, "Keep that up, and I'll die a happy man."

She smiled, pleased that she was giving him such pleasure.

Then Alistair slipped lower on the bed and began a new dance with his tongue, one that had her grasping the top of his head and crying his name aloud.

All thought fled her mind. All sounds ceased to register in her ears. Her world centered on the heated bliss created by his tongue. She knew she stopped breathing, but she was beyond caring as she exploded in a sensual rush of pleasure.

Alistair caught her to him, kissing her mound, prolonging the pleasure of the release. She quivered and slowly unclenched her hands from his hair.

"Happy?" he asked softly.

She nodded. For once, the power of speech had escaped her.

He lifted himself over her, easing her legs apart with his own. The heat of his arousal as it brushed her inner thigh ignited another wave of desire in her. She opened her legs wider and offered herself to him.

He moved to enter her, the heat of his arousal demanding communion with the fire building inside her. Lauren lifted her hips to draw him in, and he leaned forward, smiled into her eyes, and kissed her lips. "Thank you," he said, as he claimed her most intimate self.

She cried out slightly, and he paused.

"It's okay," she said. "It's been so long."

"Good," he said, almost fiercely. But despite the

ferociously possessive look on his face, he moved gently and slowly, gliding inward then drawing back then moving quicker and quicker and deeper and deeper and she forgot all about anything but the feeling of being completely joined with Alistair. He'd taken possession of her from her heated core clear up to her heart.

"So good," she murmured, moving her hips faster.

With that encouragement, Alistair increased his tempo, driving her even wilder with every thrust. She was getting that crazy about-to-burst-inside feeling all over again.

"Oh, Alistair," she said in wonder as the sweet rush of release began to overtake her.

He enveloped her in his arms and raced with her. Lauren merged, heart, body, soul, and mind with Alistair and cried out even as he exploded within her and dropped to the bed, holding her as if he would never let her go.

Sunday morning, Oliver opened his eyes to a flood of sunlight, a chorus of chirping birds, and Barbara, still sleeping, curled up next to him.

He couldn't believe his good fortune.

He'd returned to his house last night and found Barbara in the back parlor, being cosseted by Columbina, who was treating her to her favorite pictures of Oliver as a baby.

That sight confirmed what Oliver already knew. He'd met the woman who would help him turn the Gotho house into a home.

Barbara stirred and her eyes fluttered open. Then as she looked around her, they grew wide. She blushed becomingly, and said, "Good morning, Oliver."

He kissed the tip of her nose. "Good morning, sweetheart."

She looked thoughtful. "So I didn't dream last night, did I?"

He shook his head. "Regrets?"

Her face lit into a smile. "None. Though as I started to tell you last night, I really do have a four-date rule before I, well, you know."

He grinned and rolled over so that he lay almost on top of her. "I did the math. We worked together two days, we had dinner Friday night, and breakfast at Brennan's. I count four dates."

"Not very professional of me," she murmured.

"Or of me." He stroked the side of one breast. "How about we supersede our consulting contract?"

She was watching him as if she were drinking in every nuance of expression on his face. He loved the way she noticed everything, the way she gave herself so completely to him, the way she made him feel as if he could do more with his life than he'd ever dreamed possible.

"Is that because you think it will be awkward to work together?" She colored slightly, and then added, "After sleeping together?"

Oliver smiled and shook his head. "Not at all. What I'm hoping"—he watched her carefully, realizing he was speaking far too soon but unable to help himself—"is that we can work together for the rest of our lives."

"Oliver?"

He brushed a stray lock of hair back from her cheek. "I know I've been goofy the last few days, but I don't regret it. It was as if some switch inside me flipped, and I became open to possibilities I've never known before. No way would I have dated a woman I was doing business with, but being with you seemed so right."

She nodded. "I understand that."

"And you have every right to think me a flake after the way I carried on about Lauren, but I think, as my brother would say, that experience was meant to be." He smiled at her. "Not as a romantic thing, but as a sign from the universe that I should let loose and live a bit."

Barbara smiled. "Maybe my godmother did one of her magick spells."

Oliver kissed her and said, "I don't think anything she could do would equal the magic of the way I feel about you." He took a deep breath, and said, "Barbara, will you marry me?"

A hint of a tear appeared in her eyes.

"I didn't mean to make you sad," Oliver said, alarmed that he had done so.

"I'm not sad, Oliver. I'm happy. I just can't believe all this has happened so fast."

"And you're a methodical, logical person, and you need some time to process the pluses and minuses," Oliver offered. He was disappointed, but he certainly understood.

She was shaking her head.

"Take all the time you need," he said. "I'll court you properly. I'll even force myself out of this bed if it makes you feel more comfortable."

She clutched his shoulders. "Don't you dare go anywhere," she said. "Yes, the answer is yes, I'll marry you!"

"I'll get down on my knees—what did you just say?"

Smiling, Barbara said, "I've never done an impetuous thing in my settled, orderly life, and, you know, it feels really good to be a little less rigid." Lifting her lips to his and wrapping her legs around his, she whispered, "I said yes, Oliver. Now let's seal the bargain."

"Starting with a kiss," Oliver said, capturing her lips, then murmuring as he drew her closer, "and never ending."

In the relative quiet of Sunday morning in the French Quarter, Alistair shifted in the bed, reaching for Lauren, yearning to further explore the passion they had found together.

Slowly he realized she was no longer in bed. He glanced to the bathroom; the door was open and the light off. A frisson of alarm shot through him, and he leapt from the bed, moving swiftly to the front room.

No Lauren.

And even more ominous, no sign of Buster.

"No!" He shouted the word and turned to race back for his clothes. As he whirled around, he spotted a piece of paper propped beside the altar on the coffee table. He snatched it up and read:

Thank you for the two best days of my life. Please don't try to find me.

Alistair crumpled the paper in his hand, then smoothed it out, trying to pull clues out of the few words. But not try to find Lauren? He bounded into the bedroom, cast one look at the rumpled covers of the bed where he knew he had given her happiness, and wondered what had gone wrong. He jumped into his shorts and T-shirt and ran up the stairs. By now, her father might have called. By now, he might even know where Lauren was.

He'd been so sated, he had slept like a brick, and slept late, too. It was after 10 A.M. Oh, no! He'd been so caught up in their passion he hadn't told her about her father, and then they'd fallen asleep arm in arm.

Inside his apartment, two things met his gaze simultaneously.

The flashing light on his answering machine.

The packet of condoms he'd rushed out to buy yesterday. Unopened. Alistair bit back an oath at his own thoughtlessness. Never once in all his years had he neglected to use protection. He had been so swept away by desire that he'd completely forgotten about being responsible. He wanted to kick himself, and yet at the same time he didn't feel as bad as he might. The idea of making a baby with Lauren appealed to him, strongly. But there would be no babies unless he found her and won her heart.

Hoping Dr. Stevens had called, Alistair hit the PLAY button on the recorder.

Twenty-five

Lawrence Stevens tried to keep his spirits up. Standing in front of a shop with a purple-and-silver sign that read BAYOU MAGICK SHOP, he glanced over at Bonita, and said, "Still closed."

She nodded, giving him a pat of encouragement on his arm.

"I hope we're not following another dead end," he said. The message left at their hotel by an Alistair Gotho had said they should come to this shop if they couldn't reach him by phone. When no one had answered their repeated calls, they had walked over from the hotel.

"The shop probably opens later on Sundays," Bonita said, quite reasonably.

Stevens checked his watch once more. "The sign says they open at ten. It's almost eleven."

"Hello, there," called a woman's voice.

Stevens turned around. A short woman with amazingly orange-and-silver hair dressed in a flowing purple caftan was sizing him up. Not another fortune-teller out to make a buck! He nodded, but didn't speak.

A white-haired man joined the woman. He looked far too dignified to be associated with a quack. Stevens studied the two of them and decided they could make the next move.

"Oh, dear, Durwood, the shop is closed," the woman said. "That is not a good sign."

"It may be or it may not be," the man said in a strong baritone.

"Oh, that's right," the woman said, "you were trying to explain to me about jumping to conclusions. But Alistair never opens his shop late."

Alistair? Stevens's ears perked up. Bonita exchanged glances with him, which meant she'd heard the name, too.

"Excuse me," Stevens said.

"Are you looking for Alistair, too?" The woman chirped the question, and studied them once more, her quick gaze darting about.

"Alistair Gotho," Stevens said.

"That's Alistair."

"Do you have a daughter, sir?" The question came from the older man. Stevens hoped he didn't try to charge him a hundred dollars for useless information à la Sister Griswold.

Still, he had to follow every clue he could. "Yes, I do."

"I thought so."

"But you told me jumping to conclusions was the

sign of a hasty mind," the woman said.

"Take a look at his red hair," the older man said. "Plus he looks just like the woman you introduced me to yesterday."

Stevens ran a hand over his head. He and Lauren had always had hair the identical color. "Do you know where she is?"

The older man shook his head. "No, but if you find Alistair, he may know."

A burly man stepped out of the store next door. Everyone in the foursome shifted to take a look. Apparently the man wasn't Alistair because neither the man or the woman called out a greeting.

"Want to buy some jewelry while you wait for the magick shop to open? I have some very nice, very rare things."

"No, thanks," Bonita answered.

The man accepted the polite rejection. He returned to the shop but a few minutes later reappeared, a broom in hand. He began sweeping the sidewalk in front of his shop in ambling strokes.

It seemed to Stevens, in the anxious state of his mind, that the man was overly interested in their party, but at the moment, he didn't trust either his logic or his instincts. He just wanted to find his daughter and make sure she was okay.

"Perhaps," Bonita said in her gentle way, "we should introduce ourselves."

The older man smiled, and Stevens noticed the corners of his eyes crinkled in a friendly way. The man seemed 180 degrees removed from Sister Griswold and her ilk. Stevens couldn't get a good reading on the orange-haired woman, but then, he doubted if anyone could.

"I'm Lawrence Stevens and this is my fiancée, Bonita Bristol."

"General Wisdom," the older man said, extending a hand.

"And I'm Mrs. Merlin," the orange-haired woman said. "We—or I, I should say—know Alistair through magick."

"We're here looking for my daughter—"

Mrs. Merlin clasped her hands together. "She is going to make Alistair the happiest man in the whole world."

"Is that so?" Stevens's paternal protective instincts shot up a notch more. Who was this Alistair and who was Lauren to him? "We'll see."

Next door the man had stopped sweeping and was leaning on the broom, not even bothering to hide his curiosity. Stevens glared at him, and the broom began to move again.

The front door rattled slightly and Stevens tensed. At last he would learn something.

The door opened and everyone on the sidewalk glanced upward to the top of the three steps.

A broad-shouldered man with hair that fell to his shoulders and the most piercing blue eyes Stevens had ever seen filled the doorway. In his hand he held a piece of cardboard and a tape dispenser. Without glancing at them, he turned to the glass of the door and held the sign in place.

"Don't touch that tape," Mrs. Merlin said.

He turned around. "I can't help you today, Mrs. Merlin. I'm having a crisis of my own."

"Oh, I know. That's why we're all here."

"All?" Slowly, the man focused his gaze on the group on the sidewalk. "General Wisdom," he said, nodding at the older man. "And"—gazing at Stevens, he descended the steps, one hand held forth, the tape and sign in the other—"you're Lauren's father."

Stevens shook his hand and introduced Bonita before asking the words he'd been waiting to speak. "Is Lauren with you?"

Alistair shook his head. "I suppose that means she isn't with you?"

Stevens shook his head, feeling sick. He'd had such hope.

"Why don't you all step inside?"

"I don't understand," Mrs. Merlin whispered to her male companion as she climbed the steps. "When other people jump to conclusions, they seem to get things right."

Alistair remained behind. Before he entered the shop, Stevens heard him say to the man with the broom, "Jo-Jo, may I have a word with you?" Perhaps the next-door neighbor knew something; Stevens would make it a point to find out.

Lauren knew she shouldn't have taken the coward's way out. She'd slipped out of bed like the proverbial thief in the night. Only she was worse than a thief who stole material possessions. She knew from her night with Alistair that she held his heart in her hands.

And where was she?

Walking away.

Eyes downcast, lost in her thoughts, she'd been walking for hours, methodically covering the blocks of the Quarter that ran from Iberville down to Esplanade and then back up the next one-way street. She'd started on Bourbon after leaving Alistair's and had now worked her way over to Chartres, which led into Jackson Square.

Lauren slowed, earning a grateful *arck!* from Buster, and looked around, locating the spot where she and Alistair had first met. The Square was coming to life, with more and more artists opening their green supply carts and setting up shop. Some were already sketching caricatures or creating street scenes with swift, practiced strokes. Lauren walked through them and the Sunday morning tourists over to where the policemen had confronted her.

She smiled wistfully as she pictured the moment Alistair had appeared on the scene. He'd spared her from arrest, fed her, given her a place to stay, and taught her that love between the right man and woman was a beautiful gift. And what had she done? Run out the door to spare herself the possible pain of a potential future hurt!

"You're an idiot," she said.

Buster hopped about on her shoulder.

"Love trouble, dear?" A woman Lauren hadn't noticed crept up beside her. "Perhaps I can help. Sister Griswold knows all—oh, it's you and that bird," the fortune-teller said disappointedly.

"Hello," Lauren said. "How have you been?"

The woman shrugged. "Some days better. Some days worse. And you?"

After having watched the woman work her marks, Lauren couldn't resist the temptation to tease the woman just a bit. "Can't you tell?"

"Of course I can." She tugged on her array of shawls. "I'm a professional, but sometimes it's nice to hear the good news from the person's lips rather than reading it from the cards. Makes it more personal."

That made sense to Lauren, even though she suspected the woman had no psychic ability and was simply skirting the question. "Well, I have a real job and an apartment—"

"Never mind all that. Get to the love part. Tell me about the man with the pretty wallet."

That comment puzzled Lauren. "I've never seen Alistair's wallet. I'm not sure if he carries one. If he had, the mugger wouldn't have given him such a hard time over his shoes."

Sister Griswold was staring at her as if she were crazier than Ruthie the Duck Lady, one of the Quarter's eccentrics. "Not him," she said. "The blond with all the cash who wanted to gobble you up."

Suddenly Lauren understood something she had yet to figure out. "You lifted Oliver's wallet and hid it in my bag!"

The sly old lady adjusted her turban, and said, "Oh, never mind that. What does it matter when all is said and done, if you've found the man of your dreams?"

"It's not right to steal," Lauren said. The old woman had not only pickpocketed Oliver's wallet, but she'd been willing to let Lauren take the rap if the man had searched then and there for it! "If you're more than a street hustler, prove it."

"Oh, very well, give me your hand."

Lauren inched her hand forward, almost wishing she hadn't made that last statement.

Sister Griswold took both her hands and crooned and muttered as she gazed at them. Then she held only her right one and traced a line or two here and there. Lauren was shifting from foot to foot by the time the older woman said, "He is waiting for you. Many friends and family are waiting for you. But you are waiting on some answer. And the answer . . ."

"Yes?" Lauren leaned forward. "What is the answer?"

"You hold the answer in your hands."

"What?"

Sister Griswold shrugged, adjusted her shawls, and said, "Now, if you'll excuse me." Then she moved away majestically, leaving Lauren standing there puzzling over her message.

Suddenly, Lauren started to giggle. Buster swiveled his neck down as if to check on her sanity. Lauren lifted her hands. "My hands, Buster, I hold the answer in my hands."

The fortune-teller was quite a shyster but in her own way she'd pointed out a useful truth. "Life is what you make it," she said aloud, then picked up her carryall and headed back toward Bourbon Street.

At long last she was going to piece together a life of her own, not the life her father expected of her or the one she'd tried to follow to please her professors or art instructors. And if Alistair would forgive her for walking out on him, she was going to see if the two of them couldn't move, a slow step at a time naturally, toward a life they created with their own hands.

The next thing she had to do was call her father. Forcing her to stand on her own two feet was the best gift he'd ever given her. Waiting to cross the next street, Lauren leaned on the light post to rest. All that pacing had caught up with her.

She glanced at a freshly printer flyer taped to the pole and gasped when she saw her own image. Quickly she scanned the brief notice. Her dad had come looking for her!

In Alistair's upstairs apartment, the intercom buzzer rang. Everyone jumped. Alistair dashed to the speaker control.

Oliver's voice came through. "Do you mind if Barbara and I come up? We couldn't get in through the shop."

Alistair buzzed them in. He'd been about to leave to begin canvassing the streets for Lauren. Mrs. Merlin had brewed tea for everyone and was in the kitchen whipping up some muffins and feeding tidbits to Midnight. Alistair hadn't had the heart to stop her. He'd never seen her so contented. The first thing she and the general had told him was that if Alistair was still interested in selling, he was interested in buying the shop. "It would make Maebelle happy," he'd said, "and if I'm any judge of finances, it's a steady source of cash flow."

Now General Wisdom walked over to where

Alistair stood near the front door. "Some campaigns take longer than others. I think you should wait here for at least the next half hour."

"I see." Alistair hid his frustration. He was the one who had stalled earlier. He'd made love to Lauren but not fully opened his heart and mind to her. He should have begged her to stay, told her directly how much he needed and wanted her in his life. He didn't want to rescue her—he wanted to walk side by side through life with her. "It's hard to sit here when I'm worried about Lauren," he said at last.

The general nodded.

"I just need to talk to her. I scared her off, moved too quickly in some ways and not effectively in other ways."

Again, the man nodded. "Time to reassess your strategy, son."

"She's afraid to love because she equates that with being abandoned. Her mother died early and she had a bum of a boyfriend and then"—he lowered his voice so Dr. Stevens couldn't overhear him—"her father let her down."

General Wisdom put one hand on Alistair's shoulder. "Men and woman are wise enough to grow beyond those hurts."

"I believe she is. But I need to talk to her." He ground one hand into the opposite palm. "I'd give up all my magickal gifts if I could just talk to her!"

"Would that be your most valued possession?"

"Not anymore," Alistair said, grateful for the solid presence of the general. He missed having his dad to talk to, and the general reminded him of his father.

"Lauren isn't a possession, but she is more important to me than anything else." He realized the general couldn't understand the import of Alistair renouncing his magickal gifts in exchange for her return—but Alistair knew.

A knock sounded and Alistair moved to let Oliver and Barbara in, knowing in his heart that he would gladly make the bargain he'd just declared.

One look at his brother and Barbara and Alistair smiled, putting aside his own troubles for a moment. He showed them in, introduced them to Dr. Stevens and Bonita, and waited expectantly. His brother hadn't let go of Barbara once, either holding her hand, or touching her arm, or putting his arm around her.

"We wanted to share our news," Oliver said. "Barbara and I are going to be married."

Alistair clapped him on the back and kissed Barbara on the cheek. Mrs. Merlin dropped the pan of muffins she was taking out of the oven on the floor with a clatter. Barbara rushed to her side and hugged her. Midnight, who had been keeping Mrs. Merlin company, moved to sample the spoils.

Oliver followed and soon had the mess sorted out.

In the midst of the celebration, Alistair glanced over at Dr. Stevens, who was gripping Bonita's hand tightly and checking his watch. Alistair pulled up a chair beside him, and said, "The general thinks we should wait a little bit longer before we hit the streets again."

"He does? And I suppose he'd say that if it were his daughter who was missing?"

Alistair nodded. "This may not be the best time to bring this up, sir, but I plan to ask your daughter to marry me."

Stevens studied him thoughtfully. "When did you meet Lauren?"

"Two days ago."

"You know about the phone call she made to me?"

Alistair nodded.

"When did you last see her?"

Alistair met his eyes. "We fell asleep together in my downstairs apartment last night."

"I see."

"You know you love her?" Bonita asked this question.

"We're perfect for one another," he answered.

She smiled.

Stevens didn't take the answer so well. "If that's the case, why isn't she here with you, the way that woman is with your brother and Bonita is with me and the lady with that orange hair is with the elderly gentleman?"

Alistair rubbed his jaw. He'd neglected to shave. No doubt Stevens thought he was a wild man with no rights to address his daughter. "I'd have to say that sometimes the river of love does not flow smoothly," he said.

Stevens nodded appreciatively and slipped an arm around Bonita's shoulders.

"I've found that to be the case myself," he said. "I'm not going to ask you if you love my daughter, but I am going to ask you if you admire and respect her."

"Yes, I do."

"And you accept her weak points as well her strengths?"

He nodded.

"And you'll love her without trying to make her into someone else?" Stevens's voice grew husky as he asked that question.

Alistair understood why. Lauren's dad knew how hard his daughter had tried to fulfill the goals he had set for her. "Lauren's come into her own," he said gently.

Bonita glanced up at Stevens and smiled. He smiled back, and said to Alistair, "You'll be good for Lauren."

The intercom buzzer sounded.

From the kitchen, Mrs. Merlin said, "Well, if we're all here, I guess we know who that must be."

Alistair headed to the intercom buzzer, then paused and turned to Lauren's father. "Would you like to answer?"

He started to rise, then stopped. "Thank you, but no. This moment is all yours."

Alistair accepted that and pressed the speaker button, telling himself it could be anyone.

"It's me. Lauren. Can I come in? And I'm sorry about the shop being closed. That's probably my fault."

Alistair smiled when he heard the stream of words. "I'm buzzing you in now," he said. Then he turned to the assembled company, and said, "I'll be right back."

He met her in the courtyard. She halted when she saw him, then as he opened his arms, she hurried forward, pausing to transfer Buster to one of the wrought-iron tables, and threw herself against his chest.

"I'm so sorry I ran away," she said.

He smoothed her hair and kissed one tear off her cheek. "It's okay. I moved too fast."

"I was afraid if I let you matter to me too much, you'd leave me, too."

"I understand," he said. "Like your mother, and Brad, then your father on the phone."

She looked up at him. "You do understand."

He nodded. "I love you, Lauren, and I promise we'll take it slow. One day at a time, if you'll let me have that chance."

"Oh, Alistair," she said, hugging him tightly. "I want to try, but you know I'm afraid, not to mention being a basket case."

"I think that's the old Lauren speaking," he said.

"You're right." She kissed him, and said, "I have learned so much. And I don't want you to let go of me, but I must call my father. I need to tell him what he did was right, making me stand on my own." She pulled a flyer from her carryall. "Look, my dad's in town. He came looking for me!"

Alistair tipped her chin and kissed her again before he said, "I know. You can tell him in person. He and Bonita are upstairs."

She tightened her arms around him, and he felt her anxiety.

"What's wrong?" he asked.

"I'm embarrassed," she said. "Here I am so happy with you and when my dad said he was going to marry Bonita, I was pretty nasty about it. Then he came all the way to New Orleans to make sure I'm okay, and she came, too."

"I think a simple apology and sincere congratulations will heal that," Alistair said, turning them toward the staircase. "Bonita seems like a woman with a pretty good heart and head."

Lauren sighed, then said, "She must be, or my father wouldn't love her."

They reached the stairs, and she said, "We forgot Buster!"

Glancing back, Alistair saw Buster had sidled from the table to a nearby banana tree. He was pecking away at some insects, looking as content as Alistair felt at that moment. "Should we leave him? Midnight is inside."

She hesitated, then as she watched him for a few minutes, said, "He seems right at home here."

"Good," Alistair said. "Let's go put an end to your father's worries."

As she walked side by side up the stairs with Alistair, his arm around her waist, Lauren felt as if her feet scarcely touched the floor. She rubbed his arm with her chin, and said, "There's something very important I need to say before we reach the door."

"Yes?"

"I love you," she said.

He gazed into her eyes, and she knew he was reading the truth of her words in her heart. "I love you, too," he said. "Thank you for a gift more special than any magick I've ever known or could ever imagine—the gift of your love."

"That is so sweet," she whispered.

Then they were at the door and Alistair opened

it. Lauren stepped through, thankful for Alistair at her side, but secure in the knowledge that she could also do this on her own.

Her father was seated next to a pretty woman with soft brown hair. Lauren walked straight toward him as he rose and moved to her.

"Lauren," he said, "thank God!"

Hugging him, she said, "Thank you for leaving me hanging on the phone."

"Thank me?" Her father looked shocked. "I came down here to find you to ask you to forgive me for that. I was trying to do the right thing, but I handled it all wrong."

"Oh, no, it was the smartest thing you ever did," Lauren said. "Though at the time I didn't think so."

Her father shook his head, looking amazed. He turned toward the woman on the sofa, and said, "I'd like you to meet Bonita."

Lauren walked over. She realized there were other people in the room but all that mattered at this moment was setting things straight with her dad and the woman now holding out a hand to her. "It's a pleasure, and I wish you and my father every happiness," Lauren said. "My dad is the greatest guy—"

"What's wrong, Lauren?" Her father asked.

"Oh, Daddy, you're the greatest dad in the world, but I want you to meet the greatest guy!"

Alistair stepped closer and her father looked from him back to her. Smiling, he said, "I already have."

"Tell, tell," said a voice that could only belong to Mrs. Merlin.

Lauren glanced around. She smiled when she saw

Barbara and Oliver arm in arm in the kitchen and Mrs. Merlin curled up beside General Wisdom on the love seat, Midnight on her lap.

"Durwood has been trying to teach me not to jump to conclusions," Mrs. Merlin said, looking quite satisfied, "but something tells me there are four very happy couples in this room right now."

Alistair clasped an arm around Lauren's waist and pulled her close.

"Happy together forever," Lauren murmured, and snuggled into Alistair's loving embrace.

What would you do if the man who got away
came back?

Lucas Hall once made Tessa Jardine feel
200 percent female . . . and 100 percent foolish
when he walked out of her life.
But now he's returned . . . and even though
Tessa's determined to resist him,
she can't help but see he's still

A GREAT CATCH

by Michelle Jerott
An Avon Contemporary Romance
Coming in September

"Buy it! Read it! You will fall in love!"
Judith Ivory